Mix-Up under the Mistletoe

Margaret Amatt

LEANNAN
PRESS
INDEPENDENT PUBLISHER

LEANNAN PRESS

First Published by Leannan Press 2024

Book Cover designed by Margaret Amatt

eBook ISBN: 978-1-914575-49-5

Paperback ISBN: 978-1-914575-48-8

CHAPTER ONE

Rafe

Early December

'*Deck the halls with boughs of holly. Fa-la-la—*'

Rafe Harrington closed his office door before any more of the song filtered in. Only a few weeks to get through before he wrapped up Christmas for another year and got back to business as usual. Sitting back at his desk, he pulled up the email he'd been reading before Marnie had decided to serenade the staff at Innova-Travel. Her repertoire of Christmas songs was impressive, if slightly annoying. But Rafe wasn't a total Scrooge, or at least he worked hard not to be. He wouldn't ban his staff from singing Christmas songs. That was way too extreme even if he did find it hard to concentrate when the rest of the office was overflowing with Marnie's festive cheer. Just because he had no particular love for the season didn't mean he had to bring a downer on everyone else.

My mother has probably said that exact phrase to me at some point.

He frowned at the screen and ran his hand around his lightly stubbled jaw before clicking on the top line of his google search. He screwed up his face as he typed the words 1-Quick Getaways and waited for the website to load on his screen. Giving that company even a few moments of airtime didn't sit well with him, but he had to know the competition. The site screamed tacky from every angle, but with the numbers of people wanting low-priced holidays, it probably didn't matter what it looked like. And Rafe had to admit keeping Innova-Travel as an upmarket brand was losing money when so many people were opting for the budget option.

We need something new. Rafe scrolled down the page. Something to keep Innova-Travel ahead of the game.

The business had expanded and still had the edge for top-end clients, but in such a competitive environment, it felt like they were missing a huge chunk of the market.

He grabbed a pen and jotted down some notes. Nothing would change overnight, but he laid out his thoughts on a couple of places he thought they could challenge 1-Quick and some of the other budget providers. After jotting down a few ideas, he clicked back to his emails, and stared at the screen. The one that had his attention needed a second opinion.

As soon as he opened the door to the main room, he located Marnie by following the sound of her voice.

'Have yourself a merry little Christmas. Let your heart beat light—'

'Marnie.' Rafe raised his eyebrow.

Marnie grinned, wheeling around to look at him. Her long black hair was pinned back at the forehead with a flashing clip fashioned like a sprig of holly. 'Sorry. Not loving my Christmas crooning? Shall I be quiet?'

'Feel free to croon away... Just not in my office. Can you come in for a second?'

'Sure, Ebenezer. But I've practically got a choir going. Sure you don't fancy joining?' She smirked as she nipped in.

'I'll give it a miss.'

'What's up?' She took a seat, adjusting her white fluffy sweater. Sequins forming a large snowflake gleamed under the down lights.

Rafe closed the door. 'We need to talk about 1-Quick Getaways.'

She pulled a face, and he mirrored it.

'Do you want to brainstorm some ideas about how we can get ahead of them in the budget market?' she said.

'Not yet. We'll need more time and a bigger meeting for that. Right now, I need to tell you about an email I had this morning.' Marnie frowned as Rafe pulled up the email on his screen. 'It's from the manager of a travel company in Manchester.'

'Oh?'

'Yeah. Apparently, a few months ago, two reps from 1-Quick Getaways visited their office. They pitched some reciprocal deals, resort distribution, the usual stuff. But then they started casually mingling with the staff, asking seemingly harmless questions.'

Marnie's keen blue eyes widened. 'And someone slipped up?'

'Exactly. A staff member accidentally handed over sensitive information. The email outlines how the 1-Quick reps were very subtle but persistent. They gathered enough intel to launch a targeted campaign that ended up costing the Manchester company thousands in lost orders.'

'That's so underhanded.' Marnie shook her head. 'Do you think they're planning to do the same to us?'

'I honestly don't know. The manager's email suggested they might have targeted other businesses in the same way. 1-Quick has a reputation for playing dirty, and this just confirms it.'

'I know they have a pretty shady reputation, but I didn't think they'd stoop this low.'

Rafe leaned back in his chair, sighing. 'Their popularity comes from selling cheap, but their customer reviews are abysmal. They're aggressive in their tactics and don't seem to care about ethics.'

'Do you think they'll try something here?'

'It's possible. They're based in London, but expanding their influence might be on their agenda. We need to be prepared.'

'So, what's the plan?' Marnie leaned forward.

'Well, the good thing is the 1-Quick bosses don't know we're onto them, so we should make an action plan in case we get a similar visit in the new year. If they see us as a ticket to the top-end market, they may well try to worm their way in. We need to make our team aware of this potential threat. No one should share any sensitive information without proper clearance. We'll also need to review our security protocols and run some internal training sessions on information security.'

'Ok, I can set that up.'

'And, according to this email, the 1-Quick people didn't make any secret of who they worked for. So, if they do turn up, they'll probably say where they're from and we'll be ready.'

'I like it. Maybe we should use it as a chance to flip the tables on them and see if we can work on a budget range.'

'Good thinking.' Rafe nodded. 'But let's sort the plan first. I need to write a script, so if anyone from 1-Quick calls, we're all singing from the same song sheet... No, not a Christmas one,' he added at the grin on Marnie's face.

'Ok, boss, but I could wow them with a few carols.'

'That might have the desired effect and send them running in the opposite direction.'

'You're such a meany.'

Rafe smirked and changed screens again, back to where he'd clicked down a rabbit hole onto a page about 1-Quick Getaways staff. 'Right bunch of grumps this lot,' he said, and Marnie laughed. 'I'm not kidding.' He scrolled further, looking at photos from a party that seemed to be there for the sole purpose of letting potential employees see what a wonderful company they were to work for, but they couldn't have chosen a group of more sullen looking people. Most of them looked like they were there under duress, not at a social event. 'Oh, look.' Rafe stopped at a picture near the bottom with a group of people at a table. He read the caption underneath it. 'There's Tilly Thorpe, admin worker. She's the only person on the whole page who doesn't look depressed or thoroughly pissed off. She's got a lovely smile. Poor girl, stuck with that bunch of misery guts. Well, if they come knocking, we'll recognise them from their dour faces.'

Marnie sniggered. 'Should I try and memorise them?'

'I wouldn't. If you look at this page too long, you'll definitely not be merry this Christmas.' He flicked onto another screen and began typing the action plan and script.

Marnie chipped in with a few ideas. She only worked part-time now as she had a young child to look after, but when she was there, she made sure everyone in the office was cheery. Every office needed a Marnie, if only for moral support. 1-Quick Getaways could definitely use one.

'Right.' Marnie got to her feet. 'I'll get on with the Easter packages.'

'Ok,' Rafe said. 'Just don't get confused by all the Christmas carolling.'

Marnie had barely shut the door when Rafe's intercom buzzed. Leaning forward, he hit the accept button, gazing out of the window over the murky Glasgow skyline as he did.

'Hi, you've got a visitor,' admin worker Katrina said.

'Who is it?' For a second, Rafe wondered if it was spies from 1-Quick Getaways already in his backyard. He hadn't had time to disseminate the script or let Katrina know that if anyone from the company turned up unsolicited, they were not to be allowed into his office and should be told he was unavailable. No way would he let anyone get away with that. They could make an appointment and behave like civilised businesspeople.

'Your sister, Genevieve.'

'Oh shoot. Is that the time?' he said. 'Give me two minutes and I'll be down.'

He was supposed to be meeting her for a coffee while she was in Glasgow. The 1-Quick Getaways screen was still open from before and he went to close it and shut down the page of grumpy-faced gits. His eyes fell on the one smiley face among them. Tilly Thorpe. He couldn't help smiling back. Something about her face was magnetic and very sweet. On second view, her smile looked a little forced, like she was trying hard to enjoy herself. The picture was dated from a couple of years ago. Maybe she'd left since then. He doubted anyone with sense would stick around an unethical company that stooped to corporate espionage for long.

He logged off and shut down the computer, then grabbed his smart wool coat from behind the door. He swung it on and headed downstairs.

'Well, hello.' He spotted Genevieve in the foyer and strode over to give her a hug. 'Long time no see.'

'That's because you're always working.' She returned his hug with a laugh.

'True.' He turned to Katrina at the desk. 'I'll be about an hour if anyone's looking for me. Unless anyone from 1-Quick Getaways calls, in which case they're not to be allowed in without an appointment.'

'Is that likely?' Katrina said.

'No, but best be prepared. I'll be sending you all a protocol email later in the day, but it's not quite finished yet. If they do come calling, ring me, or call Marnie.'

'Ok. Have a nice time.'

'Thank you.' He opened the door for Genevieve and they stepped into the cool air. The upmarket office blocks and vibrant shop buildings on Ingram Street were a sharp contrast to the grey wintery light from the overcast sky. Rafe and Genevieve walked through the bustling street, passing the Christmas shoppers, and headed towards George Square.

'I assume you have somewhere in mind?' Rafe kept pace with his sister, who, despite her heeled boots, was walking at some speed.

'Let's get a hot chocolate at the Christmas market. And there's food there too. It's where I'm meeting Elise later, so I can wait for her there.'

'Oh joy,' he said. 'My favourite place.'

'Stop it, Scrooge.'

He laughed and put his arm around her. 'Only a semi-Scrooge. I like a hot chocolate as much as anyone. How is Elise these days?'

'She's ok, I think. She never really says. Since I married Finlay, I think she finds it a bit awkward.'

'Unsurprising.' Elise had been engaged to Finlay before Genevieve and the whole thing was complicated. Genevieve and Elise had been childhood friends and were also friends with Finlay's sister. Confusing, to say the least, but it had all worked out for Genevieve and Finlay... If not Elise. 'How's married life going anyway?' he asked.

'Very well.' She tossed her long caramel hair over her shoulder. 'I think I've officially been married longer than you now.'

'Funny.' His marriage had been one of the shortest non-events in history. It still created a sore spot for his mother, who viewed his divorce as a blight on her perfect family. But he'd been young and stupid back then. Now he'd done it, he could say *been there, done that, not doing it again*. It was easier for a workaholic to be single, and weekends were never lonely because he spent them doing what he loved most – travelling. He had a Ford Ranger Raptor all kitted out for the solo traveller. Even in midwinter, he liked a weekend by a deserted loch with hiking opportunities nearby. If he sometimes craved a travel companion – well, who needed to know that?

'You know Elise is currently single.' Genevieve stopped at the kerb. 'And with her living here these days... well.'

He cocked his head. 'Seriously? You're trying to set me up with one of your friends? Isn't she some kind of man-eater?'

Genevieve looked away, smirking. 'She's just had a bad run of things.'

He frowned. 'Wasn't she engaged to Finlay because she wanted to make someone else jealous?'

'Something like that.'

'Well, I don't need you to set me up with anyone. I'm perfectly happy dating... Well, the person I'm dating.' He ignored the look on Genevieve's face. This was his go-to story, and he fobbed his family off with it all the time – especially his mum. Lovely as she was, she was determined to marry off all her children like some kind of regency mother in a period drama. Technically, she'd succeeded as both Rafe's sisters were now married, and he had been too. But it wasn't enough for Hilary Harrington. She seemed to think his happiness depended on finding the right person, but he was in no hurry to go down that road again.

'Oh, come on, Rafe.' Genevieve was still looking at him with a raised eyebrow.

The lights changed to the green walk sign and Rafe used the moment to stride ahead. As he reached the other side and rounded the corner, a brass band struck up 'God Rest Ye Merry

Gentleman'. He shook his head. How did he manage to attract so much festive cheer without even trying?

'Who exactly are you dating then?' Genevieve caught him up.

'Isn't that music lovely?' He rubbed his gloved hands together. 'So Christmassy.'

'Stop changing the subject.' She prodded him on the upper arm. 'I know you don't even like Christmas music.'

'Sure I do. I've got Marnie the in-office entertainment singing carols all day.'

'You're still dodging. Who is this person you're happy dating? Or is it just someone you made up? Again? Like you did at my wedding. You said you were bringing a girlfriend, then funnily enough, she didn't show up. You never give us names or anything. What's really going on? If you're happy being single, then fine. But why make something up?'

Why indeed? Perhaps for the exact same reason Genevieve had faked her engagement to Finlay at first. Because having his family trying to set him up was annoying. He wanted to choose for himself, but he'd lost all confidence in dating. Maybe in himself.

After rushing into his marriage, he wanted to take the time to properly get to know the right person, but that presented a conundrum. He didn't want to devote too much time to dating because it often led nowhere. The process of meeting people was so all-consuming and frequently disappointing that it was easier to get in his van and head for the hills at weekends than to face going on a date. He'd let all his dating apps lapse and never logged into any of them.

Where did that leave him? Stuck in a rut. Alone. And there was the other issue. He didn't like being alone. He enjoyed company.

'Well?' Genevieve was still throwing him looks like she expected an answer. 'Why not just tell me who you're dating? It's a shame whoever she is missed the wedding. I assume she'll be coming to Mum and Dad's for Christmas.'

'I don't think she'll be able to do that.' He thrust his hands into his pockets, smirking. It was amusing that Genevieve even partially believed he was seeing someone. He'd always enjoyed a bit of harmless ribbing with her; one of the perks of being the roguish big brother. As children, he'd had her believe all sorts of things, including bears living up trees near their house, a witch owning a tumbledown cottage on the road to school, and the existence of unicorns during the full moon.

'What are you grinning at?' She half raised an eyebrow.

'Nothing.' Though he half-wondered if she was still scared to walk past the tumbledown cottage.

'Why is it funny that your "girlfriend",' she air-quoted, 'won't be coming to Mum and Dad's? Could it be she doesn't actually exist?'

Ah... So, she maybe couldn't be so easily fooled these days.

'Hark who's lecturing me! You're the one who got drunkenly engaged and kept that going, even though it wasn't real.'

'It was real. We just didn't realise. You were the one who said even fake things were real. They were just copies of the originals.'

'Did I?'

'You sure did.'

'Well...'

'Well, what? Who is this girlfriend?'

Rafe smirked and, in his mind, quite randomly, the picture of Tilly Thorpe from 1-Quick Getaways emerged. Her smile had been the sweetest thing he'd seen all day. An opportunity for a bit of fun popped up before him. 'Her name's Tilly. Tilly Thorpe. She lives in London, so it's difficult for us to see each other. She probably won't be able to come here for Christmas. The company she works for is notorious.'

Genevieve stopped, and he collided with her.

'What the—'

'Oh my god.' She gaped at him. 'You're actually... Wow. Ok. That's...'

'Made you speechless?' Ha! *Walked into it once again.* What a cute little sister she was. He winked at her.

'So, where does Tilly work?'

'At 1-Quick Getaways. It's a rival company, so that makes things even tougher, you know? And her bosses are all really grumpy.' Rafe smiled, holding eye contact with Genevieve as if they were twelve and seven again and engaging in a staring contest. He almost burst out laughing and completely gave the game away, but somehow he kept it together. The look on her face was worth the effort.

Then she narrowed her eyes. 'Tilly Thorpe indeed. Hmm.' She took off again, heading round the corner to George Square. Christmas lights twinkled all over it and little wooden cabins with fake snow were dotted around the big wheel in the middle.

'Lovely Tilly,' he said as they joined the queue for hot chocolate. 'She has a truly beautiful smile.'

Genevieve frowned and her eyes were still narrowed like she wasn't sure if she trusted him. No doubt with good reason. She possibly still sat up late into the night on a full moon waiting for the unicorns to appear.

'I hope I get to meet her someday soon,' Genevieve said.

'Oh, me too.' He smiled, but he sincerely hoped she didn't, especially as he'd never even met her himself.

Chapter Two

Tilly

Monday, December 16th

Evening

The train screeched along the tracks, jolting Tilly in her seat like someone was shaking her. Trying to read emails on her phone on the way home never really worked. It wasn't just the constant vibration of the train speeding from central London towards Slough, but the weariness that crept in and took hold. By the time she got to her station, then took the bus and walked the remaining distance to her flat, it would be almost nine o'clock. She'd barely have time to eat before bed and before she knew it, her alarm would be buzzing. Just in time to start the journey again, only in reverse.

She pressed the off button on her phone and leaned on the window, making brief eye contact with the man opposite. She smiled, but he looked away directly and closed his eyes, appearing to fall asleep immediately. That was a talent she didn't have. Sleeping on public transport had never been something she could do easily. She was sure she'd miss her stop and have to make her way back. Barely stifling a yawn, she stared out as the city lights passed by in a haze of orange and white, punctuated here and there with Christmas colours.

The railway cut past rows of houses and blocks of high-rise flats and, as the train slowed to come into a station, the view became more focused. Tilly caught glimpses of rooms lit up, like a series of snapshots into other people's lives. Televisions flickered. Christmas trees glowed. Flashing lights adorned windows, dazzling and gaudy. Others were soft and only hinted at anyone living there. Perhaps they weren't home yet or were already in bed. Maybe in another room? The kitchen, cooking dinner for their family or soaking in a bubble bath after a long hard day.

Those lights called to Tilly. Every evening, she found herself drawn to them and the images her mind conjured of the warmth and homeliness behind those windows. Of course, she had no idea who lived there – how could she? But every little scene seemed to whisper a welcome, inviting her to join them for the split second they were in her vision.

She gazed at the buildings as they passed by like they were dollhouses. If only she could shrink to their size and join in with their lives. Warmth and safety were in there. People who had families and friends. Tilly had never had much love for Christmas, but Christmas in those dollhouses might be fun. In those make-believe worlds, she could imagine it any way she wanted.

The train rattled into her station and Tilly shook herself out of her musings, picked up her bag and exited onto the cold platform. Shivering, she pulled her collar high against the drizzly rain. In her pocket, her phone vibrated with a message, then another and another. She'd check them when she got on the bus. Her hands were too cold to attempt that now. And really, who would it be? The only people who ever called her were from work and she'd had quite enough of them for one day... Though it never stopped. Even when she was out of the office, she was always on call. Or they expected her to be.

The bus was late and Tilly tapped her toes, trying to keep warm. Some noisy people outside a pub were heading her way and her heart flickered.

Please, let them walk on by. She kept her head down. The bus came around the corner and Tilly's shoulders lightened as the doors opened and she hopped on, flicking her travel card on the pad by the driver's booth.

She took a seat and checked her messages. One from her boss about a meeting he wanted her to attend at eight the following morning.

Seriously? Should I just sleep at my desk in the future?

What was the point of even having a flat? A flat with ridiculously high rental for its size and location.

The other two messages were from Mitchell, her coworker. Tilly's heart did a silly little leap at the sight of his name. She wished it wouldn't. Office crushes were the worst, and at twenty-six, was it normal to still get them? Her hopes of making it something more had been thoroughly dashed when she'd asked Mitchell if he fancied getting a drink with her, only to discover he was already dating another colleague. The humiliation at his rejection still burned. Now Tilly had to see them both and act like she'd never asked him in the first place or pretend she'd asked him as just friends.

She leaned back, trying to think about something else, but all their interactions from the week replayed in her head and made her cringe. Not that he was mean about it, but it was so awkward, and his girlfriend was either strutting about like she was delighted with herself or glowering at Tilly like she wanted to throttle her. None of it made for a pleasant working environment. But then, she'd found a place she belonged, and that counted for something. 1-Quick Getaways was the only place she'd ever worked, and the closest thing to stability she'd experienced. If she clung to it through the storms, that wasn't a bad thing, was it? Starting over was something she couldn't face, not when her whole life had involved so many restarts already.

Mitchell's messages were both about work. *Phew*. That was a relief. He wasn't impressed by the timing of the meeting the following morning and wanted to know if Tilly knew what it was about. Like she would. The managers wouldn't tell an admin assistant anything that important. Maybe after working there since she'd left school nine years ago, she could have expected to move up the career ladder a little, but so far, that hadn't happened.

As she climbed the stairs to her flat, the usual thudding music blared from 7B. *Oh no.* That was the flat directly beneath hers. There would be very little sleep tonight – again.

Tuesday, December 17th

Morning

Bleary-eyed Tilly arrived at the office door at eight the next morning with a large cup of coffee. The second she saw Mitchell, she pulled out her biggest smile. He didn't return it, but yawned. 'These early mornings are a killer,' he mumbled. 'I hope we're not getting fired.'

'Is that likely?' Tilly took a nervous sip. After all the hours she'd put in this year, she was surely due for a promotion, not a dismissal.

'I hope not,' Mitchell said. 'Not after the info I got in Manchester. I should be getting a bloody award for that.'

'I'm sure you will. They appreciate your work.' She carried on smiling at him, but he barely glanced at her. He was unlikely to be sacked; the managers had a soft spot for him. Much like Tilly had. She gulped some hot coffee. Even with a grumpy face, there was something about him.

'In you come.' Arnie Wilcox, the managing director, opened the door. 'Sorry to call you both in so early, but something urgent has come up.'

Tilly took a seat next to Mitchell, pretty sure all she was here for was to take the minutes. She gave Arnie a little smile, and he sent her one back with an odd little quirk of his eyebrow. Tilly's cheeks felt a little hot. He was good looking but must be at least fifty, probably older, and he was married for god's sake. But he had a kind of charm brought by power, smart suits, and expensive aftershave.

'I'm doing the Scotland job already,' Mitchell said. 'I won't have time to fit anything else in, even if it's urgent.' He spoke quickly, his voice a little sharp, and Tilly understood why. Being sent to Scotland seven days before Christmas was a pretty unreasonable request. Tilly often thought some of the directives from the managers were on the harsh side. But what did she know? This was how business worked. Getting ahead obviously meant using whatever methods, even if they didn't always sit well with her. But what could an admin assistant do about it?

Expecting Mitchell to travel to Scotland on a Wednesday night and be back by Friday night with all the information they requested was bad enough, but this close to Christmas? Why couldn't they just wait until January? *Not my place to figure it out.* Perhaps Mitchell's success was against him this time. He'd excelled himself in Manchester and now Arnie wanted that to continue.

'That's exactly what I want to talk about,' Arnie went on. 'Henry has laryngitis and can't go with you now, which is unfortunate because on trips like this, it's always worth having two of you. Double the chances of getting something useful.' He gave them a tiny wink. 'I'd like you to step in, Tilly.'

'Me?' Her jaw almost hit the floor... or in her mind it did, because she couldn't actually move a muscle. 'But that's tomorrow, and I have no idea what to do. I've never done a...' What should she call it? She guessed these visits were barely disguised spying missions – chances to infiltrate the opposition and harvest as much information as possible. Not something she liked the sound of and definitely not something she had the first clue how to pull off.

'I'll give you full details on what we expect from these scoping visits. I believe you're the perfect person for the job. You always have a smile on your face; it attracts confidence. You'll be ideally placed to get the information we need. Mitchell is very experienced in these matters. He'll help you out.'

'I...' Mitchell looked at Tilly and she tried to smile at him, but his expression told her he was not impressed by this turn of events.

'What if I slip up?'

'You won't.' Arnie leaned forward. 'No need to worry. This isn't some underhand visit, and I don't want you to view it as such. It's important for our future and I'm counting on you, Tilly. You've worked here a long time.' He checked something on his computer screen. 'You've had some good ideas.'

Her cheeks heated again. Once, she'd attempted to pitch what she thought was a great idea to Arnie, but he hadn't seemed particularly interested. Now he thought it was good?

'We've taken on your suggestion about the eco-tourism and I've got some of my top people working on the idea.'

He had? But who were these people, and why wasn't she involved?

'This could stand you in very good stead for the future,' Arnie continued. 'If this trip is a success, it could lead to great places. Even better if you can persuade them to work with us.'

Tilly's heart pounded in her ears. Could she do it? Was it just a case of chatting with people and finding out what she could? She'd probably be great at that. She was good at watching and listening. Often, it was easier than joining in.

'Ok.' She took a deep breath. 'If you tell me exactly what I have to do.'

When she and Mitchell left the room, Mitchell rolled his eyes. 'Not sure why he's chosen you to do this. No offence, but you're not exactly qualified for it.'

'I know that, but...' Tilly blinked, not sure what to say. Ever since she'd asked Mitchell for that drink, he'd been off with her. How was it her fault she hadn't realised he already had a girl-friend? Before that, he'd always seemed so nice. But how often had she thought that about someone?

'And Scotland.' Mitchell let out a low groan. 'It's such a frigging long way to go.'

Tilly tried not to hear any unspoken words, but couldn't help thinking he'd added, 'and to be stuck with you' inside his head.

'Well, it'll be a good experience for me.' She brought her hands together and slapped on her smile. 'I've never been to Scotland before.'

'This isn't a sightseeing trip. You won't have time to do any-thing other than work. And Scotland is an ugly, cold place any-way.' Mitchell sighed. 'You need to study the two places we're visiting. One of them is Innova-Travel. Have you heard of them?'

'Yeah, they're pretty big.' Tilly swallowed the disappointment that she wouldn't get to do any sightseeing.

'Arnie's going out for the big guns. Innova is top of the game for the prestige market, and he wants all the information he can get.'

'How did you get it in Manchester?'

His easy grin returned, and he ran his fingers through his hair. 'Just played it cool, made friends with some of the staff, got chatting to them and we went for drinks, then I asked a few questions. Once we find their weak spots, we know where to strike.'

'I'm not sure I can do any of that.'

Mitchell smirked. 'Innova has a good reputation, but sometimes good people are easy to get around.'

Tilly nodded. That might be true, but she didn't like the sound of it. Not after what she'd been through in her childhood. Arnie may call this a scoping mission, but was it really anything other than spying? Still, it was what she was being paid to do, and she had to try her best.

Wednesday, December 18th

Evening

Sleeping on a reclining chair on the sleeper train that night proved to be as impossible as sleeping on any other form of public transport. Mitchell was flat out, wearing the ugly sleep mask they'd provided, his head lolling to the side. Tilly was glad she'd never gone on a date with him. That snoring would have been hard to get used to. But would it have been any better than the blaring music from the flat downstairs?

She'd lost touch with the dating scene, much like the way she'd lost touch with most of the friends she'd made growing up. Maybe that wasn't surprising, given how all over the place her young life had been. Sometimes she struggled with the fact she was only twenty-six; she felt so much older, and dating seemed like something other people did. People who weren't tired to the bones from working all hours and commuting. People who had exciting lives to share. People who didn't need to be ashamed of their past or their family... or lack thereof.

Tilly looked out the window into the blackness, sporadically glimpsing little dollhouses as they passed through towns. She tried closing her eyes every now and then, but sleep was as far from her as the North Pole. Occasionally, she drifted, but the train would jolt, and she'd be wide awake again. Perhaps she always slept with one eye open. A habit she'd learned as a child and never shaken off.

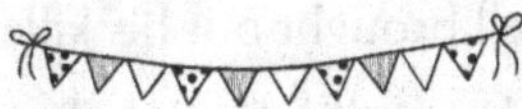

Thursday, December 19th

Morning

By the time they reached Glasgow on Thursday morning, Tilly was exhausted and completely discombobulated. She couldn't stop yawning as they got a taxi and headed for the hotel. Mitchell rolled his eyes and shook his head, no doubt assuming she couldn't see him as he was facing the other way, but she spied his reflection. They left their cases at the hotel, but weren't able to check in until later. Still in the clothes she'd put on last night, they set off for Innova-Travel's head office. Hopefully Mitchell would do most of the talking because Tilly was so bushed she was sure she'd say something stupid as soon as she opened her mouth.

Struggling to hold back another yawn, she followed Mitchell towards the glass doors of an office perfectly slotted into an old Victorian sandstone building. She glanced up, briefly observing the amazing architecture of the street before Mitchell opened the door. Inside was a very white reception area with a tall Christmas tree in the corner next to a rounded desk where a woman sat at a computer. Along the walls were a series of photographs of landscapes and one of a very dramatic house. Tilly focused on it for a second until the woman spoke.

'Good morning. Can I help you?'

'Morning.' Mitchell brought out his killer smile. No wonder Arnie chose him to do this kind of job; he could switch on the charm at the drop of a hat. Tilly had fallen for it, but when she thought logically about it, he wasn't right for her. Clearly he didn't like her as much as she'd hoped. Now, it seemed like she annoyed him more than anything.

'We have a meeting with Rafe Harrington,' Mitchell contin-ued. Tilly clasped her hands in front of her and smiled. Had he already arranged a meeting? Or was that a lie? He sounded so confident.

'Let me see.' The receptionist typed something into her computer and looked at the screen. 'I don't see anything here for Mr Harrington today.'

'Hmm,' Mitchell said. 'That's odd. Maybe we could go in and see him anyway, or if he's available this afternoon, that would be fine.'

The woman clicked away at her keyboard. 'What's your name?'

'Mitchell Hayward.'

'And what's your business with Mr Harrington?'

'Market research.'

'Which company are you representing?'

'Is Mr Harrington available?' Mitchell continued, smiling. 'It would be good if we could see him as soon as possible. We're on a fairly tight schedule.'

'Can you tell me your company name, please?'

'1-Quick Getaways,' Tilly said.

Mitchell gave her an exasperated look, but Arnie hadn't said to hide it, and this sneaking their way in didn't feel right. It wouldn't exactly foster any confidence. If they were to find out anything useful, they'd need to build up a working relationship. Surely, honesty was the best place to start. But then, when had her approach to anything ever brought success? Maybe she'd have been better off keeping her mouth shut.

'Unfortunately, Mr Harrington isn't in Glasgow this week. He's gone home to his family for Christmas. I can make an appointment for you sometime in the new year, or you can email him. He might pick up his emails during the holidays.'

'Where is his home?' Mitchell asked.

Tilly tossed him the same look he'd given her just a moment ago. Surely he wasn't considering following the man to his home?

'Nowhere near here,' the woman said. 'And I doubt he'd appreciate a work visit.'

'Of course,' Tilly said. 'And just to make this clear, we're here on a networking visit and would welcome an informal chat with Mr Harrington, that's all.'

The receptionist lifted her left eyebrow slightly, betraying her scepticism. 'Would you like me to pencil you in for a date in the new year?'

'That would be fine.' Tilly gave her a warm smile.

Mitchell glared at her again, but she kept her focus away from him as the woman clicked her keyboard. 'His first available date is January the twenty-third.'

'That's more than a month away,' Mitchell said.

'He's a busy man.'

'That's fine.' Tilly didn't drop her smile, and the receptionist smiled back.

'Great. You're in the calendar.'

'That's a beautiful house.' Tilly gazed at the aerial photo on the wall. It was like something out of *Grand Designs* with an all-glass front and a glass tower in the centre flanked by balconied terraces on either side and with a green roof, so the whole building looked to be coming out of the ground.

'It's a bespoke eco house built by Mr Harrington's parents.'

'Wow, it's gorgeous.' Tilly adjusted her glasses and squinted at the small print at the bottom of the picture. Greenacres, Glenbriar. She had no idea where that was.

'Yes, it really is.' The receptionist carried on typing. 'Ok. I've put you in for a meeting that day.'

'Thanks,' Mitchell said, his expression grim. As soon as they were on the street, he put his hands on his hips and shook his head. 'Why did you agree to that?'

'We won't get anywhere with sneaky methods.'

'What are you talking about? I'm not doing anything sneaky. It's about being smart and personable.'

'It's about building trust,' Tilly countered, and if that was what he considered being personable, it was a miracle he'd got anyone to open up in Manchester.

'And for that, we need to be smart and personable, like I said. We can't just blurt stuff out and agree to any old thing, like meeting up in a month's time. That's giving them too much time.'

'I didn't blurt it out.' Did she? 'I was just looking for a compromise.'

Mitchell shook his head. 'This is why you'll always be stuck in admin. You don't get business. There's more to it than flashing that smile and agreeing with everyone. You should have let me handle that receptionist.'

'What?' She looked away and shook her head. If she could muster the energy to get angry with him, she would try, but she couldn't. She was too exhausted. Did she agree with everyone? She didn't agree with him right now, but falling out wasn't a good plan. Not when they had another day and a half to get through.

'I bet he's sitting in there right now.' Mitchell jabbed his thumb back towards the Innova office.

'What were you going to say to him if we got in there?'

'We just need to open a dialogue. Pave a path about the positives. Test the water and gain his confidence.'

'Well, if you really want to see him at home, we could try visiting the house that was in the picture.'

'What house?' Mitchell frowned, then smiled. 'Oh, that one you mentioned to the receptionist. Is that why you were asking about it? Clever. So, you're actually sneakier than you look.'

'No, just smarter. We're not being sneaky, remember?'

He chuckled. 'Thing is, we don't know if he's actually there. His family might have built the house, but they might not live in it. And he might have gone elsewhere or nowhere. Who knows? It's too risky.'

Risky or stupid? Sneaky or smart? Crazy or worth a shot?

'Yeah, you're right.' She really was no good at this kind of thing.

'But you know what?' Mitchell's smile grew. 'That was smart, and I think you should do it.'

'What about you?'

'I need to get back tomorrow night, or my girlfriend will kill me. You can spend the extra day travelling about, if you want? I can't risk not getting back.'

Every one of his words carried a sting.

'But don't worry, I'll tell you exactly what to say and how to play it. This could be your big moment.'

Could it?

Tilly had devoted so much time to 1-Quick. When she'd got the job there, the sense of belonging was overwhelming. She'd never had anything so stable in her life. She owed them. Now, she had a steady job, a home of her own, albeit a small one, and she didn't want to jeopardise that.

Could one more day in Scotland be all it took? One day that could be the defining moment of her career... Maybe even her life.

Chapter Three

Rafe

Friday, December 20th

Morning

'Sorry to do this on the last day before the Christmas break,' Rafe said to the staff as they sat around the conference table. 'But after we had the 1-Quick spies in yesterday, I just want to check in and make sure everyone is happy with the script and familiar with what to do if they call again before January the twenty-third. Katrina did an amazing job of keeping them out yesterday.'

'I can't believe the nerve of them.' Marnie shook her head, dislodging her star deely-boppers.

'Thing is, if we were the first company they'd approached, we wouldn't have known any better. I'm not against working with other companies, but I don't appreciate their methods. They're very aggressive. We all need to be very careful with any information we give out to anyone from outside the company. This time, they straight up asked to see me, but I understand in Manchester, it was an informal chat with staff that led to the data breach, so let's all be careful with what we talk about.'

'Are we talking about customer details being stolen?' Jonah, one of the project managers, asked.

'Not in this instance. It was market research the company had carried out and showed various trends and pockets of growth in the area. 1-Quick took it all and targeted the customers with better deals.'

Jonah let out a low whistle. 'Sneaky.'

'Very.' Rafe opened a screen on his laptop and connected it to the smartboard. 'Let's go through this and get it out of the way.' He checked his watch. He was leaving early to drive to his parents' house in Glenbriar, in Highland Perthshire. The weather for that area was looking decidedly ropey, and he wanted to give himself plenty of time. Snow was forecast for the afternoon and while road closures were unusual, they weren't unheard of, especially given the location of the house. He may make it to the town but the house was some miles out and the long sloping driveway was a nightmare to negotiate in bad weather, even for the Raptor.

Everyone looked like they were desperate to get away and start their holiday and he didn't want to be the Scrooge prolonging their working day any longer than necessary. He went over the protocols as quickly as he could, praying everyone was taking them in.

'Right, everyone, that's all. If you can clear your emails and get pretty much up to date, then don't hang about later. I'm off early, and I don't expect anyone to be here late. Get home and enjoy some time with your folks.'

Everyone wished him a merry Christmas as they left the room until only he and Marnie were left.

'I'll still check emails while we're off,' he said. 'And if you need to check in, that's fine.'

She smiled. 'You need to switch off and relax. For someone who runs a travel company, you're pretty crap at taking holidays yourself.'

'Yeah. I know.' He'd barely had more than a couple of days off all year. Occasionally, he took Friday afternoons so he could drive somewhere for the weekend, but even when he was away, he checked emails and kept up to date. Switching off just wasn't in his nature.

His phone lit up just as he was shutting down the smartboard and he spied the top of a message from his sister. Opening it, he noticed she'd posted it on the family group chat.

GENEVIEVE: Look forward to seeing everyone today. Especially hoping to meet the wonderful Tilly (@Rafe). Hope she's made it up from London to spend some time with us.

He rolled his eyes and shook his head, though he couldn't help a little smile. He'd brought this on himself, after all.

RAFE: Unlikely. The staff at 1-Quick Getaways are exception-ally busy right now.

'Spying on me,' he muttered to himself. He now had a potential meeting with a Mitchell Hayward in January. Plenty of time to prepare for whatever they planned to throw at him.

Another message pinged in.

MUM: Oh, that's a shame. I'd really love to meet her. I hear she has a beautiful smile. Let's hope she gets the time off.

He shook his head and chuckled. Seriously? Genevieve had properly fallen for his story. But this couldn't go on all week. Still, if it stopped his mum trying to set him up with her friend's children over the festive period, he might eke it out a little longer. Then he and Tilly could 'split up' after Christmas. Definitely not before. He didn't want to have to act heartbroken. He'd just have to play it down and say they were still in early days. The distance was proving awkward, and he was too emotional to talk about it. At least that would give him plenty of excuses to hide in his room when he was pretending to call her.

Not that he wanted to avoid his family. He didn't mind the banter, but sometimes it got too much. His mum was well-meaning, but she didn't seem to accept that people didn't have to be married or in a relationship to be happy. And then there was his dad, who was desperate for Rafe to take on his business. While they got on well for the most part, there was a lingering sense of disquiet between the two of them. Dad was closing in on retirement and he was desperate to pass his company onto one of his children. Rafe was the obvious choice. He had the right business background, but the fact he'd started his own business and not wanted to work with his father had always been a niggling source of irritation between them. Even if Dad didn't often say so out loud, it was always there, like somehow he'd stepped off the expected path and was causing grief just by doing his own thing. Guilt nibbled at his insides when he thought of his dad having to sell the company he'd built from scratch when he retired, but it didn't change the fact that Rafe had his own business. Why couldn't that be equally as important?

Before he left the office, he toyed with the idea of emailing the CEO of 1-Quick Getaways, saying he didn't appreciate their methods, but he left it. What was the point? It was Christmas, after all. He packed away his laptop and collected his coat.

The Christmas tree in the main office twinkled, and Marnie was humming 'Jingle Bell Rock' as he went over to say goodbye. 'Hope you have a good Christmas,' he said. 'And that your wee one is suitably spoiled.'

Marnie beamed. 'Oh, he will be. Don't worry. Santa will have to visit a chiropractor after lugging his sack down our chimney.'

Rafe chuckled. 'Gotta love it for the kids, eh?'

'Sure do. I hope you have a good time too.'

'Well, you know how much I love Christmas.'

'Don't we all? As soon as you're out of here, we're putting on the Crimbo Mega-mix and getting out the crackers and party hats.'

'I might have known.'

'Seriously, have a proper break,' Marnie said. 'Take some me-time and do something for yourself.'

'I honestly have no idea what that would be.'

'Ask Santa to bring you something nice... You never know what you might get.'

'I'll try that.' He waved goodbye to everyone and left, fully expecting to hear Slade at full volume before he got to the bottom of the stairs. He said goodbye to Katrina and made his way into the cold. Snow was rare in the city but that still, almost too silent feeling had settled over the busy streets. He'd always thought it silly when people said they knew snow was coming because they could feel it, but now he understood.

His phone buzzed, and he checked it again. The family group chat had more new messages, including one from his almost-eighty-year-old grandma – who had a love of social media and texting.

GRANDMA: Ooh, I'm intrigued. I was going to stay at home this weekend and come over on Christmas Eve, but if there's a chance of meeting your girlfriend, I'm on my way over. Can you give me a lift, Genevieve?

GENEVIEVE: Sure thing. Be over soon x

Rafe groaned, passing festive displays in shop windows and catching snippets of Christmas music from inside. This was getting worse. Too late to head granny off at the pass if she was already on her way to the house.

He made his way to the subway, affectionately known in Glasgow as the clockwork orange – due to its colour more than its schedule. Though, to be fair, delays were unusual. Marnie's words fluttered back. What would he ask Santa for if he could have anything in the world? His dad would ask for him to takeover the business. His mum would ask for him to find the perfect partner. Maybe deep down he shared her wish, though he didn't think he'd leave it up to a man in a red suit to decide on his life partner. The sensible thing would be to start up his dating apps again. Maybe that could be his new year resolution – after he'd split with Tilly Thorpe.

It would be a lot simpler if she would just come to life and save him from having to make up yet more stories. Ha, what would Genevieve make of that? Did she really believe all this? Or was she now winding him up in return? That seemed more likely. Ah, well, he could always suck it up with the mince pies and mulled wine and confess. They could all have a good laugh at him. Grandma would tell him off for dragging her away from her cosy house on a wild goose chase, but at least they'd all be together.

As he entered Buchanan Street, the huge Christmas lights above were dazzling. The faint sound of the brass band trumpeting 'Once in Royal David's City' was almost lost in the low buzz of traffic and chatter. Why couldn't he fall in love with Christmas? He wanted to look around and see magic, but all he saw was glitter and consumerism. Sure, it was great for business –

people loved a festive break – but that was about the most joyful thing he saw in it. As soon as it was all over, business would do another boom with people looking to escape the January blues by booking holidays. That was what he was looking forward to, but it seemed kind of mercenary. Maybe his Christmas wish should be to find the magic in Christmas again. It hadn't always felt as flat as this.

He dropped a twenty-pound note into a homeless guy's cup before dashing down the stairs to the subway, not waiting for a reaction. He didn't need thanks or praise, but maybe it would buy him some credits with the universe and help make one of his Christmas wishes come true.

Chapter Four

Tilly

Friday, December 20th

Afternoon

Open countryside whizzed by as the train sped north. Tilly put her phone on the table and looked out in awe. For someone who worked in travel, she didn't know Scotland at all. Or anywhere, for that matter. She wanted to, but holidaying alone was awkward... and she was pretty much alone most of the time. Even now. Mitchell had left her to it, though he'd spent the previous evening in the hotel going through every way she could approach this and how best to get Rafe Harrington to open up about his latest market solutions and target groups. This was her chance to prove herself to the bosses at 1-Quick.

The journey was worth it, if nothing else. Mitchell had been right in thinking she had nothing to rush home for. Maybe she could spend the weekend here. As long as she was back by Monday morning, it would be fine.

Lifting her phone, she googled Glenbriar and flicked through available hotels. It might be fun to stay an extra night here before she went home, but everything was fully booked and the nearest availability was in Perth. That might do at a push, but maybe she should save it for another time. She needed to focus on the meeting with Rafe Harrington. Assuming she got to see him, and that was a pretty big assumption. This whole trip could be a massive waste of time and energy. But she'd narrowed down exactly what she was going to say. She'd apologise for crashing his family time but say she was passing anyway and wanted to personally introduce herself before they opened a dialogue in January. Showing a more human face wouldn't do any harm, and if she was lucky, he might grant her a short time to talk, and she would seize the moment. Hopefully she could channel some of Mitchell's determination and justify Arnie's faith in her.

He thought her smile would do the trick; Mitchell didn't. He'd said smiling and agreeing with people would get her nowhere. Who was right? Were any of them? Was this whole idea insane? Or even worth the risk?

Keeping her head down, fitting in, and not rocking the boat was what she was all about. A niggle in her mind told her this course of action might not just rock the boat, but capsize it. As long as 1-Quick got what they wanted... But what about Rafe Harrington and Innova? Why did what 1-Quick was doing feel all wrong? Neither Arnie nor Mitchell thought it was sneaky or underhand. Mitchell had done something similar in Manchester and had great success. And really, what was the worst that could happen? She got turned away. Well, fine. She would take that and move on. At least she'd tried.

As the train slowed through towns, she caught more snapshots of houses and was drawn into the imaginary worlds behind their windows, or in their wintery gardens. The view was so different from the urban sprawl of London. So much space. Open countryside and snowcapped hills were never far away. Rivers snaked their way through the valleys and lochs glinted in the distance. Just beautiful.

Tilly's bed in the hotel room had been softer than she was used to, and she'd caught up on some sleep. Adrenaline was keeping her going, but she was looking forward to having Christmas Day off, not because she was doing anything festive but because she could rest. Relaxing and doing nothing were things she'd almost forgotten about. She tried at weekends, but they went so quickly once she'd fitted in food shopping, laundry, housework, and the inevitable emails that would come in even when the office was supposedly shut.

She used to enjoy running, but now even that felt like a chore. As she watched more hills go by, she wondered what it would be like to climb them. The views must be amazing. Would she ever do that?

The countryside got steadily wilder as the train left Perth. Glenbriar was just a few stops away now. The sky was pale grey – almost white. Did that mean snow was coming? She'd very rarely experienced snow. The weather app on her phone showed a chance of showers and heavy snow over high ground and rural glens. This wasn't too rural, was it?

She opened her phone again. The whole way she'd resisted doing this, but she couldn't resist any more. In between getting instructions from Mitchell the previous evening, she'd spent some time googling Rafe Harrington. She wanted to look again, and check she'd got the right person. Not that there was any doubt. The name was hardly common. The saved search came up, and she scrolled down the photos. This, more than any other objection, made her stomach twist. Before looking him up, she'd imagined Rafe Harrington as a kindly old man who looked like Father Christmas. Why? He definitely wasn't old, and he didn't look like someone prone to a belly that wobbled like a bowlful of jelly. He was handsome – alarmingly so – and he looked tall and fit in the group photos that came up. He'd won awards and there were several pictures of him getting plaques and certificates. When Tilly looked at his headshot, she had a weird sensation in her chest like she already knew him, though she was sure they hadn't met. She stared at the photo again and it seemed to call to her, much like the twinkling lights in the houses she passed on the train. Photos couldn't tell her anything about a person. Why then, did she see someone kind, generous, caring, and loving, and not just a flat image of a man?

She knew the answer to that. It was limerence. She'd been warned about it before, and it was all linked to her upbringing. Not something she wanted to think about right now. Her mind was too full of other things. Like why approaching a man like this was a lot more daunting than an encounter with a Santa lookalike. It threw up unwanted memories of dates she'd been on. Those cringy first meetings, where she was sure to over share or say something stupid. And there it was, back to her own issues again. Her innate problem of thinking guys felt more for her than they inevitably did. She understood why it happened, but it didn't take away the awkwardness. Obviously this wasn't a date, but the level of discomfiture would be on a par with that. What if she blushed or got tongue tied?

This had disaster written all over it.

She leaned her chin on her fist and gazed out of the window. She'd got this far, and it felt quite adventurous and freeing doing something like this by herself. Even if Rafe Harrington kicked her out, so what? At least she'd shown initiative and not given up at the first hurdle.

Glenbriar Station platform was small, quaint and super cute. The view down the track was of rolling hills, all snow-capped and very dramatic. An old Victorian building on the platform was neatly painted with a blue trim. It was no longer a ticket office but a bookshop with a little cart outside under the glass canopy and a large Christmas tree beside it. Fairy lights twinkled around the window display, making the shop appear like something straight out of a Dickens novel.

Tilly resisted going in even though the lights and the warmth called to her. She'd check it out on the way back. Right now, she was on a mission, and she wanted to get it done. The tension in her body wouldn't let up until this was over and she'd given it her best shot.

She made her way off the platform and into a small car park. A solitary taxi was waiting. Was it there for someone specific or available to whoever showed up? Only a couple of other people had got off and they seemed to be heading for cars.

Risk it?

Well, this whole trip was a risk, so why not? She knocked on the window and the driver opened it.

'Hi.' She smiled at him. 'Are you available for hire or are you waiting for someone?'

'I'm available.' He had a deep and gentle Scottish accent. 'Where are you heading?'

'It's a house called Greenacres. I'm not exactly sure where it is. It's a big eco-type house.'

'I know the place. It's a few miles out though, so it'll cost a bit.'

'That's fine.' Expenses would pay for it. 'But how many miles?' This might take longer than she'd expected.

'Six or seven. Should take about fifteen minutes.'

As the taxi pulled out of the station, rain pattered against the windscreen, but it was more like sleet. Within a few minutes, it was coming down thick and fast and the wipers were working overtime.

Tilly's heart fell with every passing metre. They left the town and headed along a country road. Where was this place? Should she ask the driver to wait for her once they got there? She didn't want the meeting with Rafe to be too long, just an introduction and a chance to chat to him. She went over the speech in her head she'd rehearsed with Mitchell. Gain his confidence and trust first.

Easier said than done.

'This is it here, lass.' The driver pulled in at the side of the road, then down a winding driveway.

'Are you able to come back for me?' she asked.

'When?' he glanced up, a little puzzled. 'Aren't you here to stay?'

'No... I just have a meeting.'

'Ah right. Here's my card then. Give me a call when you're done.'

'Thanks.' She took the card, paid, and got out. The sleet had turned to snow and fat flakes were falling, lying silently on the path. It was like a Christmas card, only she was living in it. Except her business here wasn't exactly joyful.

Finding the main door proved tricky as the house curved around and she took tentative steps along the path, now frosted with snow. She had her suitcase with her, which must look ridiculous and not at all professional. Lights flickered at a window, and she spotted a beautiful Christmas tree beside a door. This was another dollhouse she wanted to open and play with – the biggest one ever. What was it like inside? Her chest ached at the thought of coming home to a place like this, full of family and love.

She'd reached the door.

This was it. Raising her hand, she held her breath. She had to do it.

After another brief hesitation, she rang the doorbell.

No going back now. It wasn't like she could go anywhere else. She wasn't entirely sure exactly where she was. For a few seconds, she was sure no one would answer and the tension in her body lifted. If she turned and ran, could she catch the taxi? She could tell Arnie she'd tried, and no one was in.

Then she heard voices, and the door clicked open. A young woman smiled at Tilly from inside, and her heart and mind froze. Surely this was Rafe's wife. Of course he'd be married. He probably had children. Just because Tilly was a loner didn't mean everyone else was. Why had she not thought about that? The woman in his office had said he'd gone home for Christmas and that inferred going to be with family.

Oh god.

'I'm here to see Rafe Harrington.' Tilly tried to channel Mitchell's confidence, though most of her wanted to turn and run. She pulled out what she hoped was her best and most assured smile.

'Oh. He's not back yet.' The woman frowned slightly though her lips were still curved upwards. 'Are you Tilly?'

'Um...' Tilly stared at her, her pulse quickening. How the heck did she know that? 'Yes.'

'Tilly Thorpe?'

Tilly nodded. What on earth? Had Mitchell somehow got hold of Rafe Harrington and his whole family were prepped for her visit?

'Oh my god.' The woman held up her hands like she was about to cheer, a grin splitting her face. 'This is so awesome. In you come. Get out of the snow.'

Awesome?

What?

'I can't believe my brother,' she said. 'Sometimes he's... Well, never mind. Let me get Mum. She'll be over the moon. Just drop your case there and come on into the kitchen. It's lovely and warm. Dad's out walking the dogs, but I don't think he'll be too long. It's getting wild out there.'

Completely side-swiped, Tilly did what the woman said and followed her. This wasn't the welcome she was expecting.

'Is Rafe...?'

'He'll be here soon. Oh my god, I'm being so rude. I haven't even introduced myself. It feels like I already know you from what Rafe told me. I'm Genevieve, his little sister.'

'Um... Pleased to meet you.' Tilly smiled and was about to hold out her hand to shake it when Genevieve pulled her into a hug. *What the hell?*

She must be missing something somewhere.

'Oh, Tilly. This is just brilliant.' Genevieve's embrace was warm and kindly. She patted Tilly's back. Not used to this kind of thing, Tilly felt like she should pull away and explain that she didn't know what was going on, but something about it was so comforting that she couldn't move. Why was Rafe's sister pleased to see her? And what had he told her? How could he have told her *anything*? Tilly had never met him. Something weird was happening here, but she had no idea what. Was this a trap? His way of getting back at 1-Quick by having his family be incredibly friendly and welcoming? Perhaps to lull her into a false sense of security.

But he didn't know I'd be here, did he?

Still frowning and trying to mentally fit things together that didn't want to fit, Tilly pulled back.

Genevieve released her and smiled. 'You look exhausted. Was the trip up from London a complete nightmare?'

How did she know all this stuff?

'It's a long way and I don't sleep well on public transport,' Tilly replied.

'Oh, I totally get that. I couldn't either. Take a seat.'

The kitchen was a huge open-plan room that somehow perfectly combined space-age with rustic. The combination of sleek metal and wood was aesthetically pleasing. Tilly sat on one of the high barstools. The work surface stretched out like a canvas and could have been plucked straight from a Christmas food magazine. Under-cupboard lighting glowed, highlighting bowls of nuts, plates of biscuits, and trays of gingerbread squares.

The air was alive with the scent of spices and freshly baked treats, but it wasn't overpowering, just warming. Tilly could almost relax here if it wasn't for the strangeness of the situation. Classical Christmas music drifted around, and she felt like she was featuring in her very own Christmas film.

Genevieve opened the fridge door. 'What can I get you to drink? I don't know about you, but it feels like hot chocolate weather.'

'If you really don't mind.'

'Of course I don't. I'll just heat up some milk and go grab Mum. She's been dying to meet you. And if Grandma's awake, I'll get her too. She came here especially to see you. She'll be so excited.'

Tilly furrowed her brow and sucked on the inside of her lip. Why would Rafe's mum be dying to meet her? And his grandma had come especially to see her? This had to be a wind up, surely.

Genevieve put a jug of milk in the microwave, then said, 'Give me a minute; I'll just get Mum and see if Grandma's awake.'

What should she do? Tell her she didn't understand why they were being so welcoming? Or would that make her look rude? She wanted to make a good impression, even if this was a trap.

But it didn't seem to be, unless Genevieve was a really good actress, which was possible.

Or am I doing it again?

The childhood trauma was really rearing its head today. Was this the attachment issues showing up again? Maybe she was seeing things the way she wanted to see them and imagining Genevieve liked her more than she actually did. Tilly's old therapist had warned her about her tendency to do that in romantic situations, but it was entirely possible she was doing the same here. Now she knew about it, she identified it everywhere in her life.

'Tilly! Hello, hello.' An older woman, who was very like Genevieve, almost ran into the room. Tilly didn't have a chance to get off the stool before she was engulfed in another hug. 'I'm Hilary, Rafe's mum. So delighted you could make it. We weren't sure if you would, but this is a wonderful surprise.' Her perfume was delicate and calming. What must it be like to have a mum who hugged like this when you came home for Christmas?

What must it be like to have a mum at all?

Tilly had no family. Well, unless you included her sister, but Tilly didn't, not after what Ellie had done to her as a child. Some things were unforgivable. Even at Christmas.

She smiled at Rafe's mum, not sure what to say.

'Very pleased to meet you, dear.' An elderly lady with a walking stick shuffled forward and gave her a brief hug and a peck on the cheek. 'Such a beautiful smile indeed.'

Genevieve let out a little laugh as she scooped chocolate powder into the hot milk and whizzed it with a little hand-held electronic whisk. Tilly frowned. Were they laughing at some private joke? Soon, the hot chocolate was frothy and looked delicious. Genevieve poured it into four tall glasses with little round handles. 'Cream?' She smiled at Tilly.

'If you don't mind.'

'Not at all.'

Tilly was almost holding her breath as Rafe's mum and granny sat beaming at her like they'd never seen anyone so wonderful. This moment would surely crash down around her at any second. Perhaps they'd poisoned the hot chocolate or were waiting until Rafe got back so they could tell him how she'd imposed on them. Memories flooded back of childhood days with Ellie. All those times they'd had chances to live with nice people in foster care. Ellie had ruined those chances one by one. She wasn't here to ruin this moment, but something surely would.

Tilly would have a taste of something wonderful only to be thrown from the house and have the door slammed in her face; an all too familiar scenario.

Genevieve squirted the cream on top of the hot chocolates and handed a glass to Tilly. Outside the window, the snow was getting thick. How long would Rafe be? Tilly checked the time; she was on a tight turn around if she was to get back to Glasgow and then get the sleeper train home. Her fleeting idea of staying an extra night had evaporated. She should get away as soon as she could.

'It's very pretty here.' She watched the snow fluttering down, mesmerising her for a moment.

'We're so lucky with this spot.' Hilary sipped her hot chocolate. 'It must be quite different from what you're used to.'

'It is. I haven't seen snow for a long time. And when it snows in London, it's hardly ever as thick as this.'

'Well, you can enjoy it here,' Rafe's grandma said.

'I'm not sure how long it'll last,' Hilary added. 'It normally clears up after a few days and it'll be a miracle if it's still here for Christmas day.'

'Yeah, we hardly ever get a white Christmas,' Genevieve said.

Tilly took another sip of her hot chocolate. Much as she would like to enjoy sitting here watching the falling snow, it wasn't going to happen because she couldn't relax. Something bizarre was going on. Why were they all looking at her like that? Like they were actually pleased to see her.

Just my imagination. Attachment issues gone wild again.

'How do you normally spend Christmas?' Genevieve asked. 'Do you go to see family?'

Tilly shook her head. 'I don't really have a family.'

'Oh dear,' Hilary said. 'We didn't know that.'

Well, they wouldn't, would they?

'That's sad,' Genevieve said.

'I'm used to it.' Tilly gulped some of the cream from her hot chocolate. 'I never knew my parents. I was brought up in a children's home.' Ellie had scuppered any chance of being fostered long term or adopted with her desperate need to sabotage anything good. And not just for herself, for Tilly too. So they'd been stuck in the home every Christmas. Not exactly the stuff of dreams. After a while she got used to it, but watching Christmas films and reading Christmas books where everyone found the magic of Christmas and happiness at home with their family always hit a sore spot.

'That sounds so lonely,' Genevieve said. 'Thank goodness you met—'

'Hello!' a man shouted from somewhere in the house.

'That's Rafe,' Hilary said. Both she and Genevieve got to their feet while her grandma continued to sip her hot chocolate, barely taking her eyes off Tilly. 'Wait until we tell him you made it.' Hilary almost ran to the door.

Tilly watched them, her eyes wide and her heart thumping. He was here.

Crunch time had arrived.

Chapter Five

Rafe

'I am so sorry,' Genevieve said before Rafe even had the chance to put his bag down.

'About what?' He slung the bag off his shoulder and put it down beside a small case in the entrance hall.

'For not believing you about Tilly.'

'Oh that... Well, you know that—'

'It's ok,' Hilary said. 'She's already here. A complete shock, of course, but a wonderful one.'

'She's so nice,' Genevieve said. 'I love her already and I'm so glad she met you. She seems so sweet and...' She shrugged. 'Like someone who needs a hug.'

Rafe frowned and shook his head, trying to take in what they were saying. He ran his fingers through his hair, raking out some of the damp snow. 'What do you mean, she's here?'

Was this their idea of a joke? As jokes went, it was quite a good one, and he probably deserved it, but he wasn't about to fall for it.

'You didn't know either?' his mum said with a clap of her hands. 'She must have wanted to surprise you.'

'Yeah, yeah.' Rafe pressed his fingertips into his cheeks and pulled a fake shocked face. 'Am I surprised enough yet?'

'Don't joke.' Genevieve took his arm. 'Because she is genuinely here. So if you didn't know she was coming, you really will be shocked in a minute.'

'Of course I didn't know she was coming and I know she's not here, so you can stop the joke now, Ok? You've had your revenge.'

'Why would I want revenge?' Genevieve and Hilary exchanged a look full of meaning, and Rafe wasn't sure what to make of it. But clearly they planned to milk this charade until he caved and confessed he'd made up his relationship with Tilly Thorpe.

'Listen. About Tilly...'

'Ta-da!' Hilary threw open the kitchen door.

Rafe's eyes almost popped out of his head. He gaped and silently mouthed, '*what*?' Was this possible? Why was she here? It was actually Tilly Thorpe. The same woman he'd seen on the 1-Quick website a couple of weeks ago. Her smiley face now had a rabbit in the headlights look and she was sucking on her lip and fiddling with a ring. Across the kitchen island sat his grandma, her mouth stretched wide into a smile like she'd just bought him the biggest remote-control car in the store for Christmas and was about to hand it over.

'Mum... How?' Had his mum and Genevieve somehow engineered this? Had they lured the poor woman here so they could prank him? Surely no one would have gone along with that.

'Nothing to do with me,' his mum said with a grin. 'She came here herself. Such a wonderful surprise for us all.'

'I can explain.' Tilly rose to her feet.

'No need to explain,' Grandma said. 'It's wonderful. Come and give the girl a kiss; she's missed you terribly.'

'What?' both Rafe and Tilly said at the same time.

Genevieve laughed. 'Oh my god, are you embarrassed?' She glanced at Rafe. 'Should we leave you alone for a private reunion?'

'Actually, yes. Can you give us a minute?'

'Are you for real?'

'Let's do it, Genevieve,' their mum said. 'We'll have plenty of time for a catch up later. Let's give them a moment. It must be hard not seeing each other for so long.'

'Does that include me?' Grandma asked.

'Yes, Mum.' Hilary bustled over and helped the older woman off the seat. 'You two take as long as you need.'

'Just be good,' Grandma said.

Rafe bit his tongue as his mum closed the door behind her and his grandma. He gazed at Tilly, who was still smiling though a little vaguely, and she looked back, holding eye contact. It was almost painful but not all bad, kind of electric.

'What's this all about?' He unbuttoned his coat, trying to sound casual, like this sort of thing happened every day.

'I could ask you the same thing.' Her cheeks reddened a little. 'Why do your family know who I am?'

'You first. Why are you here?' He removed his coat and hung it over the back of a barstool.

'Do you even know who I am?'

He nodded. 'Tilly Thorpe and you work for 1-Quick Getaways, which doesn't fill me with confidence.'

She half-nodded and blinked like she was surprised he'd done his research.

Yes, I've done my homework. But it still didn't explain anything.

'So, are you going to tell me why I have an admin assistant from 1-Quick Getaways waiting for me at a house you shouldn't even know about, never mind be in?'

'Um, yes.' She fidgeted with her ring a bit more and Rafe saw for a moment what Genevieve meant about her being someone who needed a hug. She looked completely lost. 'I'm not here as an admin assistant. I was sent with a colleague to meet you yesterday.'

He folded his arms. 'Oh yeah?'

'Yes.' She took a deep inhale. 'I just wanted to beg for a moment of your time to talk to you and open up a dialogue. I have some ideas on how we—'

He held up his hand. 'No. I'm not opening up a dialogue with a 1-Quick employee. And the fact they've sent you to my family home makes me certain I never will. These underhand methods go against everything I stand for and I won't ever work with a company that condones business like that. Corporate espionage is bad enough in itself, but this—'

'It's my fault,' she said. 'The managers didn't find out this address. I did. And it was pure chance. I didn't even know if you'd be here. I just wanted to talk to you and show you that we're friendly.'

Rafe huffed out a laugh. 'You're joking me, right? You think tracking me down at my parents' home and infiltrating my family Christmas is friendly?'

Her smile faded and died. She covered her mouth. 'Sorry. When you put it like that.' Her voice cracked. She turned her back to him and lifted a red coat. 'I should go. And I apologise for the mistake.'

'Apology accepted.' It was Christmas after all, and if she was just an admin assistant, then people higher up should be taking the flak. 'How are you travelling? I didn't see a car.'

'I'll call a taxi.'

'Ok. I'll leave you here and give you a moment to call, then if you wouldn't mind waiting in the hall.'

'Right.' She pulled out her phone. Her eyes were covered by large glasses that reflected the kitchen lights. Without her smile, the sadness of her expression cut him deep. Was he being unreasonable?

No!

She shouldn't be here. For all he knew, she was just a great actress playing her role to tug on his heartstrings. But her eyes betrayed her. Even through the glasses, he saw pain, and he knew she wasn't doing this out of malice. A longing stirred in him to take her, hold her and soothe the pain away, but he couldn't do that. *Not my place.* She didn't belong here.

'How did your family know who I was?' she asked quietly.

Rafe rubbed at the back of his neck, the absurdity of the situation pressing heavily on him.

'I, um... It was a mix-up. I'll leave you to call the taxi.'

As he turned to go, the top of his head collided with something in the doorway. Mistletoe? Who the hell hung that there?

Honestly, his family was the limit sometimes in the lengths they'd go to for matchmaking. He wouldn't like to pick which one of the three women who'd just left the room had hung this here. He resisted the urge to rip it down, and also shoved away stray thoughts about kissing anyone under it... No, definitely not Tilly. She was a 1-Quick spy, and he certainly wouldn't be kissing her under the mistletoe anytime soon.

CHAPTER SIX

Tilly

Tilly's hand shook as she pulled out her phone and swallowed back a lump in her throat. Tilly Thorpe didn't cry about stuff like this. What was the point? Crying got her nowhere. When she'd cried as a child after Ellie ruined things for them, Ellie accused her of being too soft. And she couldn't afford to be soft now. Not when she needed a calm mind, so she could leave here, and soon. It wasn't like this had ever been a great idea. If only Rafe's family hadn't welcomed her in like an old friend. Being treated as someone they cared for and were happy to see made the situation so much worse, but she still didn't get why. How could it be a mix-up?

No time to figure it out. She just needed to call a taxi and get far away from here. This scenario felt all too familiar. How often she'd left foster homes under a veil of sadness with a burning in her gut, her whole body gripped by helplessness and Ellie's smug face grinning at her.

Ellie wasn't here to scupper this, but Tilly had done it herself by being here in the first place. She didn't belong here. When the meeting with Innova came up in January, she wouldn't be part of it and just as well. She needed to get far from Rafe Harrington and his family. Her head pounded and her chest stung. She cringed over and over as she put the taxi number into her phone. Why hadn't she anticipated this? She'd imagined the best possible outcome, but of course that was never going to happen. She was nothing but a 1-Quick spy. She'd infiltrated his home, intruded in his family life, stepped inside one of the dollhouses, and expected to be allowed to stay. But it wasn't for her. It never was. These snapshots of other people's lives were nothing more than glimpses into a passing reality. She didn't know how to get herself into a world where hot chocolates with family and hugs in the kitchen were real.

No one was answering. The call rang off without even going to voicemail. She tried again in case her clumsy fingers and misty eyes had made her put in the wrong number.

What must the Harringtons think of her? Hilary, Genevieve and Rafe's grandma had been so nice. Now they'd be raging. They'd shown her so much hospitality, but she was nothing but an unwanted trespasser at their family Christmas.

Still, the call wasn't connecting. Tilly glanced out the window. The snow was heavier now and the thin layer on the ground was growing. What should she do? Try to walk? How far was it to get to Glenbriar, and would she make the train if she went on foot? It would be tight. It left in an hour.

She called again, pacing towards the window, and looking out over the long and very white garden. Beyond it, hills rolled into the distance, swathed in fir trees that were snow-covered like an iced Christmas cake. Could anything be prettier?

The call connected.

'Hi, I wonder if you could come for me at Greenacres and take me to Glenbriar.'

Some static on the line cut off the first part of the man's words. 'Five o'clock is the earliest time I've got, lass. And the weather isn't getting any better. I'm not sure the road'll be passable by then.'

'Oh... Right. Five is too late. Um, ok. Thanks.' She ended the call. How would she get back to the town for her train?

There must be other taxi companies. She could make a start and call them as she walked. But first, she needed to retrieve her case from the hall. She opened the door Genevieve had led her in and made her way back. Her heart leapt a mile when she saw Rafe standing there. She'd assumed he would be with his family, probably complaining about her. He glanced up from his phone and smiled – actually smiled. Ok. That was unexpected. Her already shaky heartrate spiked, and she held her breath.

'Everything ok?' he said.

'I'll leave you now. I just need my case.'

'Here.' He lifted it, extended the handle, and passed it over to her. 'You can wait in here until the taxi comes. No point going outside in this weather.' He peered through the narrow side window that ran up the length of the door. 'It's getting heavy. I hope the taxi can get down the driveway; it's pretty steep. He might get down then not get out again.'

'The taxi isn't coming. Or at least I haven't found one that can.' Tilly fastened her coat. 'I'll walk while I look for another company or see if there's a bus. I need to catch a train in an hour and if I wait for the taxi, it'll be too late.' She reached for the door handle.

'Wait a second,' he said. 'You can't walk to the station from here. Well, you can, but it'll take over an hour and it's definitely not a sensible idea in this weather.'

'I'm sure a bus will go past, or I'll hitch a lift or something.' Though she didn't really like that idea.

'There are no buses out here.' He frowned at the view beyond the window again and ran his hand around his jaw. 'I can't let you go out in that. It wouldn't be right. Let me take you to the station.'

'No,' she said very quickly. 'I can't. I shouldn't be here at all. No way am I going to drag you away from your family anymore.'

'I can't in all conscience let you walk to the station. I have a Raptor that'll get through this. It won't take long.'

She didn't want to ask what a Raptor was. 'No, really. I feel terrible.'

'Well, don't.' He shifted closer to her, so that he was blocking the door with his considerable height and broad shoulders. Running his fingers through his hair, he watched her for a moment, and her cheeks burned under his scrutiny. 'I have a confession to make.'

'What do you mean?'

He sighed, and the expanse of his chest, under his ribbed sweater, rose and fell. 'When I heard 1-Quick were scouting for information and looking to expand their reach, I looked at their website. When I was scrolling, I saw your picture.' He glanced at his feet and the corners of his lips turned up. 'Your smile... It spoke to me.' He raised his eyes to her face again. 'I know that sounds stupid.'

Tilly kept her eyes on his, listening, but barely comprehending where this was going.

'Later on, my sister was quizzing me about girlfriends and asking if I was bringing anyone here for Christmas this year.' He pinched the bridge of his nose. 'So I made up a silly lie to tease her and said I had a girlfriend and she lived in London.' With a helpless shrug, he held out his hands. 'And her name was Tilly Thorpe. Sorry.' He pulled a face. 'I never expected to meet you, so I thought it was a harmless thing to say.'

'But...' Tilly frowned. 'So, they thought I was your...'

'Girlfriend, yeah.'

'Wow.' Tilly wasn't sure what else to say. The whole situation was crazy. Beyond crazy. It was impossible.

'Of all the people... and then you turn up.' His eyes snared her again, and he shook his head like he almost didn't believe she was real. Maybe she should pinch herself and check.

'It really is a mix-up, and a weirder one than I thought.' She gave him a little smile.

'It's pretty embarrassing,' he said. 'Now you see what a sad case I am.'

'I'm sure you're not.'

He pulled an uncertain face. 'I definitely shouldn't get off scot-free. So, let me give you a lift to the station, ok? That might go some way towards me making up for using you without your knowledge or consent in my deception.'

'Ok.' She couldn't deny how much easier it would be if he drove her. And he didn't seem quite so intimidating or annoyed now. In fact, he seemed decent... Nice even, like how she'd imagined him from his picture.

'I'll just tell my mum I'm giving you a lift. She'll have a million questions, but they can wait. Here.' He handed her a little black keycard. 'Jump into the Raptor. I'll be there in a second.'

Tilly headed across the snowy drive and saw a large black and very shiny pickup style truck parked there. As she approached, the doors clicked open without her touching anything like it sensed her – though obviously it was the key it sensed, but still, it felt like magic. This must be the Raptor. She jumped in. Could anything more bizarre happen today? She needed to get on the train and back to London, away from this wild place. But her heart wept a little. How beautiful it would have been to stay here.

Don't! It's not possible.

She knew better than to torture herself with false hope. The door on this dollhouse would close and she'd be back on the outside where she belonged.

Rafe closed the house door and trotted across the drive into the car. He cut a handsome dash in his outdoor wear and Tilly tried to ignore a little spark in her tummy she was starting to feel every time she saw him.

'That wasn't pleasant,' he said. 'Mum, Grandma and Genevieve all want to come out and speak to you, but I asked them not to. I didn't have time to fully explain. They think we're breaking up. God knows what they'll think when they find out we were never actually together.'

Tilly couldn't begin to imagine, but that part of the problem was his. She'd be long gone by the time he had to explain. The wheels spun a little as he manoeuvred the Raptor up the hill.

'What will you tell the people at 1-Quick about me?' he asked.

'Nothing. I don't think I'll even mention that we met.' She looked out the window, her chest heavy again. 'I shouldn't have come.' But Mitchell knew she had and would want to know how she got on. Her stupidity wouldn't be rewarded with a promotion for Christmas. She might even be sacked for this cockup, and where would that leave her?

'You're tenacious, I'll give you that.'

'I'm not really.' That definitely wasn't a name she'd ever been called before.

'Then why did you do it?'

She let out a sigh. 'Because I'm totally inexperienced at this kind of thing. I thought my boss would be happy if I made contact, but I doubt he will be now.' How could she have been so stupid?

'It's water under the bridge. Don't let it bother you.'

How kind of him, but the whole situation was cringeworthy. Occasionally, she'd thought some of 1-Quick's methods unethical, but she was never sure who was safe to talk to, or if it was her place to say. Arnie always seemed approachable, but she couldn't be certain the directions were straight from him or from someone above him. Now instead of speaking up, she'd jumped under the 1-Quick cloak and was as bad as anyone else.

'You just go home and enjoy Christmas. Don't think anymore about this,' he said.

'Hmm,' she mumbled. 'It's not exactly my favourite time of year.' Though maybe if she lived in a winter wonderland like this, she might change her mind.

'Me neither,' Rafe said.

'Really?' She turned to look at him. 'But your family seem to love it.'

'Yes, they do. Maybe I should make more of an effort, but it just seems like such a lot of work for just one day. A bit like having a wedding every year.'

'I wouldn't know.' Tilly looked out the window again. 'I've never had a wedding.'

'I have, and it was a lot of money for... Well, we didn't exactly stay married long enough to make it worth it.'

'You're divorced?'

'Yup.'

At least he'd made it that far. Her relationship record was as pitiful as the rest of her history. Being alone was pretty much standard for her now. It saved her the pain of break ups when potential lovers got annoyed with her being clingy and needy, or falling too fast and rushing them into places they didn't want to go.

Rafe pulled up outside the station in the little car park. 'Here you go. You should make your train in plenty of time.'

'Thanks,' she said. 'And I really am sorry for all the hassle I've caused you.'

'Don't worry. I'm glad you did. It was nice to meet you in person.' He looked at her and his lips curled up. She couldn't help but mirror him. 'Tilly Thorpe.' As he said her name, his smile grew wider. 'I apologise for using your name the way I did.'

'Well, you must have been nice about me because your family were so kind. I should have thanked them before I left.'

'I'll let them know.' His eyes held hers, and she found herself unable to move. She didn't want to leave him so soon. It felt like she'd only just found him, and even though she didn't know him, there was something reassuring about his presence.

'Ok,' she murmured, not sure if the word had come out.

'Take care,' Rafe said. 'Who knows, maybe our paths will cross again.'

'Maybe.' But would that be a good thing? Not if it made her chest ache the way it was doing right now.

She opened the door, took her case, and got out. For a moment, she looked back at Rafe. A lump swelled in her throat. She swallowed it down, shut the door and almost ran towards the platform. She must not look back.

Let him go.

They should never have met in the first place.

And yet, they had. She trundled her case onto the platform. The little bookshop was closed for the day and all she could do was look in the window… as ever.

She glanced at the overhead departure sign and her heart fell a thousand miles.

Cancelled. Cancelled. Cancelled.

All the trains were cancelled due to the bad weather. No way. What was she going to do?

There were no places to stay; she'd checked earlier, and the nearest ones were in Perth, about twenty miles away. Could she get a bus? Would they still be running? The snow was still falling, and the light was fading. She'd read that it got dark up here around four o'clock in December. There was only half an hour of daylight left… Then what?

She was stranded alone in the cold, with no idea what to do next. Sitting down on a bench under the canopy, she put her head in her hands, barely holding back tears. They wanted to come, but she didn't let them. Crying alone was pointless. She'd been there, done that too many times. No one would come. No one ever did. There was no one to comfort her when it all got too much. There never had been and most likely never would be.

Some voices and laughter made her look up. A group of young people had made their way onto the platform. They moaned and shouted when they saw the trains were cancelled, then burst out laughing and left, slapping their arms around each other's shoulders. Tilly swallowed back more tears. These people had people. But she only had herself.

She'd have to use that and do something. No point sitting here, moping. She got to her feet and took a deep breath. She could do this.

Chapter Seven

Rafe

'I 've just looked at the website and lots of trains are cancelled,' Hilary said over the phone, and Rafe turned the in-car volume down. His mum sounded a little hysterical.

'What?' he replied, glancing up at the thick, swirling snow.

'Yes. So don't let Tilly go. Whatever happened to cause you to split up doesn't matter now. We can't have her stuck. Is this on loudspeaker?'

'Yes, but Tilly's already gone for the train. I'd better go and see if she's ok.' She may be a 1-Quick spy, albeit an unwilling one, but she was also a person, a woman trying to carry out an impossible task to impress managers with their own agendas. A woman with a beautiful smile and sad eyes. Eyes that were the windows to her soul, and he sensed something troubling in there. He couldn't, in all conscience, leave her out in this.

He threw open the door of the Raptor.

'Hurry and make sure she's ok. She obviously still cares about you. She made the long trip to be with you for Christmas, didn't she?'

'No, that's not what happened. Tilly isn't my girlfriend, and she never was. I saw her picture the day I met Genevieve, and I made up a story as a joke. No way did I expect her to turn up at the house. We've never even met before today.' Fat snowflakes gathered in Rafe's hair, and he raked them out, heading for the entrance, still with the phone at his ear, though it was now silent.

'Mum?'

'I don't get it... Why did she turn up at the house then?'

'Because she works for a rival company and they're trying to get information about Innova.'

'It didn't seem like that. She didn't strike me as a cut-throat undercover agent. She was a dear.'

'Yeah, well. That's the truth.'

'Truth maybe, but the whole situation seems more like Christmas magic, if you ask me.'

'What are you talking about?'

'Like it was meant to be.'

'No, Mum. That's nonsense. Because she's not my girlfriend.'

'Maybe, but she is a person and right now, she's a person in trouble.'

'I'm on my way.'

'Oh gosh, hurry. What if she gets stranded?'

'If she's there, I'll help her out.'

'Yes. Bring her back. It's getting dark and the poor girl looked lost enough.'

'I will.'

'And be sensible driving. Cressida and Tina have just arrived with Alexander, and they said the driving conditions were dreadful.'

He glanced around and saw Tilly with her head down against the snow, heading off the platform towards the exit.

'I'll be extra careful. I've just spotted her. Need to go. See you later.' He ended the call. 'Tilly!' he shouted.

She looked over, saw him and made to keep on walking. He jogged to catch her.

'Hey,' he said. 'Is your train cancelled?'

'They're all cancelled from this station,' she said. 'For the rest of the day.'

'What are you going to do then?'

'Why do you care?' She took off her glasses and wiped the snow from them with her glove, though it didn't seem to make much difference. Her dark, wavy hair was encrusted with flakes like jewels.

'Because I'm a human being.'

Shaking her head, she looked away. 'I'll see if I can get a bus to Perth. The trains might still be running from there, or I might be able to get accommodation.'

He thrust his hands into his pockets. 'I doubt the buses will be running now either.'

'Well, I'll stand in a doorway all night.' She threw out her hands, then put her glasses back on. 'It's my own fault. I shouldn't even be here.'

'Come back with me. My parents' house has lots of rooms.'

'No way.' She shook her head. 'I can't do that. I've already done enough. Turning up was bad. Now I've dragged you out in the snow. I can't bring any more stress and misery to your family.'

'You won't be doing that. In fact, my mum, for one, will be more stressed and miserable if I leave you here.'

Tilly held her hand over her mouth. 'She shouldn't have to think about me. She doesn't even know me.'

'My mum is a very kind and caring woman. She liked you when she chatted with you. She won't rest easy unless she knows you're ok.' He rubbed the back of his neck and let out a sigh. 'And neither will I.'

'After all the trouble I've caused.'

'Let's put Innova and 1-Quick aside for a moment. Forget about them. What's left?'

She gave him a desperate little headshake. 'I don't know.'

'Two people,' he said. 'One who has nowhere to stay, the other who has plenty of space to accommodate her. Surely it's a no-brainer.'

'But we're not just two people, are we? The circumstances matter and I...' She raised her eyes to the falling snow, and it caught in her eyelashes like frozen tears.

'Please, Tilly. I'm happy for you to come back with me. You can have a room in the house where no one will bother you. Then, as soon as the snow clears, you can leave. Or if you want to join us, that's also fine. You decide. All I want is to make sure you have somewhere safe to be.'

'Then I should at least buy some food, so I don't have to scrounge off your family.'

He smiled, and the tension slackened in his chest. Thank god, she appeared to be coming around to the idea, because if he left her here, she might freeze to death. No way could he leave her without knowing she had somewhere warm to go.

'You saw the kitchen earlier,' he said. 'There's enough food in there to feed an army for several weeks. You won't be scrounging. And to be honest, I'd like to hit the road as soon as possible. It's getting dark, and this weather isn't getting any better.'

She drew in a deep breath. 'Ok. If you insist.'

'I absolutely insist. I'm on the point of abducting you.'

A small smile played on her lips, but still didn't quite reach her eyes. 'I suppose it would be better if I came willingly.'

'That would be preferable.'

'Thank you.'

'No need. Now, come on. Back to the car.'

They jumped into the Raptor, and Rafe shook the snow from his jacket. He reversed out of the space and made for the exit. The Raptor's giant tyres handled the snow well, but a lot of smaller cars would struggle in this, and it wasn't letting up.

Streetlights popped on alongside the Christmas lights as he drove down the main street of Glenbriar.

'This is a sweet little town,' Tilly said. 'I'd never even heard of it before.'

'Yeah, it's a nice place to live.'

'Do you normally live here?'

'No. I have an apartment in Glasgow.'

'Is it expensive to live here?'

'Oh yeah. Houses here are sought after and there's always a lot of demand for them.'

'My flat has a ridiculously high rent. It's in Slough, which is good for commuting, but the flat itself is in terrible condition. It's an old building, and it's not well kept. The walls are paper thin, and I have really noisy neighbours.'

'That doesn't sound nice.'

'It's horrible.'

Rafe kept his eyes on the road, but his heart twisted. At times like this, he thanked his lucky stars for how fortunate he was.

'Sorry,' she said. 'I don't know why I said all that. You probably don't want to know.'

'Sure, I do. Seeing a new place gives you a different perspective. That's part of the reason I enjoy travelling. You can learn so much from other places and other people. Even if it just serves as a reminder of why you love your home... or not in your case.'

'I'd like to travel more. Coming here on my own is about the most adventurous thing I've ever done. For someone who works for a travel company, I really don't have much experience of other places.'

'It's hard when you're working,' he said. 'I haven't taken time off to travel properly for ages. This thing is all kitted out for me to do weekend trips though. I've got a tent that fits over the back and onto the roof. So most of my travels are within driving distance at the moment.'

'Wow... I've never done anything like that.'

'I think you'd enjoy it. You must have an adventurous spirit.'

'Must I?'

'Well, you attempted a risky mission. Most people wouldn't even have considered it.'

She shook her head, and he flicked his gaze sideways, glimpsing the tail end of a smile aimed at him.

He glanced in his rearview mirror and caught his reflection in the fading light. His lips quirked slightly. Maybe his mum was right and the reason Tilly was here was something out of their control... Christmas magic? He huffed out a laugh and Tilly turned to him.

'What?' she said.

'Nothing, sorry. Just thinking about the craziness of all this.' He didn't believe in Christmas magic. Right now, he needed to concentrate on the road. The snow was still falling, and things were getting dicey. He couldn't afford to be distracted, even though Tilly's smile had that effect and there wasn't much he could do about it.

CHAPTER EIGHT

Tilly

Friday, December 20th

Evening

Tilly swept her hand over her damp hair. Outside was almost pitch black now, and the snow swirled in the headlights like she and Rafe were entering a vortex. It felt like she was doing exactly that, being sucked into the unknown. Everything that had happened in the past few days seemed almost unreal and if Rafe stopped the car now and she got out to discover she was on another planet or in a different dimension, she'd almost believe it.

'I really can't apologise enough,' she said. 'What I did was so stupid.'

'Forget about it,' Rafe said.

'I can't. It's the reason all this is happening. I should explain myself.'

'You already did.'

'Not properly.'

'You wanted to prove a point to your boss or show him you had initiative. Something like that.'

'That's true, but I took a gamble that could have gone so wrong. I worked out where your house was from a picture at the Innova office.'

'Ah, very clever.'

'That's what my colleague said. He thought it was the perfect plan to visit you.' Now it was dark it was easier to talk for some reason. 'But he didn't want to come himself as he couldn't risk not getting home on time. So I did it on my own.'

'Sounds like he was too chicken to try.'

'Or had more sense.'

Rafe let out a little laugh. 'Maybe. You must be a dedicated employee. I hope they recognise that.'

She doubted it. In all her years there, she'd blended into the background, doing what she was told, trying to please people, and desperately clinging to the fact that she had somewhere of her own. Yes, clinging... What she did best.

'How long have you worked there?' he asked.

'Since I left school, which was like nine years ago.'

'You're obviously very loyal.'

'I guess so. I try to do whatever's needed. The workload has got more and more recently, but sadly the wages don't go up, and

I'm still an admin assistant, even though I've covered other roles when people are off sick.'

Rafe made a huffing sound. 'Pardon me for saying so, but it doesn't sound like a particularly pleasant environment to work in. Of course, you'll know I'm not a 1-Quick fan anyway, but the more I hear, the more they go down in my estimation.'

'I suppose I've got used to it.'

'But you shouldn't have to, and expecting an admin assistant to do anything other than the job you're trained for seems wild to me. I'm all for people working their way up, but with adequate support and training. And then the wages have to reflect that.'

That sounded like music to her ears. Surely this was the way managers should think. Memories flickered around her head. Those times she'd wondered about ethics. Occasionally, she'd internally questioned managerial decisions, but it wasn't her place to challenge them openly.

'Do you enjoy what you do?'

She let out a sigh. 'I wouldn't say enjoying it is the right word.'

'It's not my call, but have you considered other jobs?'

'Not really'

'Then maybe you should. I wouldn't expect any employee to do anything other than the job in their contract unless the circumstances were extreme, in which case I'd at least negotiate an interim settlement with them until something better could be formalised. I certainly wouldn't send them on a snooping mission. Not that I'd send anyone on one of them because I don't agree with them.'

'They only sent me because the person who was meant to go ended up being ill.' Shaking her head, she laughed. 'My boss thought my smile could charm you.'

'Oh man.' Rafe facepalmed. 'He got that right. Your smile charmed me before I even met you.'

'Which is very weird, especially considering the cock-up I made of this.'

'Stop beating yourself up. It doesn't sound like any of it is your fault. You were sent to do an unethical job, you clearly weren't given adequate training, and you were abandoned by your superior to do the job on your own.'

'I've been so, so stupid,' she groaned.

'You made a decision based on the options you were given, none of which were any good, and you did what you thought best for the business. Your employers should be pleased with your loyalty, if nothing else.'

'I guess we'll see.' She rested her head back. If only Arnie was as understanding as Rafe. Rafe had a knowledgeable aura that came with power. He definitely knew how to talk the talk, but he seemed so much more genuine and caring.

'It's been quite a day, hasn't it?' he said. 'I still can't get over the fact that you, of all people, turned up. Out of everyone in the world I could have pretended was my girlfriend, I chose you and then you showed up.'

'It's mad, isn't it?'

'More than.' He leaned forward and squinted out the window. 'Uh-oh, what's this?'

Ahead was a steep upward sweep of the road. Red rear lights flickered in it and an engine revved.

'I think they're stuck.' He pulled the Raptor in behind them. 'Let me see if they're ok.' He unclipped his seatbelt and got out.

Tilly waited, watching in the beam of the headlights as he spoke to some people heavily wrapped up. Should she be surprised at how nice he was? Shouldn't the CEO of a successful company be more arrogant and self-centred? That was her general experience. She couldn't see any of the management staff at 1-Quick or other companies she'd dealt with helping out someone who'd behaved like her. Or jumping out of their warm car on a freezing night to help a stranger who'd broken down.

Her chest was still tight, and she couldn't release the tension. What would his family make of the situation? They'd all think her a total idiot for turning up on his doorstep. Who did that? But he'd said she could have a room and stay in it. That was what she'd do. She wouldn't intrude anymore. They wouldn't want her gatecrashing their family time. Listening to them in other rooms in the house wouldn't be much different from watching other people's lives from the train.

Rafe opened the door beside her, and she jumped. 'Sorry,' he said. 'I didn't mean to startle you. I'm going to help clear a path around these people and then give them a push.'

'Can I help too?'

'Sure. I've got a shovel in the back, and I might have something else we can use.'

Tilly followed him around to the back of the Raptor. Its black paintwork stood out against the whiteness of the snow. It was weird how light it felt despite how dark it actually was. The snow seemed to have a luminous quality. And it was silent, eerily so. She shivered a little as she stood beside Rafe. He opened the tail-gate and raked about. For someone who used this for travelling and adventure, it was amazingly neat and tidy – like an advert for an outdoor explorer.

'You look prepared for everything,' she said.

'Thanks.' He grinned as he reached for something. 'I like to think so.' He pulled out a full-size shovel and a fold-up trowel. 'Which would you prefer?'

'I'll take the small one. You can probably work the shovel better.' She'd never had a garden, or had to dig anything up.

'Ok.' He handed her the trowel. 'We need to move as much snow as we can from around the wheels so they can get a grip on the road. Then we'll give them a push and hopefully that'll get them moving. They're nearly home. Apparently, their house is just another mile along. If we can't get them moving, we'll get them into the Raptor and take them home. They can walk back for the car another time, though it's not the safest place to leave it.'

Tilly smiled at the two people who were using long sticks from the roadside to move some of the snow from around their tyres.

'Thank you so much,' one of the men said. 'I'd rather not be stuck out in this.'

'Definitely not.' Tilly shuddered at the thought of what she'd have done if Rafe hadn't offered her a place to stay... But she still couldn't shake the feeling that she shouldn't be here at all.

She scraped away at the snow around the front tyres, trying not to watch as Rafe shovelled great mounds of it. But she couldn't keep her eyes away. He was quite something to watch, especially when he took off his jacket. That sweater clung to a broad chest and shoulders. Even in the narrow beam from the headlights, she saw just how fit he was. Not that she should be noticing.

Eventually, after what seemed like hours of scraping, Rafe suggested the driver got back in. He, Tilly and the young passenger positioned themselves around the car and with a bit of huffing and a lot of engine-revving, they got the car moving to the top of the hill where the road levelled out.

'In you get,' Rafe said to the passenger. He jumped in and Rafe closed the door. The driver opened his window and called his thanks.

'Well, that was a first.' Tilly folded up the little trowel.

'Always carry a shovel in the back of the car in winter,' Rafe said. 'One of the first driving rules around here.'

'I can't even drive,' Tilly said. 'I've never needed to.'

'It's kind of essential up here.' He took the trowel from her and loaded it into his boot. 'The good thing is, if we get stuck, I have a tent and all the equipment in this car, so we can camp out with a fire if necessary.'

'That sounds very adventurous,' Tilly said. 'And cold.'

'Probably, and let's hope we don't have to do it. This is already an unexpected diversion. We should get going. Mum will be frantic.'

Tilly jumped into the Raptor and closed the door, imagining what it would be like huddling in a tent with Rafe on a night like this. She'd never camped even in good weather, and she wasn't keen to start her tent experience in thick snow, but the idea wasn't wholly without merit. It was certainly fun fantasising about it, and for a few moments she swapped her dollhouse daydreams for winter camping ones. Rafe pulled off and his heavy-duty tyres seemed to have only the slightest judder on the hill before they reached the flatter section. The other car was nowhere in sight, so presumably the people had gone on safely.

'My other sister arrived just as I reached the station,' Rafe said. 'Apparently, she and her wife had quite a ropey journey.'

'Oh... Do you have a big family?'

'Just two sisters, both younger. Genevieve, who you already met. She's married to Finlay and my other sister is Cressida. She's married to Tina, and they have a baby... Well, I suppose he's a toddler now. Alexander. He's a funny wee thing.'

'And they're all at your parents' house for Christmas?' Tilly's chest tightened a little more.

'Yeah. My mum loves this kind of thing. Genevieve and Finlay just live in the village so they can go back and forward, but it's nice when we're all together and no one has to worry about driving home.'

'I'll keep out of your way and not bother anyone.'

He flexed his hand on the wheel. 'If that's what you want to do, then, of course, but you're more than welcome to join us. Everyone in my family is very sociable and happy to have company. But you decide.'

She already had. Once she was safely in the room, she'd stay there. A memory stirred, similar to the one she'd had earlier about her sister. It grew and more joined it, like a snowball rolling through her mind. She saw a journey from the children's home to a foster family. Maybe it was one journey or maybe it was a collage of them all squashed together. Whichever it was, she recalled how a little seed of hope would spring up as she and Ellie sat in the taxi. Maybe this family would be the one. Maybe here they would find the love and acceptance families were supposed to bring. But her eyes landed on Ellie and her heart sank. What was going through her sister's mind behind that sneering smile? Plans for how she could ruin their chances this time? Why did she always do that? Didn't she want a family? She scuppered every chance they had with her bad behaviour, stealing, sometimes violence, running away and constant defiance.

Eventually, when it was too late to be adopted, Tilly had realised she didn't have to stay with her. The years of being loyal had got her nowhere. As the big sister, she'd wanted to stay with Ellie and make sure she was ok, but Ellie had never cared about anyone except herself... And she hadn't even done a great job of that. As soon as Tilly left the home, she'd cut ties and never looked back.

She'd kept track of Ellie from afar. Sadly, it was no surprise to learn that Ellie had ended up in prison just months after leaving the home and had been in and out ever since.

With a few shallow breaths, Tilly rid herself of these thoughts. This wasn't a foster family, and she had nothing to prove, no one who could scupper anything... Except herself and she'd possibly done that already.

Rafe turned the Raptor into the driveway. At the bottom of the curving driveway, Greenacres was lit up like a Christmas beacon. Lights glowed in the windows, promising warmth and shelter. The vacant cavities in Tilly's heart filled with heat like frothy hot chocolate had been poured in to fill every gap; its nurturing qualities made her chest swell with hope. Soon the dollhouse would open, and Tilly would be allowed back in.

But how welcome will I be?

Rafe parked up and got out. Tilly followed, not sure what to do or say... to anyone. How could she justify being back here?

Rafe opened the door and let her go in before him.

'Just leave your case there if you want,' he said. 'I'll tell Mum you're back and we can get a room made up for you.'

'Don't put her or anyone to any trouble.' Tilly placed her case back where it had been just an hour or so ago. 'If there's bedding or sheets, I can do it myself.'

Rafe looked at her and his gaze was intense; she wanted to look away, but she couldn't. His pupils had magnetic powers, holding her fast. He tilted his head and gave her an almost pitying smile. 'It's ok. No one will mind. Mum loves having guests.'

Fiddling with the cuff of her top, Tilly followed him down a curving corridor. Sounds of chat and laughter came from a room to the left.

'Can I wait out here?' Tilly asked. Was she still breathing? This was horrible. She was an imposter, and there was no escape route. Maybe this was how Ellie had felt about going into foster homes. Maybe she didn't see a chance for love, but somewhere scary with unfamiliar people she didn't feel equipped to impress. Was that why she'd fought it? At least in the home, everything was familiar.

'Of course. Or you can wait in here, if you like.' Rafe opened a door to a small room lined with bookshelves. A sofa was placed at one wall and had lots of cushions and a big fleecy blanket on it. 'I'll speak to everyone and explain what's happened.'

'Thank you.' Tilly kept breathing purposefully and took a seat on the sofa. This room was the stuff of dreams, but she couldn't relax, not when she knew what Rafe was doing. What the hell would his family make of this?

Chapter Nine

Rafe

Rafe closed the door on Tilly. He clung to the handle for a moment, his chest feeling a little bruised. She looked so alone and desolate, like a fish out of water. A far cry from the woman with the beautiful smile. But all of it added up to a person who sparked something inside him. Curiosity, perhaps, maybe concern. This was a weird situation to be caught in, but she seemed almost panicky about seeing his family again. She needn't be, but if she really didn't want to see them, he could protect her.

He entered the living room to soft easy listening Christmas carols. His mum loved to play tunes like these in every room at this time of year. The buzz of happy chat alongside the music made him feel like he'd strolled into a festive café. The Christmas tree twinkled in front of the glass wall. Come summer, those doors opened onto a huge patio, bringing the outside in, but at this time of year, they were safely closed, keeping the wintery weather firmly outside.

The family sat around on the large corner group of sofas. His mum was beside Cressida, and his grandma beside Tina. Little Alexander stood at the coffee table, banging his fist on it, and Genevieve leaned forward, shaking a little teddy at him. Rafe's dad, Geoff, sat next to Genevieve's husband, Finlay, and without hearing what the two men were saying, Rafe guessed they were chatting about golf or rugby. Rafe closed the door behind him.

'There you are.' His mum looked up and spotted him. Two black labradors and a French bulldog jumped up from the fireside and bolted towards him, their tails wagging like mad.

'Hello, hello.' Rafe patted them all. Horace and Dax were his parents' labs and Mitzi was Genevieve's French bulldog. 'Go back to your beds, you mad dogs, go on.' He laughed as they ignored him.

'Thank goodness you're back,' Hilary said. 'I was just about to phone you.'

'Yeah. It's pretty treacherous out there now. A guy was stuck on the steep section near the turn off to Dalarvin.'

'Thank goodness, you're all safely here for the weekend.' Geoff got to his feet and hustled the dogs back to their beds. 'It's great to see you, son. I hear you've had a bit of drama this afternoon.' His dad embraced him, clapping him on the back.

'Yeah, just a bit. Hey.' He leaned over and hugged Cressida, then Tina. 'Good to see you both, and you.' He bent down and ruffled Alexander's curly hair.

'Car,' Alexander said.

'If you say so.' Rafe grinned at him.

'I think he's trying to say your name,' Tina said, 'though most people seem to be called "car" at the moment.'

Rafe sat on the arm of the sofa next to his grandma.

'So, what happened to Tilly? Did she get on a train?' Hilary asked.

'No, she didn't.'

'Where is she then?' Genevieve lifted Mitzi onto her knee and cuddled her.

'The poor girl.' Grandma shook her head.

'She's ok, she's in the book room.' Rafe gave Grandma a gentle pat on the shoulder.

'She's here?' Geoff gaped at him.

'Yeah, she is.'

'Oh, thank goodness.' Hilary splayed her hand on her chest and let out a sigh. 'But why is she in the book room? Bring her in here.'

'No, she doesn't want to come in. All of this has been a bit strange. For both of us. Neither of us has acted in a way we're proud of.'

Genevieve pulled a face. 'I can't believe you made up a story about her and then she turned up here. It's mental.'

'It seems very odd to me,' Geoff said. 'I've been in business a long time and I'm only too aware of the ridiculous tactics some businesspeople will use, but to turn up unannounced like that was completely below the belt.'

'She must have had her reasons,' Hilary said. 'She looked like a poor little lost soul.'

'We've discussed it all and come to an understanding.' Rafe focused on his dad as he spoke, knowing he'd be the hardest to convince.

'She could be a skilled actress,' Geoff said.

'That wasn't an act.' Grandma shook her head.

'I agree,' Genevieve said.

'If she works for a rival company with no ethics, then I wouldn't trust her,' Geoff continued. 'Even her being back here is suspicious. How did she wangle that?'

'I invited her,' Rafe said. 'She didn't want to come back with me. She wanted to get a bus to Perth, but they won't be running in this weather. It was this or let her spend a freezing night alone in Glenbriar.'

'You did the right thing,' Hilary said.

'You did.' Geoff nodded, then flattened his lips and frowned. 'We couldn't have her freezing, but we have to be very careful about what we say around her.'

'Oh, really, Geoff,' Grandma huffed. 'She seems a sweet little one to me.'

'It could all be an elaborate ploy.' Geoff's eyebrows knitted together. 'We don't know anything about her except where she works, and that speaks for itself.'

'Normally, I'd agree with you,' Rafe said. 'But not this time. She talked to me on the way here and I believe her. She's sorry for coming here. It was an unwise decision, but her bosses sound like a right bunch of tossers. Sorry.' He pulled a face at Alexander, then leaned over and gave him a wee tickle. Alexander screamed and giggled.

'Thankfully, he doesn't understand that word yet,' Cressida said.

'Just as well,' Rafe muttered, sitting back on the sofa arm. 'So, anyway, I feel bad for Tilly. She's upset about what she did. She's loyal to the company and no matter how misguided that may be, she undertook this trip with good intentions.'

'I hope it doesn't backfire or come back to bite,' Geoff said.

'Rafe's right,' Genevieve said. 'Tilly seemed really worried about something. I thought she was tired from the travelling, but she was probably nervous because she wasn't one hundred per cent in on what she was doing.'

'Bring her in,' Hilary said. 'She can join us for some food and drinks.'

Rafe shook his head. 'She wants to be left alone, so we should respect that.'

'As long as she's not running off with anything,' Geoff said.

'Like the family jewels?' Cressida sat up straight with a mischievous grin on her face. 'I didn't know we had any. Where are they?'

'I meant information more than physical items.'

'She won't,' Rafe said; despite everything that had gone on that day, he trusted her. 'Can we make up a room for her?'

'Of course.' Hilary got to her feet. 'I can do that right now.'

'I'll help you.'

'No, you sit and relax. I'm happy to do it. I'd love to see Tilly.'

'Please, leave her just now. I said she could be alone.'

'Ok. I will.' Hilary patted his arm. 'I'll go and sort a room for her.'

Rafe shifted into his mum's vacated seat next to Cressida and put his arm around her. 'I never had a proper chance to say hello. How are you?'

'All good.'

'And you, Tina?'

'Yeah, I'm good. Relieved to be here in one piece. That was quite a drive.'

'Driving in the snow isn't much fun,' Rafe agreed. 'And look.' He leaned down to where Alexander was now sitting on the floor, banging a toy car on the carpet. 'You've found the car.'

'Car.' Alexander looked up and giggled, big dimples pressing into his chubby cheeks. 'Car, car.' He banged it on Rafe's hand.

'Is that a car for me? Thank you. I hope you're still on the nice list.'

'*You're* the only one in the house who isn't,' Genevieve said. 'As usual.'

'What? I've been good this year.'

She raised an eyebrow and stroked Mitzi, who was now curled in her lap. 'You think fibbing to your little sister about your relationship status is good? And inventing a girlfriend from a picture of someone with a nice smile?'

'She does have a nice smile, doesn't she?'

Both Cressida and Genevieve looked at him with wide eyes.

'Do you actually fancy her?' Genevieve asked.

'No.' The word came out a little too fast. This situation was bad enough without any more complications, but he couldn't deny there was something intriguing about her. 'Maybe just a tiny bit,' he whispered so his dad wouldn't hear, and winked like he might be joking. A strange urge was growing deep within him, gnawing at his insides and tugging at his heart. An urge to discover why that beautiful smile didn't reach her eyes and what he could do to make that happen.

'Ooh, the intrigue,' Genevieve said.

Hilary returned to the living room and leaned on the back of the sofa behind Rafe. 'I've made up a room for her. It was already made up, in fact. I just added towels and some snacks. I wasn't sure if Aunty Lil would make it over, so it was on standby, but she's not able to come, so it's all ready for Tilly. Should I go and tell her?'

'I should do that,' Rafe said.

'At least let me come with you. I feel like it's my duty to welcome her into the house. It's sad thinking of her sitting in there all alone and I'm neglecting her.'

'We're just respecting her wishes, Mum. She won't think badly of you for doing that.'

'I suppose not. She just looked like she needed a good hug.'

Was it wrong that he wanted to be the person administering that hug? The thought of taking her in his arms and holding her close set off little fires inside him. What in hell's name was that all about?

He flexed his fingers and got to his feet. 'I'll go and speak to her.'

His mum looked at him with pleading eyes.

'Ok, Mum. You can come too.'

Chapter Ten

Tilly

With this many books to choose from, Tilly would never be lonely again. She could live in this room quite happily for the rest of her days. Someone had a penchant for romance novels and Tilly smiled as she read the back covers. Why did all the heroes look like Rafe in her mind?

The door opened, and she almost threw away the book she had in her hand, only just keeping hold of herself and slipping it back onto the shelf before turning around to see Rafe and his mum.

He knocked on the open door with an apologetic smile. 'I should have done that before opening the door, shouldn't I?'

'It's fine.' Tilly gave a little shrug. 'I was just looking at the books. I hope that's ok.'

'Of course it is.' Hilary came across the room with her arms spread wide. 'Oh Tilly, Tilly. Come here.' She took Tilly in her arms and wrapped her in a hug. 'I'm so glad you're back here with us. I was worried sick when I heard the trains were cancelled.'

Speechless, Tilly relaxed into the hug. Tears welled in her eyes again. They'd been so close to the surface the past few days.

Blaming it on tiredness was her go-to excuse, but this time it felt like so much more. Hilary rubbed her back and Tilly had to work hard not to let out a sob. Why was this woman being so nice to her? After all she'd done? She knew from experience that people who behaved badly were rejected, with good reason. And she'd behaved worse than anyone today.

'You're not to worry about a thing while you're in this house,' Hilary went on. 'Rafe has explained everything, and we fully understand. Sounds like you work for a bunch of tyrants.'

'Mum.' Rafe's low voice cut into her monologue with a warning edge.

'Thank you.' Tilly made her best attempt at a smile.

Hilary stepped back, still holding Tilly's shoulders, and looked her over. They were about the same height. Average. Tilly was pretty average in everything really. Average height, weight, looks, income, et cetera. Nothing to make her stand out from the crowd.

The half-open door swung inward and two black labradors pushed their way in, sniffing around and wagging their tails; their huge eyes gleamed with adorable please-pat-me expressions.

'Seriously, you two?' Rafe said. 'These dogs are so nosy. Tilly, meet Horace and Dax.'

'Hi.' She leaned over and patted them. They both seemed to smile. One of them sat while she smoothed his velvety head under her palm.

'You treat this house like your home,' Hilary said. 'You may only be here for a day or two, but don't be a stranger. You're welcome to join us at any time.'

'I really don't want to intrude.'

'It won't be an intrusion, but if you prefer your own company, we'll respect that.'

'Thank you.'

'Do you want to have a look at the bedroom?' Rafe said. 'I'll get your case if you do. Or you can stay here and read the books if you prefer.'

'Could I take one up with me?' she asked.

'As many as you like,' Hilary said. 'I have far too many and haven't even read most of them. I really need to make more time for it.'

'I liked the look of this one.' Tilly pulled the one she'd hastily shoved onto the shelf back out. It had a shirtless man on the front. The picture cut off at his neck and she imagined Rafe's face fitting perfectly.

'Oh, don't let Rafe see that one.' Hilary's cheeks reddened a little. 'He doesn't need to know what kind of books I read.'

Rafe looked away and smirked. 'You read whatever you want. It's entirely up to you.'

Hilary winked at Tilly, then nodded at the book and mouthed. 'Good choice.'

'I'll get your case and put you two back in the lounge.' Rafe left the room, taking the dogs with him. Hilary followed him out and Tilly clutched the book close to her chest, stupidly imagining she was actually hugging Rafe; somehow that was satisfying and comforting – not really how she should feel about hugging the CEO of a rival company, who only a few hours ago she'd been planning to extract vital information from. But if she did as he suggested earlier and took business out of the equation, she saw a nice guy standing in front of her. Someone she could easily like. Exactly the kind of person she dreamed of and wished would walk out of one of the dollhouses and into her life. But why here? Why now?

'We have a lot of bedrooms in this house,' Hilary said. 'We like to have family and friends around and to be able to offer them places to stay. Geoff is in the renewables business, so everything is heated in the most cost effective way. To keep everything economical, we make sure all the rooms in use are together rather than spread out. I hope that's ok. I don't like the idea of you being stuck in another part of the house anyway. Even now, I like to keep my babies close. I know you're not technically one of them, but while you're under this roof, I'll be taking care of you.'

Tilly swallowed back another lump in her throat. Was this for real?

'We're all in what Geoff calls the west wing. I think it's because he used to love watching the TV show with that name.'

Rafe caught up with them, carrying Tilly's case as they headed up the stairs.

'The doors have numbers on them. I know it looks a bit like a hotel,' Hilary went on, 'but we find it easiest this way. All the doors look the same and in a corridor like this, guests often get confused.'

Tilly saw why immediately. The corridor curved around, and rows of doors went off it to one side.

'Your room is here. Number five. You're next to Rafe. He's in number four and no one's in room six.' Hilary opened the bedroom door and Tilly gasped.

'Are you alright?' Rafe asked.

'I just didn't expect the room to be so beautiful... Well, not that I thought it would be bad. It's just so gorgeous.' She'd have been happy in a plain room with a bed and a blanket, but this was like something out of a magazine. A modern styled bed with a rustic wooden headboard dripping with fairy lights took centre stage. Fluffy blankets and cushions adorned the bed, and a distressed-wood end table was laid with a tray of snacks.

'Mum likes her *How to Hygge* book almost as much as those romantic ones.' Rafe put Tilly's case just inside the door.

'I hope it didn't take you long to set this up,' Tilly said.

'Not at all. I already had the bed made up for Geoff's sister in case she wanted to come over, but she can't make it now. I just popped on some lights to make it a bit festive and I've left you snacks, in case you're hungry. You're welcome to have dinner with us later, of course.'

'Or you can have a tray up here if you prefer,' Rafe said.

'You're all so kind...' Tilly gazed around the room, hardly daring to believe she was here, inside the dollhouse world. She wanted to hug them both but didn't dare. 'I don't want to make any extra work for you. So, don't worry about feeding me.'

'Nonsense,' Hilary said. 'Like we'd have a guest here and not feed them. I'll not have that.'

Tilly caught Rafe's eye. He gave her a brief shrug and pulled a face indicating his mother had spoken and he wouldn't disagree.

'Well, you take some time in here if you like,' he said. 'Or do whatever you want. It's entirely up to you.'

'There's a small shower room in here too.' Hilary pushed the door open. 'If you'd prefer a bath, then along the corridor, just after bedroom eight, is the main bathroom. Feel free to use it.'

'I really can't thank you enough,' Tilly said. How big was this house? More than eight bedrooms!

'No need.' Hilary put her arm around Tilly's shoulder. 'You just keep warm and don't hesitate to ask for anything if you need it.'

'Thank you.' Tilly only just held back the tears. She was getting worse. Why so emotional?

'Come on, Mum, let's give her some space.' Rafe ushered his mum from the room.

Tilly sank onto the bed, and it seemed to beg her to lie back, so she did. The soft blankets engulfed her like she'd landed in a cosy nest. So dreamy. Turning onto her side, she propped herself up and opened her phone. So much had happened today and none of it had got her anywhere with the job she was supposed to be doing.

Expecting to see a text or an email from Mitchell, checking in with her, she frowned at his lack of communication. Nothing. Why was it when she didn't want anyone from work to contact her, she had several messages? But the day she felt like someone should at least have checked she was ok, there was nothing.

No request for updates or anything. She half wanted to message both Arnie and Mitchell and let them know how she'd got on, but the other half talked her out of it. Maybe it was best to say nothing about anything that had happened here.

She let out a sigh. Other than going on the world's most insane wild goose chase, what exactly had happened here? Nothing that she wanted to share with them. This adventure had landed her in a beautiful room in a house with a loving family. Somewhere she most certainly didn't belong, but she could think of worse places to be. If she could switch off from work for a while, she might even enjoy herself here.

Who knew how long she'd be stuck? Maybe the snow would stop, and the roads would be clear by morning. She had to get back to work on Monday, but part of her just wanted to snuggle up and hibernate here for the winter. Under different circumstances though. She still couldn't rid herself completely of the creeping guilt of being here at all. But it was such a comfort knowing people were downstairs, and she wasn't alone.

She lifted the book she'd taken from the book room and started reading it, stifling a yawn. Exhaustion was creeping up on her. It had taken its toll the last few days and she could quite happily close her eyes and drift off in this wonderful soft nest.

Tilly's eyes opened to a knocking sound. Blinking, and trying to fix her glasses which were at a weird angle on her face, she rolled over, taking a moment to remember where she was and why her stomach felt wobbly despite the deep contentment in her body amidst these wonderfully soft blankets.

'Tilly,' a low voice said from the other side of the door. 'Are you ok?'

Shit. She was in Rafe Harrington's house. Struggling to unwrap herself from the mass of blankets, she pushed them aside and tried to flatten her hair before opening the door.

'Hi.' She pulled it open, adjusted her glasses so they were perfectly straight, and hitched on her smile.

Rafe returned it with a side-quirk of his lips. 'We're about to have dinner if you want to join us.'

'Oh...'

'Or shall I bring you something up?'

'I don't want you to go to any trouble. Maybe I could come and get something, but I don't think I should eat with your family. I'll just get in the way.' She glanced away. Why were tears so close to the surface today? The cork had well and truly popped since she got here.

Rafe didn't reply, but she was hyperaware of his eyes on her. Even without returning his gaze, she felt them x-raying her.

'I don't know what to say,' he said after a moment. 'I can give you all the assurances in the world that my family will be happy to have you join us, but I don't think you'll believe me.'

She willed herself not to cry.

'Hey.' He reached out and placed a warm hand on her upper arm. 'I'm sorry. I didn't mean to upset you.'

She shook her head and flapped her hands in front of her face, forcing out the words, 'You didn't.'

'Then...' His fingers gently applied pressure to her arm, rubbing her with the pad of his thumb. 'Of course you're welcome to come and get food and take it wherever you like. It just seems so lonely.'

The pain in her chest cracked, and she let out a little sob.

'Tilly?' he said, his voice questioning. 'What's wrong?'

'I'm so sorry.'

'Please, don't be. Here, do you need a hug?'

'I...' Did she? She had no idea. 'Probably.'

Before she could fathom what he was doing, his arms were around her and she was resting her head against a wide, firm chest. 'Everything's ok.' He rubbed his hand over her back in a soothing circle.

'Is it though?' she sniffed. 'I feel so...' She wasn't sure how to describe it. 'Adrift.' The word popped from nowhere. And she wasn't sure that was what she meant. Because despite the muddled situation, Rafe's arms were anchoring her better than anything she could remember.

'I get it. Business travel is never easy to start with, and this has got to take the cake for weirdness. I wish I could convince you that my family don't want to add to your problems. They genuinely care what happens to you now. We're all invested in your wellbeing.'

She closed her eyes, controlling her breathing; it seemed to want to come in fits and starts. Why did this hug feel so good? Why did *he* feel so good? Normally, no one was around to give comfort for anything, and it was so gorgeous to have someone treat her like this. Some of the weight dropped from her shoulders as he continued to gently massage her back.

Wind whistled past the window outside despite what she assumed was top-level double glazing. It sounded wild, but she was in the safest, warmest place she could imagine.

Thank my lucky stars I landed here.

How could she have stayed outside on a night like this? She brushed away the thought of what might have happened had Rafe not come looking for her. Of course, she wouldn't be here at all if it weren't for her own stupidity, but right now, it seemed like this was exactly where she was meant to be.

'Ok,' she whispered, pulling back and using the heel of her hand to wipe away the tears from under her eyes. 'I'll come down for dinner.'

He smiled, relaxing his grip on her but not fully releasing her. 'Good. Come and join the chaos.'

Their gazes met, and Tilly was caught in a tractor beam, tugging her closer. Did he have some hidden power commanding her to come to him? She'd obey in an instant. Why deny how attractive she found him? Where was the harm? Looking wasn't a crime. Having a crush wasn't either. Not if that's all it was.

If she didn't know better, she might think he felt something for her too, but that wasn't a road she was prepared to travel. Oh no. She mustn't do that. She *did* know better. Therapy had taught her to be on her guard whenever she was faced with possible romantic encounters. That's when limerence reared up and took over, feeding her all sorts of fake ideas. This shouldn't be classed as a romantic encounter, but... Well, she definitely felt something for him. Maybe just gratitude. And that definitely wouldn't be two way.

'I, um, should tidy up a bit,' she said.

'Sure.' He still didn't release her completely, watching her with an almost puzzled expression. 'Come down when you're ready.'

She smiled, and he finally dropped his hands, letting her go. If she hadn't been prepared for it, she might have toppled over. Dizziness washed over her, and she was suddenly lightheaded. Maybe just because she hadn't eaten much all day.

'You really do have a beautiful smile, Tilly,' he said, then with a little grin of his own, he left her to get ready.

Taking steadying breaths, she returned to the bed and sat on the end.

He thinks I have a beautiful smile.

He hugged me and looked at me like I was someone who mattered to him.

Why was he being so nice? Making himself so damn loveable? Just like his whole family. Tilly made her way to the bathroom, took off her glasses, and gave her face a wash. She dabbed it dry and applied some make-up. Something was needed to hide her blotchy eyes. Her naturally curly dark hair looked wild after getting wet earlier, but she didn't have time to do much about it. Raking in her bag, she found a claw clip and pulled her hair back into a messy updo. The finished result was far from perfect, but it would do.

Hallmark movies had never been her thing, but she'd watched odd bits of them occasionally, when trying to force herself into being festive – not that it had ever worked. But here she was, bang in the middle of one, or so it seemed. This house was like a film set lavishly decorated with greenery, ribbons, gold glittery baubles and even sprigs of mistletoe hung in doorways. The grand stairs had evergreen garlands all the way down the banister and Rosemary Clooney crooned 'The Christmas Song' gently from a hidden speaker.

At the half-open door to the dining room, Tilly paused, hearing voices. Should she go in…? Or knock? Or turn on her heel and run?

Hilary's voice rose above the others and too late, Tilly realised it was because she was at the door on the other side. She opened it fully and Tilly pulled a smile, hoping it looked like she'd just arrived and hadn't been standing like a ninny for the last few moments.

'Tilly!' Hilary beamed at her, then gave her another wonderful hug. 'I'm so pleased you decided to join us. I've set you a space, right beside Rafe. He'll be delighted too. Now in you go.'

Thrust into the limelight, she couldn't exactly back out now, but she wasn't sure where to look. Rafe got to his feet and pulled out the chair next to his. 'Here you go.'

'Thank you.' She took the seat and made a bit of a business about tucking it in before looking up at the family.

'Let me introduce you to everyone.' He went around the table and Tilly put faces to the names he'd told her in the car earlier. Genevieve gave a little wave when Rafe reached her.

'We've already met,' she said. 'And Tilly, I'm so thrilled you're here for real.'

'Nice to meet you,' Geoff Harrington said. He was very like his son, only with almost white hair and a less imposing figure, though he still looked in good shape and his smile was very charming. 'I hear you work for a travel company too.'

'Um… Yes.'

'But we're not talking shop,' Rafe said.

'I know, I know,' Geoff said with a grin. 'Old habits die hard.'

'*Die Hard*?' Cressida said. 'Please tell me you're not going to make us watch that again. It is so not a Christmas movie.'

'Uh-oh,' Rafe said aside to Tilly. 'We have this argument every year.'

'And *is* it a Christmas movie?' Tilly asked. 'I've never seen it.'

Rafe let out a half laugh. 'If Dad gets his way, you can watch it with us and decide for yourself.'

'Really? Surely it either is or it isn't.'

'It doesn't exactly have the usual Christmas themes, but it's set at Christmas, so it's open for debate. As you can see.' He raised his eyebrow across the table to where his dad and his sister were still arguing about it, though both were laughing.

Rafe lifted a bottle of sparkling wine from the centre of the table. 'Fancy some of this?' he asked Tilly.

Should she?

His eyes pressed her to say yes.

'Ok, a little. Thank you.'

He poured some into her glass. Tilly's mind strayed back to what his mum had said about him being pleased to have her next to him. Why would he? He certainly didn't seem upset about it, but did he particularly want her beside him?

Hilary returned to the room and Tilly caught her eye. The older woman's lips turned up as her gaze moved from Tilly to

Rafe. She put her hands together and tapped her fingertips as if silently applauding.

What was she up to?

Tilly chanced a half glance at Rafe and caught the end of what could have been an eye roll. He shook his head, pouring himself some wine.

Was Hilary trying to set them up? Maybe she wanted the situation Rafe had invented to be true.

Did he?

More to the point, do I?

That would be mad. They hardly knew each other. Was this just her seeing what she wanted to see? Clinging to anyone who showed her kindness and concern? That was what her previous boyfriend had accused her of being – too needy and too clingy. And he was right. A therapist had confirmed it. Since her early years, she'd dreamed of being part of something like this. Dreamed of the dollhouse opening and letting her step inside and be part of the world. Now she was here, but she couldn't afford to get too attached because this couldn't last. When the snow melted and disappeared, she'd be going with it. She was nothing but a fleeting winter visitor.

Chapter Eleven

Rafe

'Once we get Alexander down for his nap, how about we have a game of charades?' Cressida said.

Candles flickered on the tables alongside empty plates and cracker debris. Rafe sat back and something brushed against his shoulder. For a second, his heart stopped. Had Tilly stroked him? Turning his gaze, he realised it was nothing but the tissue crown from the Christmas cracker he'd propped haphazardly on his head. His movement must have been enough to knock it off. Taking it in his hand, he slipped it onto the table, glancing at Tilly, who was still wearing her crown. Seeing the joy on her face when she'd snapped a cracker with him had thrown technicolour across his monochrome vision of Christmas.

'Not charades,' Genevieve moaned.

'You love it.' Finlay nudged her with a smile.

Tilly caught Rafe's eye, and he realised he was still looking at her. Her cheeks were a little rosy, perhaps from the prosecco his mum had given her, and her lips quirked up. A tiny sparkle appeared in her eyes; that was better than she'd been earlier.

Being no stranger to his mum's matchmaking tactics, Rafe guessed exactly why she'd insisted Tilly sat next to him. And he didn't mind. He'd meant what he said earlier about fancying her a bit. Who wouldn't? That smile got him every time, and she seemed like a sweet, sensitive soul. But those sad eyes. How could he top up that smile, so it reached them? But that wasn't his place. His mum might imagine a fanciful outcome for them, but he was too sensible to let it happen for real. He was happy enjoying her company and making her feel welcome for a short while, but as soon as the snow melted, he'd give her a lift back to the station and let her get on with her life.

'Do you like charades?' He leaned back a little so she could answer without everyone hearing. This whole event was possibly a charade for her.

'I don't think I've ever played it,' she said.

'Oh, you'll love it,' Cressida pitched in, and Rafe barely held back an eye roll. His family really were a bunch of nosey parkers. 'We can do a Christmas theme. Remember the year, Rafe, you were trying to do Santa on his sleigh, and we all thought you were acting out sitting on the toilet?'

He put his head in his hand and screwed up his lips. 'You seriously had to remind everyone of that.'

Tilly giggled, and he threw her a look, but when his eyes met hers, he burst out laughing.

Suddenly the sparkle blazed in her pupils, and she wasn't a little mouse, but a radiant star. 'I bet that was quite a sight.'

'Oh, it was,' Cressida said. 'He looked constipated.'

More giggles erupted from Tilly.

'Seriously?' Rafe said. 'I was about twelve.'

'No, you weren't,' Genevieve said. 'I was about fifteen when that happened, so you must have been at least twenty.'

'Well, twelve, twenty... It's in the same ballpark.' He gave a nonchalant shrug at her look of protest.

'It is to me,' grandma said. 'I'll be eighty next year, but I still feel like I'm in my twenties. The body just doesn't play ball these days.'

'Doesn't seem to stop you though.' Rafe raised his eyebrows.

'True.' She necked the remainder of her wine and poured some more.

'Let's go into the living room and do some charades then.' Hilary got to her feet and lifted some plates.

'Let us clean up, Mum.' Rafe got up and took the plates from her. 'You've done enough already. Go and relax.'

'Ah, thank you, son.' She patted his arm. 'You can come with me, Tilly.'

'I should help.' She pushed back her seat.

'No.' Rafe piled up some more plates as his sisters did the same. 'Keep Mum and Grandma company. That'll be helping enough. We'll clean up.'

'If you're sure.'

'He is.' Hilary helped Grandma to her feet. 'And you haven't met Mitzi yet.'

'Who's that?' Tilly asked.

'She's Genevieve and Finlay's French bulldog. She and the boys get on very well.'

'I see,' Tilly said as they headed out of the room.

'They have so much energy…' Grandma said, and their voices trailed off.

'Ooh,' Genevieve said as soon as they were out of earshot. 'You and Tilly are so cute.'

Rafe gave her a look. 'Don't let's go there.'

'Why not? You said yourself you liked her. This is a chance. Grab it.'

'I wouldn't advise that,' Geoff said. 'Don't go grabbing a strange woman. You don't know where she's been or what she's up to.'

'That is a hideous way to put it,' Cressida said.

'Yes, Dad,' Genevieve said. 'She seems really nice. Just quiet.'

'Which makes me even more suspicious. I don't doubt she's a nice person, but quiet people don't normally act the way she did.'

'Let's just be nice to her.' Rafe stacked one last plate on his pile. 'She's really upset about causing us any trouble. When really, it's nothing for us to add another place to dinner or let her join us for a few hours. Let's face it, if she really was my girlfriend, you'd do that anyway.'

'Indeed, and I certainly don't have a problem with that,' Geoff said. 'I just think we should be guarded about certain things.'

'All the more reason not to talk shop then,' Rafe said.

'Pity really. I have a lot of things I'd like to discuss with you.'

'I'm sure it can wait until after Christmas.' Rafe left the dining room for the kitchen, carrying the pile of plates, with Genevieve following.

'You dodged that nicely,' she said.

'Yeah.' He laid the plates on the kitchen counter and opened the dishwasher. 'I don't want him to ask me to take over the business again. I can't.'

'He really wants you to.'

'I have my own business to focus on and that's all I've got time for at the moment. Don't you fancy it?'

'I don't really have the expertise. And I enjoy what I do. Running a big business like that is not for me and Cressida doesn't want it either.'

'Same. I could do it, but what about Innova? I belong there. It's my baby and I don't want to give it up. Sure, it's not as big as Dad's business, but I'm getting there, and it doesn't feel right to walk away from it.'

'I think you should stick with it. Even though I don't like the idea of an outsider taking over Dad's business when he retires, I guess I'll have to accept that when he does.'

It was one of the reasons, Rafe had deliberately not used his name for the business. He didn't want to end up in this situation. Would Harrington Energy Solutions be the same without a Harrington at the helm? He didn't like the idea of handing it over to someone out of the family either, but it didn't change his personal feelings on taking it on either. It just left him with a bad taste in his mouth. Neither choice was good.

When the washer was loaded and the dining room tidy, Rafe and the others made their way to the living room. He barely held back a laugh when he spotted Tilly sitting on the floor by the Christmas tree, being licked and slobbered over by the three dogs. Joy spread across her face, lighting it from top to bottom. Dog therapy had clearly worked wonders. Hilary beamed at him, then sidled over.

'She's in love,' she said.

'What?'

'Tilly.'

'Is she?'

'With the dogs. Look at them. Have you ever seen anyone so happy?'

'Oh... Yeah. She looks very... um, happy.'

Hilary patted his arm. 'Don't be jealous. I think she quite likes you too.'

'Mum, seriously?' Though his gut did a weird little flip-flop. Did she like him? As in *like* like him?

Oh god. That would not be sensible.

This was Christmas fever taking hold and making him think stupid things. Possibly the fact he hadn't dated for a while was an issue too. Tomorrow, he needed to go for a run or pump some iron, release some of the physical tension gripping his system, and dispel the pent-up energy. Nothing he might like to do with Tilly should feature in that plan. Sleeping with the enemy wasn't a great idea at any time... though she didn't really look like the enemy anymore. A tiny moment of doubt flickered through him. What if his dad was right, and Tilly was faking all this to lure him into doing something stupid? But he brushed it away. Crazy as it may seem, he trusted her. But it wouldn't be the first time he'd been fooled by a lovely smile.

He took a seat on one side of the large L-shaped sofa, expecting his mum to sit beside him, but she continued over to Tilly and chatted with her. Tilly extricated herself from the dogs and Hilary helped her up, laughing as the dogs tried to lure her back down again with their pawing and shuffling. Once Tilly was on her feet, Hilary pointed to the empty seat next to Rafe. Brushing down her clothes, Tilly came over and sat by him.

Can Mum be any more obvious? But he was in control. He dealt with people all the time, and Tilly was just another person.

'You're getting on well with them,' he said.

'They're so cute and cuddly. I've never really spent much time with dogs.'

'That's city life, isn't it?' he said. 'I miss having a dog. These guys are always fun to be around.'

'Shuffle up.' His mum appeared and waggled her hand, indicating for him to move even closer to Tilly.

Silently grinding his teeth, he did as his mum wanted, not drawing attention to her blatant matchmaking or the fact there was plenty of room for her without him moving. It was simpler just to let her play this game, but it meant he was closer to Tilly than was sensible. His thigh brushed hers and his body reacted like a teenager. Christ, he had this bad. He crossed his legs and Tilly glanced at him. Her smile was back. She exhaled gently and her chest heaved under her cream sweater. Ok, so he really shouldn't be looking there. Her warm thigh pressed against his again and her shoulder nudged him. She blinked and switched her focus back to the room, but she didn't move or attempt to pull away.

Geoff topped up the drinks, and the family chatted for a while as Tina put Alexander to bed. Rafe breathed very deliberately, until his legs relaxed. Once that happened, he found the touch of Tilly's thigh rather pleasant. It became almost natural. Like she was meant to be here at his side.

He tossed back some more prosecco, trying to numb the inappropriate feelings jumping around inside him. But unbidden, his eyes latched onto her again, and she gazed back. It would be so easy to slant his head to the side, lean in, and kiss that precious smile. Was she thinking something similar? She blinked like she was clearing her mind, then looked away, and fiddled with the ends of her dark hair.

He restrained from leaning his arm along the back of the sofa behind her. Such territorial acts should be reserved for women he was dating, not strangers who worked for rival companies, but the need to touch her burned strong. His fingers twitched, and he gripped the stem of his glass tight.

Tina returned carrying a baby monitor and gave Cressida the thumbs up.

'All ok?' Hilary got to her feet.

'He's sound,' Tina said.

'Wonderful. Well, I found the box of prompts you made.' Hilary smiled at Rafe.

He leaned his head towards Tilly's ear, the simmering fire in his chest urging him to get closer. 'Mum keeps the strangest things. We must have made those prompts about twenty years ago.'

Tilly smiled at him and momentarily her teeth grazed her lower lip – such an adorable action that sent lust barrelling through him, making him want to dip in and kiss her right there and then.

Master this.

Why was she affecting him like this? Curse this dry spell, making him feel like a horny teen.

'You're lucky.' She gave him a little shoulder bump. 'She values you all so highly.'

'That's true. But it's what Mums do, right?'

Tilly gave a little shrug, like she wanted to disagree, but Hilary opened a small box and said, 'Who wants to go first?' Tilly's attention instantly turned to her.

Rafe sipped his drink. What was Tilly's story? Maybe her home life hadn't been as good as his growing up. Should he ask?

Or was it better not to and keep it as none of his business? He could hardly keep things purely professional now, but he could maintain sensible boundaries. Though how long they'd last, he didn't like to say.

Finlay volunteered to go first, and the game started with the usual guessing of how many words, then syllables. The wild acting got steadily worse as the evening went on and more drinks were consumed.

Tilly declined a turn the first time around, but Rafe took his chance, put his glass onto the coffee table and tugged out a card. *When Santa Got Stuck Up The Chimney.*

Why did this feel like history repeating itself? Time to bring out the constipation face again... Tears of laughter streaked down Tilly's cheeks, as he strained and pushed. She took off her glasses and wiped them, still chuckling as he returned to the seat.

'That was so funny.' She replaced her glasses.

'I think you should take a turn too, then I can have a good giggle as well.'

'Ok.' She picked a folded card from the box, read it, and took her place in the middle of the floor. Rafe sat back, leaning his arm along the sofa as he'd wanted to do earlier, watching her. What was she doing? She made several false starts, turning away and laughing, before gathering herself and making wide gestures with her arms. Then she pointed to herself, crossed her arms over her chest, and flapped her hand at the Christmas tree. Her eyes landed on him and her finger hovered in his direction before she made the wide arm gestures again.

Genevieve and Cressida were shouting out suggestions nineteen to the dozen, but Rafe frowned. 'All I want for Christmas is you,' he said.

She nodded, and their eyes connected again. 'Yes.' The noise in the room momentarily stopped and Rafe's ears buzzed. The connection was powerful, and those song words seemed to intensify it.

'Oooh!' Genevieve laughed, picking up the box. 'You two.'

Tilly took her seat back beside him, and he moved his arm just in time.

'Thank goodness you guessed it.' Her cheeks were very pink, but the room was warm. 'I'm not very good at that kind of thing.'

He kept his eyes on her and smiled. 'You seemed good to me.'

'You definitely got the message across.' Hilary leaned forward for her glass, beaming at the two of them as she sat back.

'Oh... I didn't mean—'

'It's ok.' Rafe brushed his shoulder with hers. 'Just my crazy family.'

She nipped her bottom lip with her teeth again, like she was trying to hold back a giggle, and nodded.

Heat seared in Rafe's chest like heartburn. Prosecco could be bad for that, but this was something else – something Tilly-related. He half wished she really had come here as his girlfriend, then he could go upstairs with her after and make love to her until his body and soul were fully and deeply satisfied. Many strange things had happened today, but that wouldn't be one of them.

Eventually, the game lapsed into chat until people started yawning. Rafe stifled his as best he could but there was no fighting it.

'We should get some sleep,' Cressida said. 'Alexander always wakes in the night and gets up early.'

'I'm calling it a night too.' Hilary got to her feet. 'And Grandma's already given up on us by the looks of things.'

She was leaning over to one side on a cushion, snoring gently.

'I'll wake her,' Cressida said. 'Grandma.' She gave her a little poke.

'What?' She blinked her eyes open. 'I wasn't asleep, just resting my eyes.'

Rafe smirked and stood up. 'Well, I'm going to bed to rest my eyes in there.'

'I'll go too.' Tilly followed him immediately. 'I can't thank you all enough for having me.'

'Think nothing of it.' Hilary put her hands on Tilly's cheeks and kissed her forehead. 'It's an absolute pleasure.'

Tilly blinked as if shocked, but smiled.

They headed up the stairs together, Hilary helping Grandma.

'You'd think in a house this size you'd have downstairs bedrooms or a lift at the very least,' Grandma grumbled.

'I'll carry you if you like,' Rafe said.

'No, I absolutely don't. I'd be petrified.'

He laughed and winked at Tilly.

'Goodnight to you both,' Hilary said through another yawn as she reached the top of the stairs.

'Night, Mum. Grandma.' Rafe gave them both a kiss and a hug.

'Night,' Tilly said.

'And be good,' Grandma added.

'Um... Ok.' Rafe furrowed his brow. Had Grandma been reading his mind? God forbid. No one needed to know what was happening in there right now. He gave her and his mum a little wave as he and Tilly turned the other way towards their rooms. 'Sorry about them,' he said as he reached his door. 'They don't mean anything. It's just their way.'

'It's fine,' Tilly said with her most beautiful smile.

Rafe leaned his hand flat on his door. 'Sleep well, Tilly. And rest easy. Everything turned out ok today, didn't it?'

'Your family are so kind.'

'Well, I'm glad you tracked me down. You've definitely added to the Christmas chaos today.'

The beautiful smile grew, lighting up her whole face. Rafe internally fist pumped. There it was, right up to her eyes. Shining.

'Thank you... For everything.' She held his gaze for a moment, then blinked. 'Especially your stuck Santa impression. I'd have missed out for sure if I hadn't seen that.'

He huffed out a laugh and shook his head. 'Glad it made you happy. Yours wasn't too bad either.'

Her cheeks coloured again. Intriguing. Did that mean she was feeling something too? He doubted he was all she wanted for Christmas, but maybe she wanted something from him, or to do something with him... A kiss? A cuddle? A bit more? What was on her mind? If only he could prise it open and find out. Not that he should act on it. This situation was messy enough.

With one last smile, he opened his door. 'Goodnight, Tilly.'

'Goodnight.'

He went inside, loosened the neck of his sweater, then hoisted it off over his head and tossed it into the washing basket. In the room next door, Tilly would be undressing for bed too, and he had a weird sense that she was just right there on the other side of the wall, less than three metres from him, tugging off her top and rolling down her jeans, like they were undressing together.

Stop it.

But he couldn't stop imagining the scene. Even as he lay in bed, listening to the wind whipping the snow past the window, Tilly's face swam in his mind. Was she awake too? What thoughts danced through her mind this cold winter's night? Was she thinking about him and how warm it would be if they were cuddled up together? He let out a groan. Could he just shut this down?

It felt like he'd barely closed his eyes when he awoke to a crying sound. For a moment he thought it was still the wind, but slowly he recognised it as a baby. Alexander must have woken. Other distant voices drifted vaguely into his conscience and the crying stopped. In another life, he was a married man with kids. If his marriage had worked out, he could easily have had two or three children by now. Instead, he'd given up that idea and focused on his career, but more and more, it felt like something fundamental was missing. The thought was keener and sharper than it had been for a long time.

His thoughts drifted to the room next door and his eyes closed to thoughts of Tilly once more.

CHAPTER TWELVE

Tilly

Saturday, December 21st

Morning

Tilly pulled a fleecy robe over her shoulders and slipped her feet into a pair of white fluffy slippers. Hilary Harrington had thought of everything. This place was better than a five-star hotel. She left the little shower room fresh as a winter rose. Thankfully she'd put a reserve set of clothing in her case. The dull leggings and plain grey sweater weren't exactly the glamorous, sexy garments she wished she'd packed for an unexpected weekend with Rafe Harrington, but they'd have to do. After that, she had nothing clean, which meant she *had* to find a way back to London, preferably today. She stretched her arms, her muscles slightly tense. The thought of returning to London was high in her mind, but the thought of staying here pushed its way in, waking fluttering snow fairies in her tummy. Pinpointing exactly why wasn't tricky. Rafe's face rose to the surface of her mind and the snow fairies danced, reminding her of the night before. All those smouldering glances. The way his accidental touches sent bolts of electricity to every nerve end. This was bordering on dangerous territory.

Don't get carried away or imagine this to be anything special.

She had to take care. Swatting the visions away, she crossed the beautiful bedroom and opened the curtains. The floor-to-ceiling window was actually a door onto a little veranda, but no way was she getting out there today. Thick snow blanketed the floor right up to the door, making it impossible to open. The garden and countryside beyond sparkled white. Sun lit up ice crystals that glittered like pixie dust, and pure blue skies contrasted with the white landscape. Icing-sugar-like snow encrusted the branches of tall pine trees.

She wrapped her arms around herself, drawing the robe close as goosebumps slid along the back of her neck. If only she could cocoon herself in a blanket and sit and watch this all day. Of course, she couldn't actually do that. A groan escaped her lips, but she still couldn't drag her eyes from the stunning landscape. Somehow, she needed to find transport to get her to London, either today or tomorrow. Surely something, somewhere, would be running. Wouldn't snow ploughs come along and make the roads safe to travel on?

The 1-Quick office was open right up until Christmas Eve. They didn't even finish early. Scrooge or what? Apparently, the company CEO thought they shouldn't even close on Christmas Day and he'd already stopped giving them Boxing Day off. People's holiday needs didn't stop for Christmas, which meant they shouldn't either – or so he said – which meant Tilly still had to work on Monday and Tuesday. She'd be off on Wednesday for Christmas Day and then back on Thursday for the Boxing Day rush. Pressure built in her brain with every thought she added to it. How could anyone find this time of year fun or relaxing with a schedule like that? Having Wednesday off was barely worth it. And with a Monday morning looming just two days away, she couldn't afford to linger. Arnie wouldn't accept her being snowed in somewhere in the Highlands as a reasonable excuse, when technically she shouldn't even be here. No reason she gave was likely to go down well.

She sat on the bed and opened her phone, checking the train app. All trains in this area were cancelled. *Seriously?* What about buses? Same story. Only a handful of buses were running on the main roads, and none were currently stopping in Glenbriar. She wasn't sure if she could even get from Greenacres into the town anyway. Rafe had said it was too far to walk in this weather and if the taxi journey had been anything to go by, he wasn't joking. A trip that took ten minutes in a car must be at least an hour's walk, and she didn't have boots or waterproof clothes. Would the Raptor get through this? It had those big thick tyres, but the snow looked deep.

I can't expect him to go out in this.

How could she? It would put him at risk and no way did she want that. Taxi drivers would be the same. None of them would want to risk it out here, and who could blame them? Tilly didn't drive, but she didn't fancy even being a passenger in this.

A low hum of people chatting outside her room caught her attention. Were they going downstairs? She wasn't sure what she should do. Stay here or go down with them? They'd said she was welcome, but was expecting breakfast an imposition? Had they only said those kind things because they had good manners but actually couldn't wait for her to leave?

She clutched to the hope that it was real. Last night had been such fun, and she'd felt so included. Hopefully, it wasn't a fantasy that had died overnight.

Rafe's room was next door. Should she knock and ask him if she could go downstairs with him? Or was that too clingy? She glanced up at the door to her little shower room and then along the wall. The layout suggested he had a matching shower room in his bedroom. Had he been taking a shower just through the wall from her? Why did that feel so intimate? An x-rated movie had started rolling in her head in monochrome. Rafe, with a tanned body, toned abs, and muscular shoulders, like the shirtless guy on the front of the book she'd borrowed last night, was showering before her, water cascading over him as he ran his fingers through his hair. As her internal voyeur cam moved lower, she gasped and shook her head.

Oh my god.

She had to shut that down. But how? Last night on the sofa, they'd been so close. Just how good had that felt? When he'd hugged her, she'd felt safe and cared for. But the daydream she'd just had was something else.

Or was it just further evidence of her clinginess? Her imagination filled in gaps with wild suggestions, miles away from the reality he was living. A guy like him was easy in his own skin, carefree around other people, and sitting next to her probably hadn't put him up or down. She let out a little scoff and gave herself a mental shake. Time to stop this. Why did she always read all sorts of things into situations? She'd imagined all the looks. He didn't like her any more than any other woman. Why would he?

Just concentrate on getting back to London; this will all blow over and none of it will matter anyway.

The thought pushed her into getting the rest of her clothes on quickly. She opened the door and glanced into the corridor. Voices were still chattering somewhere in the house. Not being familiar with the layout, she couldn't work out exactly where they were coming from. Now was the time to be brave and go downstairs and find out. Slowly, she made her way to the top of the grand, sweeping staircase. It was modern in design but, like everything in this place, the contemporary, mixed with rustic, gave it a charm all its own. She stopped for a moment, running her fingertips over a poinsettia and pine garland on the banister. Such gorgeous festive décor. Hilary must enjoy this kind of thing to have spent so much time on it. Tilly hadn't bothered with a single decoration. Even if she loved Christmas, she couldn't imagine finding the time to go all out like this.

She edged through the half-open door into the kitchen, following the smell of bacon and the sound of happy chat and clinking crockery. Most of the family were there, sitting chatting, or at the worktop making drinks and popping slices of bread in the toaster. Tilly swept around, mentally ticking them off. No Geoff and no Rafe. Without him, it felt weird going in. She took a deep breath. Everyone kept saying she was welcome. Now was the time to test that.

Just one more step.

'Morning,' Hilary said with a bright smile and Tilly froze before she could move further into the room. 'Did you sleep well?'

'Yes, thank you,' Tilly said. And come to think on it, she really had. Surprisingly well, all things considered. The peace and quiet had been second to none. The lack of blaring music and traffic replaced by roaring gusts and the faint tinkle of wind chimes had been just the tonic. She'd even managed to forget about work in the aftermath of such an enjoyable evening.

'Looks like you're stuck with us for a while longer,' Genevieve said. 'No one's getting out of here yet.'

'Oh dear.' Tilly made her way into the room.

'Yeah,' Cressida said. 'Take a seat.' She pointed to the table where Genevieve and Finlay were sitting with Grandma, and

Tina was putting Alexander into his highchair. 'This area has been badly affected.'

'This glen has always been good for snow, even if the village wasn't affected,' Genevieve added as Tilly took a seat next to her. 'I remember quite a few days off school.'

'Do you?' Cressida said. 'I remember Mum sending us in all weather.'

'Really, girls,' Hilary said. 'You were older when we moved here, Cressida, you didn't have as long at school as Genevieve.'

'Yeah, but I remember that time the school bus skidded going around a corner and nearly hit the sweet shop on the main street.'

Hilary frowned and gave a little shake of her head.

'Funny how memories change as we get older.' Grandma chuckled as she spread jam on her toast.

'I'm not making that up,' Cressida said.

'Morning, everyone,' a voice behind Tilly said, and she turned instantly. Rafe stood at the door, looking delicious in a chunky cable-knit sweater and jeans. He'd taken off his boots and had on thick cosy socks.

Uh-oh. How could she even attempt to kid herself on that she didn't fancy him?

'Morning,' Tilly said along with everyone else.

'Quite some weather out there, huh?' He raked up his slightly damp hair, giving Tilly a smile that could have melted most of the snow.

Mitzi came bounding in, slipping and scratching a little on the wooden floor as she made a beeline for Genevieve. Genevieve scooped her up and cuddled her. 'Did your naughty uncle let you get all wet and not dry you properly?' she cooed.

Cressida picked up Alexander's cup from the floor and put it back in front of him. 'We've just been talking about the weather. It's going to cause some disruption.'

'Lucky we're not going anywhere.' Genevieve put Mitzi down and dusted off her clothes.

'I need to get back to London,' Tilly said. 'Either today or tomorrow. My boss will kill me if I'm not at work on Monday morning.'

'Dear, dear,' Grandma said. 'He sounds like an eejit. Fancy expecting someone to get from here to London in this weather.'

'Yeah,' Tilly agreed. 'But I can't impose on you all anymore and I've also run out of clothes.'

'The clothes aren't a problem,' Hilary said. 'I can wash everything.'

'I'll put them on with my things after breakfast,' Genevieve said. 'I need to wash this stuff now.'

'Um...'

'And we can lend you anything you need. I'm sure between the four of us' – Hilary gestured to herself, Genevieve, Tina, then Cressida – 'I'm sure we can find something that fits.'

'And there's always me,' Grandma said. 'I have some very fetching floral skirts.'

'Mother,' Hilary said. 'I didn't include you because I know you didn't bring much yourself.'

Grandma chuckled and gave Tilly a cheeky wink.

'And you're not imposing.' Genevieve patted Tilly on the arm. 'We like having you here, don't we?' Her gaze fell on Rafe and Tilly felt her cheeks burning like someone had slapped her.

'Of course we do,' he said breezily.

'Why don't you just call in sick? Feign a stomach bug. That'll buy you forty-eight hours, minimum,' Cressida suggested.

'That's the easiest thing to do.' Rafe padded into the kitchen and cut a thick slice of bread.

Tilly shook her head at his back and let out a little huff. 'Are you serious? You're a CEO.'

He pushed his bread into the toaster, then turned to face her, leaning on the work surface and folding his arms in a casual way that still exuded sex appeal. 'Uh-huh?' His grin looked equal parts questioning and wicked.

'Well, would you want your employees doing that?'

'He's very naughty.' Grandma shook her head. 'So, he probably does it himself.'

He smiled one of those megawatt smiles of his, melting Tilly some more. 'I'm not just a CEO, I'm also a human being. And, let's get real, people do it. Everyone knows that. We've all done it at some point in our lives.'

'Told you,' Grandma said.

'Yup,' Cressida added. 'Sometimes it's the only way.'

'I haven't done it,' Tilly murmured, fiddling with the cuff of her boring sweater.

'First time for everything.' Grandma winked at her.

'I think you should do it,' Genevieve said. 'Then you can relax and not have to worry about getting back.'

'It's going to be impossible anyway,' Cressida said. 'You might manage it, but you might also cause an accident for yourself or someone else.'

'That's true,' she said. 'I'll have to think about it.' Though she was pretty sure she wouldn't relax if she ended up staying here. Her brain would never stop badgering her with guilty thoughts of where she should be and that would block anything pleasant that might happen.

'You shouldn't put yourself at risk.' Rafe lifted his toast from the toaster, plated it, and joined Tilly at the table, which was already set with pastries and a selection of spreads. All of it looked so yummy Tilly wasn't sure what to choose. 'I wouldn't expect anyone who works for me to do that, but I understand how you feel.' He took the empty seat next to her. 'You're a conscientious employee, which is great. You don't want to feel like you're letting anyone down.'

'Exactly.'

'But I'm inclined to think they've let you down.' He offered her a plate laden with pastries and she lifted a croissant.

'Maybe they have.' She sighed and reached for the jam.

'It's probably not my place to say it.' Rafe spread a liberal amount of butter on his toast. 'But from what you told me yesterday, it sounds like they've been abusing your loyalty. Of course, I don't advocate tit-for-tat behaviour, but it makes me wonder why you're so happy to give without getting anything back. Even respect. They should be prepared to accept your word and your predicament without threatening behaviour. If an employee of mine called in to say they were snowed in, we'd work around it. They could work from home or, if that wasn't possible, make up the time elsewhere. We'd agree on something that was fair.'

'I don't see anyone at 1-Quick caring enough to do that. They're more likely to say it's coming off my pay and still make me work the time back.' Tilly cut her croissant in half rather aggressively.

'That's unacceptable, but I know it happens all too often.' He offered her a small bowl. 'Clotted cream?'

'Is that normal on croissants?'

'It's Christmas. You can overindulge on anything you fancy without feeling guilty.'

She flicked him a little smile and their eye contact grew intense. Normally, she didn't even bother with breakfast. There just wasn't time. But she got the feeling his words carried a hidden meaning. What else did he want to overindulge in? She almost groaned out loud. There she was doing it again 'Ok.' She took the bowl from him, twitching a little as her fingers brushed against his hand.

'Just see how things go today,' he said. 'We'll keep an eye on the weather and watch out for the snowploughs.'

'I guess that's all I can do; maybe I'll get out tomorrow.'

'If it clears at all and the trains or buses start again, I'll give you a lift to the station.'

She bit into her croissant and gave him a little nod of thanks. The warm buttery pastry combined with sweet jam and rich cream was so divine she almost let out a moan of pleasure. Catching a stray croissant crumb with her fingertip, she brushed it from her lips and into her mouth.

Rafe raised his eyebrows as he held his toast to his mouth and Tilly savoured another bite. His lips probably tasted as good as this. But she wasn't supposed to be thinking about things like that. She looked away, steering her thoughts to her predicament. While trying not to do anything rash made sense, she couldn't shake the feeling she was doing something wrong if she didn't spend every second at least trying to be back.

'You're one-hundred per cent replaceable at work,' Cressida said. 'I'm sure they can survive a couple of days without you.'

'Give me the phone number,' Grandma said. 'I'll call them and tell them the situation. That's one thing about growing old, I'm not easily intimidated. What's the worst that can happen?'

Tilly chuckled with the others. Nothing would happen to Rafe's lovely grandma, but Tilly wasn't sure Arnie would extend that courtesy to her. Of course, he could survive without her for a day or two, but it didn't wholly remove the queasy sensation in her stomach. That job was all she'd ever had. She didn't know how to do anything else.

Geoff came in clapping his hands, looking ruddy cheeked. 'It's gorgeous out there. Just dried the lads. They're getting warm by the fire now.'

'You look frozen.' Hilary took his arm as he approached the Aga.

'It's bracing, alright. I'll take the camera out later and get some pictures. I've not seen it like this for a while.'

'Would you like to go for a walk?' Rafe asked Tilly. 'We could find some boots that fit you, I'm sure.'

'Yeah, I'd like to. It's so beautiful.'

'What size of feet are you?'

'Five.'

'I think that's the same as Mum. She has loads of boots. I'm sure she'd be happy to lend you some.'

Tilly bit into her croissant again. She wasn't going anywhere for the next few hours at least, so she could afford to relax and enjoy this. The fairies in her tummy fluttered again, making their way into her chest, sending tingles through her nervous system. Enjoying herself here meant spending time with Rafe and that thought was really doing things to her body... and her brain.

CHAPTER THIRTEEN

Tilly

Saturday, December 21ˢᵗ

Morning and Afternoon

Snow crunched under the fur-lined walking boots Tilly had borrowed from Hilary. What was it about ruining virgin snow with big clumpy footprints that was so satisfying? Defiling the pristine landscape should be a crime, but it didn't take away the fun of being the first to make a trail across it. Finlay and Rafe had strayed onto a different path, examining animal tracks and trying to work out what they belonged to. Tiny little bird tracks made swirling circles around the leafless bushes and bird tables.

Tilly clapped her arms around Hilary's bright pink snow jacket. Even with that, a warm fleece scarf and insulated gloves, there was still a bite in the air Tilly wasn't used to. Crisp winter air filled her lungs, taking the cold inside her, but far from being painful it cleansed her deep. Squinting towards the bright but cold sun, she shielded her eyes, trying to see as far as she could. This landscape was unfamiliar to her, but she couldn't imagine it being anything other than a winter wonderland.

'Tilly,' Rafe called, and she glanced over her shoulder.

'Yes.'

'Watch this.' A mischievous grin played on his lips. He lifted a thick wad of snow and lobbed it at Finlay, who was in front of him on the path.

'What the?' Finlay turned around, shaking his hood. 'Right, that's it.' He scooped up a ball of snow from the top of a tall stone planter and pelted it back at Rafe.

'Oh, for god's sake. Take cover.' Genevieve grabbed Tilly's arm and pulled her behind another planter. 'This will be carnage.'

Tilly ducked down behind the planter, peeking out to watch, unable to stop smiling.

Rafe and Finlay tossed more snowballs at each other, laughing and pretending to be deadly serious in their aim... or maybe they were deadly serious. They were definitely very competitive and using a lot of effort.

'Boys will be boys,' Genevieve said with a smirk. 'I'm not getting involved in this.'

'Me neither.' Tilly chuckled at them. They looked like a pair of big kids. She didn't remember doing anything that silly even when she was a child, let alone now.

'If we run, we can catch Cress and Tina,' Genevieve said.

They'd walked on ahead with Alexander toddling in between them.

'Should we?'

'Yeah.' Covering her head, Genevieve ran down the path and Tilly did the same, expecting a snowball to hit her at any second.

Cressida looked behind and rolled her eyes. 'They're worse than Alexander.'

'Don't I know it?' Genevieve looked over her shoulder at her husband and her brother. 'And Finlay's so competitive.'

'So's Rafe.' Cressida rolled her eyes. 'This could go on for a long time.'

Laughter and shouts echoed through the air as the snowball fight continued.

Tilly turned around and saw Rafe behind her, facing the other way and tucked into the edge of the house like he was waiting to ambush Finlay. She scooped up a handful of snow, her gloved fingers tingling. 'Here you go,' she laughed, sending a snowball flying towards him.

'Oi.' He jumped back as the snow hit him and Tilly turned away, giggling with the others. 'Which one of you did that?' he shouted, pulling out the high collar of his snow jacket and shaking it.

'Alexander,' Cressida said.

Genevieve put her arm around Tilly's shoulder, laughing so hard she looked like she might double over. 'That was hilarious.

Nice shot. Went right down the back of his jacket by the looks of things.'

'Thanks.' Tilly glanced back at Rafe, who dodged another incoming projectile from Finlay.

'You've got a good aim,' Tina said.

'That was my first ever snowball.'

'Beginner's luck, maybe.'

'I've always wondered what it would be like in the snow.'

'I guess there isn't a lot of it in London.'

'Hardly any. We have had it occasionally, but never a lot, and... well, I don't really know anyone who would want a snowball fight.'

'Shall we build a snowman?' Genevieve said. 'You won't have done that before either.'

'Definitely haven't.' Tilly said.

'Let's do it then.' Genevieve turned to Finlay and Rafe, who were still charging about behind them like they were on a combat mission. 'Hey guys. *Do you wanna build a snowman?*' She sang the iconic line from *Frozen*.

'Sure,' Rafe chuckled, his breath creating a cloud in the frigid air.

'A proper one?' Finlay said. 'Like a sculpture.'

'Oh, sure, it's an art form. Shall I demo?' He packed up a little ball in his hand, then rolled it along a low wall. The snowball grew as he pushed it, the flakes clinging to his gloves.

'Don't throw that.' Genevieve shielded her face.

'I'm not sure I can even lift it, never mind throw it.' He rolled it off the wall and onto the ground to collect more snow. Finlay was doing another one on the grass beside them, exposing a long and rather out-of-place green stripe. 'But if I find out who threw that snowball before, I'd give it a go.'

'It was me,' Tilly said. 'So, let's see you try?'

He drew back a little and narrowed his eyes, clearly not expecting that. He'd obviously thought one of his sisters had done it. 'I'll think up a better punishment for you.'

'Oooh,' Genevieve said in a sing-song voice. 'Sounds a bit kinky to me. Remember the safe word.' She winked at Tilly.

'Not funny.' He raised his eyebrow at her and dumped the snowball on the ground. Finlay picked his up, barely getting it off the ground, and staggered towards them.

'This weighs a tonne.' He heaved it on top of the original snowball.

'Let's do some shaping,' Genevieve said. 'So much for your fancy sculpture. This doesn't look like anything.'

Tilly joined in, moulding the snow, running her gloved palms over it. 'Like this?' Her eyes caught Rafe's. Why had that come out so suggestive? Kind of like she was smoothing her palms over the contours of his body.

'Looks perfect,' he said.

'Aw, you two,' Genevieve said, 'are too cute.'

'What are you talking about?' Rafe frowned at her, but his lips were curled up at the corners, implying his innocence.

Tilly's cheeks were overly warm considering the temperature. As her hands moved over the snow curves, her mind carried on racing down a different path completely. It wasn't a snowman in her thoughts anymore, but a very hot man. The one she'd imagined showering that morning. The one just metres away from her.

'Good for you, Tilly.' Genevieve clapped her hands together to knock the snow off them. 'I love the way you're embracing Christmas with the crazy Harringtons. It's all about making memories.'

'Snow isn't Christmas,' Rafe said. 'It's statistically more likely to snow at Easter in Scotland than it is at Christmas.'

'Oh whatever.' Genevieve rolled her eyes. 'We have snow now, and we're all here together enjoying it, so that's definitely Christmassy.'

She had a point. For the first time in the midst of snowflakes and laughter, Tilly had a sense of what the magic of Christmas really meant. It wasn't about snow or 'stuff' but being part of something bigger. Despite the cold, warmth seeped into the chambers of her heart in a way she'd never anticipated. She'd made her first happy Christmas memories.

She smiled at Genevieve, then Rafe and the corners of her lips sagged. Already a sharp edge had formed around the memories. Because that was all they would ever be. Short and sweet glimpses of a brief moment she'd once spent with a lovely family.

After taking numerous photos of the snowman and some of Alexander knocking him down, everyone moved on. Rafe fell into step with Tilly.

'I apologise for my family's none-too-subtle attempts to set us up. This is the reason for my lying about my relationship status in the first place.'

'It's ok,' Tilly said. 'They mean well.'

'I know, but if it starts to irritate you, just tell me. I can't promise I can make them stop but I'll try.'

'I'm flattered they would even think it's a possibility.' She huffed out a puff of air as he held her gaze.

He tilted his head and a slight frown flickered across his brow. Had she said something she shouldn't?

'I don't see why not,' he said with a little shrug. 'Single guy, single girl and all that. It doesn't seem that impossible to me.'

Tilly smiled, not voicing the list of objections that had already started rolling like film credits in her mind. It was nice thinking for a moment that being a couple with him wasn't an impossible idea. All the inappropriate thoughts she'd had earlier returned, only this time he wasn't someone she fancied just for his hot body. He was so much more. Like a sped-up film, a whole stream of possibilities rushed before her, life events she hadn't considered for herself before now. A house with a garden, a wedding, babies, children, family holidays, love, belonging. Quickly, she shut them all down. Daydreams like that were fed by limerence and led nowhere but heartache.

'You know what you were saying earlier about the bosses at 1-Quick letting me down?' she asked. If she talked about work, it might stop her thinking about all these other things. Remembering why she was really here might also keep her mind on the straight and narrow.

'Yeah.'

'Well, the more I think about it, the more I realise they have done. A few months ago, I came up with an idea for how we could improve things. They listened to it and said it was something to think about in the future. Then it was never mentioned again until the other day when Arnie said it was good and he wanted to carry it forward. I wonder if he only said it to butter me up for coming here.'

'Very possibly.'

'You also wondered why I was so loyal to them.'

'I do. I mean, it's a great quality, but I can't condone their methods, so I find it hard to understand your loyalty.'

'I've worked there since I left school. Maybe it's a case of not knowing any better. It's a stable job, and the qualifications I've done have all been work based. It feels risky giving that up for something new.' Would she get anything else? After finding a place that accepted her, she wasn't in a hurry to start looking for somewhere that might reject her.

'Sounds like a better-the-devil-you-know situation, but I really think you're up against it at 1-Quick. I can't speak for all other businesses everywhere, but I'm one hundred per cent certain you could get a new job somewhere else where you'd be treated better, and you'd probably be a lot happier.'

She drew in a breath as she considered. He was probably right. Maybe this was the wake-up call she needed. Would a magical day in the snow be her epiphany moment? When better for it to happen than at Christmas?

'What was the idea you suggested?' he asked. 'You don't have to tell me, of course. Or if you like, you can officially pitch it to me, and I might consider backing it at Innova. You could turn the tables and feed me information about 1-Quick instead of the other way around.'

'Are you serious?'

'Why not? I'm always on the lookout for good ideas. But if you think it's unethical, I completely understand.'

'I would like to tell you, but...'

'If this isn't the right time or place, then I'll happily set up a proper meeting to discuss it in the new year, though you might have left 1-Quick before that.' He gave her a little wink, leaving her in no doubt that was exactly what he thought she should do.

'Yeah. Not sure how that'll go. But I don't mind telling you informally. I trust you.'

'I'm glad.' He tilted his head a little. 'Because I trust you too.'

She smiled. 'Even with my dodgy connections.'

'Even with them.'

'Ok, well, the idea...' She fiddled with the fingers of her wet gloves.

'You can give me the gist of it. I'll be able to tell you straight away if it's something we'd be interested in.'

But what if he hated it? The pain of his rejection might be too hard to bear. His expression was gentle though, and his pupils were wide in his icy-blue irises; they seemed to be inviting her to talk. 'Well, it was an idea to add a series of eco-friendly budget packages aimed at attracting environmentally conscious travellers. It's not only a popular area, but it's important for the planet. The packages could include stays at eco-certified hotels, sustainable transportation options, and activities that focus on nature conservation and cultural preservation.'

He gave her an encouraging nod.

'We could partner with local businesses and communities to ensure that every aspect of the trip is sustainable, from organic dining options to community-based tourism projects. The goal would be to make responsible travel accessible and affordable without compromising on quality.'

He smiled and gave her a gentle nudge. 'It sounds great. And look around you.' He pointed towards the house. 'You're at the home of an eco-warrior. I'm actually shocked with myself for not thinking about something like this myself. I've been thinking about how to crack into the budget market, and this could be the edge I'm looking for. They should have listened to you.'

'You like it?' She could hardly believe it.

'Yeah, I really do.'

Behind them was a scurrying sound, and Tilly swung around to see the three dogs bounding through the snow. Geoff followed at a half run. 'Guess what?' he said.

'What?' Rafe asked.

'I've found the old sledges. How about we have a go this afternoon?'

'Aw brilliant.' Rafe rubbed his gloved hands together. 'Will this be another first for you?' he asked Tilly.

'It would... But I'm not sure I can go on one.'

'Why not?'

'Well... Aren't they a bit scary?'

'It's up to you, but I wouldn't want you to miss out. You could try a short run. There's a field beside the house that's on a slope. It's not too steep, but it's quite long and has some bumpy places. I remember sledging down it as a kid right through a gap in the fence at the bottom and ending up in a stream. Not my finest hour and it was bloody freezing.'

'Not exactly selling this, are you?' Tilly laughed as they made their way around the back of the house. She would be glad to get inside and warm up again, especially if they were going out later.

Back at the house, they hung their damp coats and gloves in a warm utility room with an extractor fan that Geoff explained to Tilly was working on banked energy saved from solar panels in a special battery.

Hilary had put on another amazing spread for lunch and Tilly was almost able to forget what had brought her here and just enjoy herself. Should she let Arnie know where she was? The thought had barely entered her mind when she pushed it away again. She still had a whole day to figure out how to get home. Sunday train services weren't as frequent, but as long as they were up and running again, she'd be fine.

She didn't hold back on filling her plate with sausage rolls and delicious little filo pastry tarts. The cold had given her an appetite, and she needed to build up her energy for the afternoon.

Rafe sat opposite her at lunch, eating his selection of finger foods with more than half an eye on Tilly. She knew it because she couldn't stop looking back. Perhaps he was sizing her up. Was it because he liked her idea? She couldn't exactly stop him from stealing it or using a variation of it. Ideas couldn't be copyrighted after all. But was that the only thing on his mind? His gaze dropped more than once to her lips, and she returned the favour. God, he really was handsome.

'No sledging for me,' Grandma said. 'Those days have long gone. Thankfully,' she added to Tilly with a wink. 'I get to stay indoors where it's lovely and warm.'

'I'm happy to stay here too,' Hilary said. 'I don't have a burning desire to get cold and wet. You can borrow my jacket and boots again, Tilly. I'm sure the fans in the utility room will have dried them out.'

They had, and Tilly pulled them back on after lunch and stepped back into the snow with the others. She put her hand over her shoulder, reaching for the hood that was stuck down her back, wriggling her neck as she tried to free it.

'Allow me.' Rafe stepped up behind her and gently tugged it out. Goosebumps prickled up her spine. His proximity was warm, and kind of alarming, not because she was scared of him, but because the sensations he elicited in her were confusing at best. Her skin tingled beneath the layers of clothing, and she wanted to close her eyes and slip into a dream where his soft touch didn't stop there. But it did, and he stepped away, running his fingers through his hair.

'Thanks.' Tilly adjusted the hood on her shoulders.

Rafe gave her a brief smile, and they fell into step with the others.

'This field doesn't belong to us,' Geoff said as they crunched through the snow towards the top of a rolling plain of snow. The edge of what was presumably the fence stuck up around the perimeter. 'But we know the farmer and he's always been happy for us to use it.'

Rafe had said it wasn't steep, but it wasn't exactly flat. Thick woodland flanked it at the top, the tree branches weighed down by snow. At the bottom end was a more obvious fence, presumably the one Rafe had ploughed through as a child. In some places, winter bushes grew around it and in other parts, it was wide open.

Tilly's pulse quickened as she tried to imagine rushing down at breakneck speed. The cold air bit at her cheeks, and she tugged the collar of Hilary's jacket. A few snowflakes seemed to fall, though it could have been from the overhanging trees. A gloomy grey had covered the blue skies of the morning.

'Looks like more snow is coming,' Geoff said. He, Rafe, Cressida and Genevieve all had large plastic sledges in either pillar box red or royal blue.

'It's amazing these things have lasted,' Genevieve said.

'That's plastic for you,' Geoff said. 'If you want durability, there's nothing better, though of course that isn't always good.'

Genevieve dumped her sledge on the ground, then smirked at Finlay. 'You first, then I'll hop on top.'

'There's an offer I can't refuse,' he said with a smirk, climbing onto the sledge. Genevieve clambered on top, leaning back so he got a mouthful of hair. Tilly barely had a chance to laugh before they were off, whizzing down, towards the open section of fence away in the distance.

Geoff and Rafe got onto a sledge each and followed. Tina sat on with Alexander, and once she'd decided he liked it, Cressida pushed her off.

'Don't you fancy a go?' Cressida asked after she'd filmed Tina and Alexander shooting off.

'It looks a bit scary, but if Alexander can do it, I should, shouldn't I?'

'Only if you want to.' Cressida patted her back. 'No point in forcing yourself. There's a shorter slope on the side here.' She climbed a little further and pointed. Tilly followed to look. 'It's a bit messy at the bottom with all the dead bushes, but you should be able to stop before that.'

Tilly had no idea how to stop. At the sound of voices, she turned around. Geoff, Finlay and Rafe looked to be having a race back up, running with their sledges while Tina and Genevieve walked behind helping Alexander. When they got back to the top, Rafe grinned at Tilly. 'Want a go?' He was a little short of breath.

'I'm not sure.'

'I suggested the shorter run.' Cressida pointed to the other side of the hill.

'Um... It looked a bit better, but I don't know how to stop.'

'Come on with me if you want,' Rafe said.

Her heart pounded in her chest. Together? With him? How close they'd be. He'd have to hold her, and she'd be at his mercy – which didn't bother her one bit. She craved it.

'Ok.' Her voice was small, but he smiled and gently put his hand on her back. The touch sent a shiver through her, even with all these layers on.

'Come on then.' He placed the sledge at the top of the shorter run. 'This one is actually steeper,' he said. 'It'll be quite fast.' He sat down, holding the sledge in position with his feet. With a deep breath, Tilly positioned herself in front of him. With his firm body behind her and strong arms around her, she felt like nothing could harm her. His hot breath landed on her neck, and she trembled, every nerve end tingling, but before she could fully enjoy the sensation, they were off, hurtling down the slope.

Wind whipped through her hair, and her screams and laughter rang out as they raced downhill. Rafe's arms held her tight, his strong legs wedging her in.

'Oh my god,' she squealed, clinging to the rope. They approached the bottom of the hill, and panic surged through her veins. 'Watch out!'

'Fuck,' he yelled.

With a sudden lurch, the sledge careened off course, veering close to a snow-covered bush. Tilly's heart leaped into her throat as they crashed into it.

The sledge rolled over and Tilly found herself lying on her back in the snow, Rafe on top of her and a flurry of flakes dripping on them.

'Christ, I'm sorry about that.' Rafe pushed himself up to move away.

Breathless and exhilarated, Tilly pushed her glasses straight onto her nose, then put her hands up, and slipped them around his neck.

'What are you doing?' He looked her in the eye.

'I just...' She blinked. 'This will sound really stupid, but I wish I *had* come here as your girlfriend and that all this was real. I haven't had this much fun in years... maybe ever.'

'I wish that too,' he murmured, gently moving a strand of damp hair from her forehead. 'I can't stop thinking about you, and I don't mean as anything to do with 1-Quick.'

'Same.' She tugged off her gloves and let them fall to the ground, pressing her cold fingers against his warm skin. 'Will you kiss me?'

'What?' His eyes widened and Tilly's cheeks scorched. Why had she said that? What kind of idiot was she? As if she hadn't done enough stupid things in the past couple of days.

'I, um, thought this bush was mistletoe.' Her voice was barely a whimper.

He frowned. 'I don't think so. It doesn't grow around here.'

'Oh... Well, I didn't know... I—'

'How about we pretend it is?'

'Could we?'

'Yeah. In fact, I was wrong. It's definitely mistletoe, and it's demanding that we use it.'

She smiled, unable to draw her gaze from him. He tilted his head slightly and slowly slipped her glasses onto the top of her head. Then he dipped in and pressed the most sublime kiss onto her lips. The warm touch woke every frozen nerve end in her body. He slid his hand under her head, cradling her as he plied her with more gentle kisses. All soft and on the surface, but enough to wake her heart from a deep slumber. She was alive with need now, like she'd never been before. And hungry. Without thinking, she opened her mouth to him, and he responded. She held him close as he ravished her lips, willing this moment to last for a very long time.

Chapter Fourteen

Rafe

Rafe kissed Tilly firmly, almost desperately, a deep sense of urgency rising inside him. Snow dripped from the hedge above and he vaguely registered the rhythmical drops landing on the back of his head and neck like someone was flicking him to get his attention. But good luck with that, because they weren't getting it. Tilly was everything in the here and now, and all that mattered was stealing more of these delicious kisses. She didn't seem to want him to move either. He was wedged on top of her, but her hands were clamped so tightly around his neck he couldn't get up without a huge effort. And why should he? This was infinitely more pleasant. The heat and decadence of their combined lips was like nothing he remembered experiencing.

And I've kissed a few women.

Perhaps it was the completely unorthodox location.

He freed a hand from its glove and traced his fingers around her jaw, loving how it moved so hungrily as she kissed him. Her lips parted again, allowing him deeper access, and he took it, sweeping his tongue against hers. Her nails clutched the skin at the nape of his neck. Electricity roared through him, and she gave a little whimper, moulding closer to him. The fire in his gut would be more than enough to melt the surrounding snow.

What the hell were they playing at?

But he couldn't stop. The tension that had been intensifying since the previous day was pouring out now. This was a whole new level of magic. The forbidden aspect was thrilling – he was kissing a rival spy, someone who shouldn't even be here, who he didn't really know, and yet... The danger was still there. Was his trust justified? What if this was all part of an act? It wasn't unheard of for people to sleep their way to the top. Was she buttering him up for her own reasons?

He continued kissing her, finding the answers in the way she responded to him. This wasn't fake. Together, they were making enough heat to scald themselves even in these subzero temperatures. How better to keep warm in winter?

'Rafe! Tilly!'

Voices were shouting nearby. Possibly from the top of the hill. Could people see them from up there? Would they come down?

'Shit,' Rafe muttered, pulling back. Tilly's eyes were closed like she didn't want to wake from a dream. 'People are coming. Let's save this for later.' He moved off her and helped her to her feet. She looked almost dazed, her hair dishevelled and her gaze unfocused.

'Later?' She fumbled for her glasses that had fallen off the top of her head, wiped them quickly, and put them back on.

'Well, only if you want to… Though maybe we shouldn't.' He straightened out his jacket and ski trousers, then bent and picked up the sledge.

'I—'

Tilly didn't get a chance to finish as Finlay bolted over the small embankment they'd veered off.

'Are you guys ok?' he said.

'Yeah, all fine,' Rafe said. 'That was an unexpected detour.'

'I thought you'd got stuck.'

'We kind of did.'

Tilly flashed him a look, her eyes wide and desperate.

'That hedge didn't want to let us out.'

'And no injuries?' Finlay said.

'Don't think so. You ok?' He smiled at Tilly.

She nodded, her mouth slightly open, and ran her fingertips over her pinkish cheeks. Rafe hadn't shaved that morning and she'd clearly got some stubble burn, though hopefully it would look like she was rosy-cheeked from the cold.

Finlay turned and waved, giving the thumbs up to unseen people. Obviously, everyone had been panicking about them. How long had they lingered down here?

Rafe bent down, picked up Tilly's gloves and the one of his own that was lying in the snow, and handed hers back. She took them with a brief smile and put them on.

Then he clambered up the embankment, turning to check she was following. She was picking her way up, taking her time, looking unsure. 'Here.' He thrust out his hand, and she grabbed it. He tugged her up with him.

Finlay was nudging something with his foot just a few steps ahead. 'You snapped this baby Christmas tree on the way down.' He rolled it over with his boot.

Rafe looked at the tiny thing now bent flat on the ground and gave a jerk of his shoulder. 'I think that's what knocked us off course. Not much we can do about it now.'

'Can't we save it?' Tilly asked.

'Na, it's properly broken,' he said.

'There are loads of them.' Finlay gestured around at the taller trees before walking on.

Of course, he was right, but Tilly's face fell, and Rafe's heart sank a little with it. 'We could take it back to the house,' he said. 'And decorate it. Our own little Christmas tree.'

Finlay glanced around and raised his eyebrow as if to comment on the use of 'our', but he said nothing, only smirked, and carried on up the hill. No doubt he'd be straight to Genevieve with that juicy morsel of gossip.

The smile had returned to Tilly's lips. Those lovely, kissable lips. 'Well, ok, I don't usually bother with a Christmas tree. In fact, this'll be my first one.'

'This is a day of firsts for you, isn't it?'

She nodded. 'It really is.'

He stooped down and detached the tree from the tiny section that was still attached to the root, then shook the snow from it.

'Not a bad shape actually.' He held it up and examined it. 'A little sparse. Needs some TLC.'

His eyes moved instantly to Tilly. *Yup. Same applies to her.* A bit of TLC would work wonders on her, he was sure, and he'd quite like to be the one administering it. With another smile, he headed upward, ignoring the speculative looks on both his sisters' faces as they met them near the top of the hill. Was it so obvious what he and Tilly had been doing? Had Finlay already passed on his bit of gossip? Or were Cress and Gen just hoping for a Christmas miracle? Something was going on, otherwise why kiss Tilly? What madness had come over him? Lust. If only he could go to the gym. Running up that hill should have dispelled some of the restless energy, but it didn't seem to have done anything. The feelings hadn't gone. He'd kiss her again in an instant, maybe even in front of his family. He almost didn't care... Except for her. She didn't need more complications, not when she only just seemed to be coming around to being here at all. With that in mind, he squashed the rising desires.

Something cold and wet brushed his cheek, then his forehead, and he blinked. Snowflakes blew in the wind.

'Is that coming from the trees?' He held out his hands.

'I don't think so,' his dad said. 'Looks grey over that way.'

Already it was coming down heavier, the flakes getting thicker and colder by the second.

'Let's get back,' Cressida said. 'Alexander is getting cold and hungry.'

'Me too,' Finlay said. 'Well, maybe just hungry.'

'You're always hungry.' Genevieve gave him a little poke.

The walk back was tough going as the wind picked up, hurling more snow at them. Alexander started to cry, and Cressida zipped him inside her jacket to keep him warm. Tilly was shivering too.

'Keep behind me,' Rafe said. 'It'll stop the snow from hitting you.'

'What about you?'

'I'm fine.' A white lie, but she didn't need to know how hard the wind bit his neck. It was good for him and stopped his mind from wandering to places it shouldn't.

When they finally reached the shelter of the house, Rafe went with his dad to put the sledges away in the large garage, while Tilly took the baby tree into the house.

'That turned into a bit of a nightmare.' Geoff stacked a sledge on a free shelf.

'Yeah, not half.' Rafe tossed the next sledges on top of the first one.

'You had any more thoughts about taking over the business?' Geoff asked in a casual way that didn't fool Rafe one bit. He'd been waiting for a moment alone to pounce.

'Yeah, Dad, I think about it a lot, but it's not the right move for me. I've spent a long time building my business from nothing. I know I'd be taking on an even bigger business, but it isn't mine. And I don't want to sound selfish...' Though he was sure he did. 'But—'

Geoff placed a hand on Rafe's shoulder. 'It's ok, son. I understand. You've done so well for yourself. I just thought I'd check in, but I don't blame you for not wanting to. I'd have been exactly the same at your age. You've got to follow your own path.'

Rafe frowned, then smiled. He hadn't expected that. 'Thanks.'

'I take back what I said about Tilly too. She's a good soul and I can see she's not up to any funny business. Not unless you count wanting to land you as a date.'

'Meaning what?'

'She only has eyes for you.'

Rafe looked away, running his fingers through his damp, snowy hair. 'Maybe. But it's not exactly a realistic option, is it?'

'No? You were fine with the whole long-distance, she works for another company thing when you made up the story to your sister. Before you'd actually met Tilly.'

'I was, wasn't I?'

'Yes, you were. And don't forget that. Don't let a good person get away on a technicality.'

But it wasn't that simple. Rafe couldn't deny he felt something for Tilly, but they hardly knew each other. Even if she liked him in return, it was too soon to do anything crazy.

But what about that kiss? Was he just desperate after a dry spell? A niggle said there was more to it than that.

They returned to the house through the blizzard, shielding their faces. 'This isn't letting up, is it?' Rafe said.

'I think Tilly might be around for another few days,' Geoff said.

'I'm not sure that'll please her.'

'It might.' Geoff slapped him on the back as they reached the door.

Once inside, they took off their ski jackets and trousers and hung them in the utility room. Delicious smells wafted from the kitchen. Hilary looked like she'd opened a hot chocolate factory and had jars laid around the table with sprinkles, chocolate coins and crushed candy canes. A vat of milk was warming on the stove, and everyone was sitting around rosy-cheeked.

Rafe took a seat next to Tilly, smiling at her as he sat. She returned it a little shyly, almost like she didn't want anyone to see the level of heat passing between them, but he felt it all over, from the tip of his nose to deep inside, in all the places he shouldn't really be sensing it. Not with so many people present. Their eyes linked, remembering the kiss, the soft touches, the promise of more.

'I doubt I'll get to church tomorrow,' Hilary said. 'Which is sad because the lovely little nativity is on, and we do a fundraiser where we serve Christmas soup and a sandwich lunch after. But in this weather, I won't be going anywhere.'

'Do you think I'll be stuck here tomorrow?' Tilly asked Rafe aside.

'Looks like it.'

'I might have to pull that sicky after all.'

'Or tell them the truth.'

'But what if they say I should never have come here?'

'They don't know your personal business. You could have used the trip to Glasgow as a base to visit some friends over Christmas. They can't stop you from doing that. You weren't to know it would snow like this.'

'But Mitchell knows where I went. He's bound to tell them.'

Rafe gave a little shrug. 'And does he know all your personal business? How does he know you didn't change your plans last minute?'

She let out a sigh, rested her chin on her palm, and stared ahead. 'It's just that... Well, I don't really have anyone. They'll know it's a lie.'

Rafe tilted his head and frowned slightly. Tilly stirred her hot chocolate absently. 'Nobody knows anything unless you've told them.'

'I've never told him anything about myself, but that's the point. There's nothing to tell.'

Was that true? She must have friends, family, hobbies. 'If you've told them nothing, they know nothing. What they assume isn't your problem. Tell them you're visiting friends, and now you're stuck. As soon as the roads are clear, you'll go back.' As the words left his lips, a sharp pain accompanied them. He didn't want her to go back. He wanted her with him here, spending Christmas with him, carrying on what they started. But that was selfish and mad. She had her own life to live.

'Who wants cream?' Hilary asked, walking around the table with a can.

Rafe held up his hand like a primary school child, then took hold of Tilly's and held it up too.

'How do you know I want it?' she said.

He raised an eyebrow. 'Just guessing.'

She smiled. 'You guessed right.'

Yes, he had. And it wasn't just cream she wanted right now. Her eyes betrayed her, and he was with her. One way or another, they had unfinished business.

'Where did you put the tree?' he asked once he had a warm mug of hot chocolate cradled in his hands.

'Your mum gave me a pot for it. It's in the utility room.'

'Ah, that lovely little tree.' Hilary took a seat next to Tilly. 'I have a box of spare decorations you can have for it too. Where would you like to put it?'

'Oh, I'm not sure,' Tilly said.

'In your room?' Rafe suggested.

'If that's allowed.'

'Of course,' Hilary said. 'Be my guest. You should help with the decorating, Rafe. I hear it was your bad steering that brought the poor thing down in the first place.'

'Pardon? My bad steering?'

'Well, it was,' Genevieve said.

'We've all heard, so there's no point denying it,' Grandma said with a smile. He didn't point out that she had a blob of cream on the end of her nose. If she was going to gang up on him, she could keep it there!

'You can decorate the tree after this,' Hilary said. 'Then we're having the cocktail making competition. Winner gets to choose the Christmas movie.'

Rafe groaned. *Great.* Cocktails were definitely not the most sensible thing for him to have right now. What would they do but add more fuel to the fire simmering low, pushing him closer to Tilly? No doubt that was Mum's plan. If only she knew what had happened under the hedge that afternoon. She'd be on the phone to the minister booking a wedding before you could say mistletoe.

'Your mum is so lovely,' Tilly said later as she carried the tree up the stairs. 'She's washed and dried all my clothes already. I really can't thank her enough.'

'She likes you,' Rafe said. 'Whether she can match you with me or not, I know she cares about you.'

Tilly turned at the door to her room and looked at him. 'Does she know about what we did earlier?'

He shook his head and leaned one hand on the wall beside her. 'No one knows about that except us. And we should probably keep it that way unless the reason you wanted to kiss me was to be nice to my mum.'

Tilly let out a little laugh. 'I can't say that even crossed my mind. I wanted to because...' She glanced back at the stairs. 'Well, you're a nice man.'

'Nice?' He shook his head, chuckling. 'Ok. I'll take it.'

'You should because it's true.' She went into the bedroom and gazed at the tree.

Rafe opened the bag of decorations his mum had given him. 'So, how do you want to do this?'

Their eyes met, and he knew what she was thinking. *Shove the decorations where the sun doesn't shine and carry on the kiss.*

'It's too risky,' he whispered, pushing the door half closed. 'My mum is likely to barge in here at any time.'

'I didn't say anything,' Tilly said.

'I know what you were thinking. It's pretty much all that's on my mind.'

She nodded and smiled at him until he was putty again. That smile did things to him. Dangerous things. Exciting things.

He moved closer, unable to take his eyes off her. If he just leaned closer...

'How are we getting on?' His mum threw open the door and marched in.

'Great.' He shoved his hand into the decoration bag. 'Just deciding what to put where.'

Soft music started playing, 'Ding Dong Merrily on High'. A carol that reminded him of Dickensian London in old films and nostalgic Christmases with the Radio Times on the coffee table – all the good dramas and films highlighted for each day.

Hilary propped her phone on a shelf, and he realised that was where the music was coming from. 'Such a beautiful little tree,' she said. 'So perfect in this room.'

'This room is perfect,' Tilly said. 'It's like the inside of a log cabin.'

'I'm so pleased you like it.'

Rafe handed her a little star. 'Pop that on the top.'

Her fingers trembled a little as she placed it on. 'My first tree decoration.'

'Didn't you do this as a child?' Rafe caught a warning look from his mother. *What?*

'No,' Tilly said. 'I grew up in a home. There was a tree in the common room, but the staff decorated it.'

'Jeez, I'm sorry. I didn't realise.' Did his mum already know that? From the look on her face, she did.

'It's ok,' Tilly said. 'But it's part of the reason Christmas has never really been a big thing for me.'

'Well, you can enjoy it this year.' Hilary patted her on the back. 'Just wait until we get the cocktails on the go.'

They finished off the tree and Rafe stood back as Tilly took a photo of it. 'That looks great.' He checked his phone. 'I've got some messages from friends I should reply to. Will you come downstairs in a bit?'

'Sure.'

'Great, see you then.' He backed out of the room, still smiling at her. His mum was on the landing, waiting, and he almost collided with her. 'What are you up to?'

'Just putting away the decorations we didn't use.'

'Did you know she'd been in a home growing up?'

Hilary nodded and let out a sigh. 'She mentioned it when she first arrived.'

'And I went and shoved my big foot in it.'

Hilary glanced at the bag in her hand, then back at Tilly's door. 'Go back in and check she's ok.'

'What?'

'Please, Rafe. Just do it. She might be upset.'

He hesitated. Should he? What if she just wanted to be alone?

Chapter Fifteen

Tilly

Saturday, December 21st

Evening

Tilly stared at the little Christmas tree, tears streaming down her face. She'd let go, and the floodgates had opened. So, this was Christmas. Or it was for the Harringtons anyway. A lovely family home full of joy, laughter, and love. She'd found the perfect dollhouse world, but it wasn't hers. She was just playing with it, borrowing it for a while. The life she had in this house belonged to a different Tilly Thorpe, one who was free to stay here, not one who had another life, a job, and a flat in London – one who wasn't supposed to be here at all.

A knock on the door. 'Tilly, can I come back in, please?' Rafe said from the other side.

She quickly wiped away her tears. 'Sure.'

The door clicked open, but Tilly didn't turn around. She stared at the little tree twinkling before her, blinking away the remaining tears, and breathing deeply.

'Hey.' Rafe put his hands on her shoulders, and she tensed. How was he so close, so quickly? 'Are you ok?'

'Not really.' She shook her head. Why lie? He may as well see exactly who she was. Who he'd kissed. Who he was dealing with.

'I'm sorry I asked about your childhood. It was insensitive of me.'

'It's not that.' She took a deep breath. 'I'll be fine. All this is just so overwhelming. Your family... That kiss. All of it.'

'I'm sorry,' he repeated. 'I thought you wanted to. I wouldn't have if you hadn't asked.'

'I did. I enjoyed it. Everything here is so enjoyable, but it's all just a passing thing, isn't it?'

'Most things are.' He quietly rubbed her shoulders. The simple movement melted the icy needles that stabbed at her heart when she thought about leaving. 'But you make your own destiny, Tilly. You decide what you want in life. Don't let others choose for you. Make sure what you choose is what you want.'

It sounded so easy when he said it like that, but for someone who'd always lived like her, she wasn't sure she could. Giving up what she'd taken time to build was a very foolish move from where she was standing.

'Do you want to join in with making cocktails?' he asked. 'Or would you rather be alone?'

'I'd rather be with you.' The truth spilled out before she could stop it.

He was quiet for a beat, then said, 'Same, Tilly. I'm burning to be with you, but it's tricky.'

'I know. I'm sorry.' She was at it again – clinging.

'No need. Let's just be sensible. Why don't you come down with me?'

Pulling herself together with a mental shake, she nodded. 'Ok. Let's make some cocktails… Yet another first for me.' God, she was getting through them today.

'Hopefully, it'll be fun.'

She caught him looking at her reflection in a mirror on the dresser next to the little tree. A hungry smile grew on his face as her eyes met his. She'd kiss him again in an instant, but that was stupid when people were expecting him downstairs.

'Come on.' He slipped his hand into hers. 'Let's go down and see if Mum needs a hand with anything.'

Tilly clutched his hand as he led the way, only letting go at the bottom of the stairs when Genevieve passed by.

'Mum's already set up a buffet tea,' she said. 'She and Grandma did it while we were out. I'm going to tell Finlay it'll be ten minutes. He might have passed out by then. Honestly, the amount he eats, you'd think he'd be morbidly obese, but it just fuels all his sports.'

Rafe led Tilly into the living room, where they sat for a while, chatting about the day with Tina and Finlay, before Geoff came to the door and announced dinner.

Hilary and Grandma had made a delicious spread for the buffet tea and Tilly filled her plate but didn't sit down. She spotted Hilary setting up another table with glasses and went over to her.

'Is this for the cocktails?'

'Yes,' Hilary said.

'Let me help.' Tilly put her plate down and helped Hilary with the setup.

'I'm so thrilled you're with us,' Hilary said. 'It means we can do this in pairs and Rafe won't be on his own.'

'Only me,' Grandma said.

'Oh, mother,' Hilary said. 'You already told me you didn't want to make one.'

'I did. And I stick by it. I'm only going to judge,' she said to Tilly with a wink. 'Then I get to taste them all without having to do one of my own.'

'You'll be making your own private batch in the corner, I expect,' Rafe said.

'Oh, shush. What will Tilly think of me?'

Tilly laughed and Hilary shook her head.

'Cressida's giving Alexander his bath and as soon as he's tucked up, we can get concocting,' she said. 'Or drinking in my mother's case, it would appear.'

Tilly nibbled her food, chatting with the others as they waited for Cressida. By the time the latter got downstairs, Tilly and the family had gathered around the island and were reading the prompt cards and laughing.

'Ok, this is going to be interesting.' Rafe handed Tilly a card with a slightly raised eyebrow.

Cressida joined Tina, who was sniggering. 'Ok, the Christmas Sparkler is coming up.'

'The what?' Cressida said.

Tina grabbed a bottle of champagne. 'You heard. Can you get the cranberry juice?'

'I actually liked the look of that one,' Genevieve said.

'Me too,' Grandma said.

'We've got Jack Frost,' Finlay said. 'Looks potent. What is blue curaçao?'

'This.' Genevieve held up a bottle filled with a sea-blue liqueur.

'Let me see that.' Grandma took the bottle from her, opened it and sniffed it. 'Oof. It's strong.'

Hilary held up her card. 'Mistletoe Martini. Rather nice by the sound of things. Gin, vermouth, and a splash of elderflower liqueur. I like it already.' She exchanged a glance with Geoff, and they grinned.

Tilly's heart lifted. She could only wish that when she reached Hilary's age, she'd have found a man like Geoff who still looked at her like that. But she didn't have anyone, unless she counted the man standing beside her, which she couldn't really. One kiss didn't make him hers. That dream would end very swiftly. Already its hours were numbered.

Just enjoy these stolen moments while you can.

Rafe showed her their card. 'The Winter Whirlwind.'

'What do we need for that?'

'Spiced rum, apple cider, and a cinnamon stick.'

'Sounds weird,' she said.

He laughed. 'Yeah, it does, doesn't it?' He reached for the cinnamon sticks at the same time she did, and their hands brushed against each other. A frisson ran across Tilly's skin. She glanced up at him and they shared a smile. Tilly's pulse raced. This was so much more than her normal one-sided crushes, fantasies, or whatever they were. Wasn't it? He was feeling something too. He'd been a willing participant in their kiss.

Rafe read the ingredients, and Tilly measured them into the shaker. Once everyone's concoctions were complete, the family gathered around the table, each with their Christmas cocktail.

'Shall we taste them?' Hilary said. 'Then we can grade them.'

'Let me start.' Grandma gave them all a wicked smirk. 'It's what I've been waiting for, after all.'

Tilly moved around the table after Grandma had taken the first taste, sipping each one through a straw and leaving a grade on the card.

'Let's see.' Hilary added up the numbers on the cards. 'Cressida and Tina, you are the winners. You get to choose this year's movie.'

They high-fived. Rafe gave Tilly a commiserative glance.

'Anyone want some more?' Cressida said. 'We could make it and you can drink the Christmas Sparkler as we watch... Drumroll... *A Christmas Carol.*'

'Can't beat it for festiveness,' Tina said.

'Good choice,' Hilary said.

'Have you ever seen it?' Rafe asked Tilly aside.

'What do you think?' she said.

'I'm guessing another first.'

'You guess right.'

'Let's get everyone comfy,' Hilary said. 'I've put a crate of blankets in the living room. If anyone is feeling chilly, just grab one.' She gave Tilly the tiniest of winks. Was she expecting Tilly to sit under that with Rafe? In front of them all? Maybe she'd be better sitting away from him. She probably shouldn't fuel this thing that was going on between them.

'You sit by Rafe.' Hilary ushered her in. 'And don't let him fall asleep. He always does that during films.'

'No, I don't,' he mumbled.

Hilary raised an eyebrow at him.

'I maybe have once or twice, but not *always.*'

Tilly sat next to him. 'Are you sure it's ok for me to sit here?' She kept her voice low.

'Of course. Why wouldn't it be?'

She gave a little shrug. 'Because of... earlier.'

He ran a finger down her upper arm, pulling back as his sisters entered. 'I'm ok with what happened earlier.'

She'd like to say she felt the same, but she wasn't sure in all honesty that she could. If ok meant she'd enjoyed it but didn't want it to stop, then maybe she was ok. If it meant they could pick it up again later, she was definitely ok. If it meant a one-off thing they weren't ever going to repeat, she really wasn't ok. But she couldn't exactly ask him in front of everyone. Maybe he was just a guy who didn't mind randomly hooking up with people and saw her as an easy target.

Hilary dimmed the lights and handed out blankets. The dogs were already piled into one dog bed, looking super cosy. Tilly smiled at their snores as a soft fleece blanket descended on her and Rafe. Almost as soon as the opening music started, he took her hand under the blanket and gently rubbed his thumb over her skin in soothing circles. 'Is this ok?' he whispered for her ears only, so low she barely heard it.

Without looking at him, she nodded. This felt all kinds of naughty, like kissing a guy in the back row of the cinema, which she'd never done either. All he was doing was stroking her hand, but something about it was so mesmerising it sent her into a dreamy stupor. How was it possible to feel this good from just that gentle contact? The film intrigued her from the off. She tried to concentrate on it and not on what his fingertips were doing to her. Her head rolled, and she leaned on him, unable to stop herself. This was bliss. If Rafe fell asleep now, Tilly couldn't stop him. She was almost dozing herself.

As the end credits rolled, so did her eyes. She could hardly stay awake. Rafe had stopped caressing her hand some time ago, but he was still holding it lightly, his head resting on hers. Was he asleep? She gave him a little nudge. Clearing his throat, he straightened up.

'Oops.' He blinked himself fully awake, moving his hand away. Hilary turned the lights up a little and offered everyone another drink. Tilly was too tired. Grandma was flat out.

'Not for me, thanks.' Tilly barely stifled a yawn. 'I should go to bed.'

The consensus was that everyone was too tired to stay up much longer. Hilary woke Grandma, who again claimed she hadn't been asleep at all. They traipsed up the stairs, chatting in hushed voices in case they woke Alexander. At the top of the stairs, they all went their separate ways, but as Rafe's room was next to Tilly's, he followed her.

'Night-night,' he said as Tilly opened her door. He lingered for a second before heading to his own door and she was aware other family members were still about, though she didn't look.

'Night.' She watched him going into his room. Something didn't feel right. Like the night shouldn't end like this, not when it had promised so much more. But what had she expected?

CHAPTER SIXTEEN

Tilly

Tilly entered her room and switched on the light, swallowing back her disappointment. What was she imagining now? Did she think Rafe was going to sleep with her? That was just plain crazy. Why would he? It all came down to her being needy and clingy again.

She pulled off her sweater and tossed it away, then unbuttoned her jeans and slipped them down. After splitting with her last boyfriend, she'd seen a therapist. The breakup had hit hard, and she couldn't come to terms with his accusations on her own. She'd sought help. When had loving and caring become needy and clingy? Sitting on the end of the bed, she tugged her jeans off her ankles. Wearing just her lacy bra and pants, she stared at the wall in front of her. The one that separated her room from Rafe's. Putting her head in her hands, she recalled what the therapist had told her. The words had hit like a train and were still raw in her mind, like she'd just heard them. Her boyfriend had been right. She was everything he'd said, and she always would be.

'Your childhood has left a scar. You have abandonment issues, so you attach to others fast. But it isn't love. It's known as limerence. You can't fully fall in love until you get to know a person. It happens to people like you because your needs were not met as a child. You feel a longing for a connection. So, you look for relationships and attach too quickly.'

She got to her feet, hooked off her bra, and kicked off her knickers. When she'd finally processed the words, she'd realised they were true. Her relationships had come about quickly, often been one-sided, and what she'd thought was natural progression was desperation. She'd pushed boyfriends to move in or take the next step, when it was far too early. Her acute craving for love and stability forced her actions.

But not anymore. Now she was careful. She recognised the signs and stepped back. She'd been hopeful about Mitchell, but she'd let him walk on by, not pushing herself forward, and taking it on the chin when it turned out he had someone else. Good sense had prevailed, and she'd saved face. Could she do the same with Rafe? Was this any different?

'People with abandonment issues often seek partners to provide them with a sense of self, security and validation.'

Yes! Exactly what she desperately wanted. It never seemed like a bad thing, but rushing the situation was what caused the problems. She picked up her clothes, put them on a wicker chair in the corner, and headed into the shower room.

She hadn't gone back to the therapist. Her words may have been true, but they hadn't helped. Tilly had felt a whole lot worse after and even now the words haunted her, as though looking for love was something she shouldn't be doing because she'd never find it... or understand it. Her past wouldn't allow her to feel love properly and all that would happen was infatuation, followed by disappointment. Wasn't Rafe a prime example? She was currently in the infatuation... disappointment would surely follow.

She started the shower, enjoying the heat of the water and the cleansing properties of the steam. She worked up a lather on her skin, rubbing in the delicious orange scented shower gel, and letting it soothe her. As she lifted the bottle to apply some more, it slipped from her soapy hands, and fell to the floor, slamming her foot on the way down.

'Ah,' she screamed, bending to grab the offensive bottle. The water blasted on her head, soaking her hair and running into her eyes. She placed the bottle on the little shelf, but it didn't take, and fell again with a slam on the shower tray. Seriously? Since when had she become so uncoordinated?

She rinsed off the foam, turned off the shower, and got out. That bottle had it in for her, and her toe was throbbing.

She grabbed a towel and wrapped it around herself. As she opened the door to the main room, a knock made her jump and squeal.

'Tilly?' Rafe's voice said in a low tone from the other side of the door. 'Are you ok?'

She opened the door, clutching the towel tight, her hair dripping, only to find him in the same predicament. How hot did he look with a fluffy white towel wrapped around his waist? The shirtless man on the book cover was nothing compared to this. His toned body was lean, but not shiny and fake. A smattering of coarse hair covered his chest, tapering down his abs, which were defined, but not so much that he looked like a bodybuilder. It was a rugged, outdoor body, rather than gym-honed. And Tilly was staring, drinking it all in.

'I... um... What are you doing here?'

'I came to see if you were ok. I heard a bang, then screaming.'

She groaned, her toes still smarting. 'I dropped the shower gel bottle on my foot.'

A grin spread across his face. 'Ouch.'

'It's not funny; it was painful.'

'Would you like me to kiss it better?'

His arm muscles looked strong, and his shoulders were broad. He was so fit... and hot. If he kissed anything, she might spontaneously combust.

Oh god, she was doing it again, but she really wanted him. He was like the most luxurious Christmas gift she could imagine, someone that was so far out of reach she wouldn't normally even attempt to get him.

'You want to? I mean...' Her breathing was shallow and uneven. Her heart was hammering hard now, and she wasn't sure what she was saying.

'I'll do anything you want.'

Their eyes met, and his pupils widened. His gaze was warm and strong, hungry but not threatening.

Was this still limerence? She was so obsessed with him she'd forgotten reality. 'I'd like to kiss you again,' she whispered. 'But I don't think I want to stop with a kiss.' And that was the raw truth. She didn't want to listen to the objections the therapist would surely be dishing out if she could hear Tilly now.

'I can make that happen.' He reached out and pushed a strand of wet hair from her face, just as he'd done earlier after they'd crashed sledges.

'Then... You better come in.' Tilly's neediness was ready to pour out, and she had nothing to stem the flow. All she knew was that she couldn't bear it if he left her alone tonight. She wanted him with her so badly, holding her and kissing her in this beautiful room with their special tree, the snow outside and wind gusting past the window.

'Give me two minutes.' He nipped back into his own room.

Tilly's body was almost shaking as she closed the door. The anticipation burning inside was like nothing she'd experienced before. She towelled her hair and ran a comb through it. No time to dry it properly. Then she sat on the end of the bed. How long had it been since she'd slept with anyone? She tried to work it out. More than a year? Would he be able to tell? Her experiences to date hadn't been that great. Maybe he'd expect fancy moves or things she'd never tried before.

With a gentle knock, he opened the door. Still wearing just the towel, he crossed to the nightstand and put something on it before coming to sit next to her.

'Are you ok?' he said. 'You're shivering. Are you cold?'

'Must be,' she said, though it wasn't that.

'Then let's get you warm.' He pulled one of the blankets from the bed behind him and wrapped it around her. She melted into his arms, and he held her close. His chest moved as he breathed steadily and deeply, and she let her herself move with it.

He placed a hand on her cheek and tucked her damp hair behind her ear. His breathing against her skin sent bolts of electricity through her, stoking the desire inside her higher and higher. She peeked up at him from the warmth of the blanket cocoon he was holding her in, and his gaze ran over her face. His fingers moved from her back to softly caress her neck, then her ear lobes. A short moan rose from her throat to her mouth until it escaped.

'I can't resist you,' he said. 'This is all kinds of crazy, but I feel like it's meant to happen.'

'Me too,' Tilly whispered.

He pressed his lips to hers and kissed her, slow, deep and intense. His mouth was softer than she remembered, and warmth radiated through her. With a contented sigh, she twisted her fingers in his hair and pulled him even closer, wanting more. The blanket slipped from her shoulders and his warm palm slid over the skin where it had been.

He deepened the kiss, erasing every inch of doubt she'd had. This was what she wanted. Nothing had ever felt better than this. They both came up for air, panting, eyes locked on each other. She'd never been kissed like that before unless you counted that afternoon, but this was so much more. The closeness and intimacy made her tummy clench and fizz.

Rafe smiled, still gently stroking her. 'I'm beginning to think you were sent here by an angel.'

'Not unless Arnie's an angel,' she said, but she grinned back.

'There's that Tilly smile. So beautiful.' He lowered his head until he was almost close enough for her to taste his little laugh. Then he kissed her again, his mouth slanting over hers, sensual and insistent, the intimate stroke of his tongue so seductive, so intoxicating, that the need inside her almost burst. She wrapped her arms round his neck and tugged him closer, letting the towel slip from around her. Her breasts brushed against his bare chest, sending tingles through every nerve end.

He continued kissing her, moving his hands across her skin, teasing them over her pebbly nipples before wrapping his arms around her.

She groaned and held her head back for a moment, before pressing her mouth to his throat and holding it there as she tried to catch her breath.

'Oh Tilly.' He lowered his forehead to her shoulder.

'That's me.' A sudden sense of power surged through her and she tossed off the blanket and the towel fully, climbing across him, so she was straddling him at the end of the bed. She bent in and trailed kisses across his chest.

'You are something else.' He gave her a wicked smile. 'And full of surprises.' He flipped her onto her back, lying her on the soft bedding. She squealed as she felt the brush of his fingers on her inner thigh, then her breathing hitched. His lips traced a line along her jaw, to her neck and then her shoulder; the sweep of his tongue sent a jolt of electricity through her.

'Oh god, Rafe.' She slid her arms round him and tugged him down so she could kiss him. How could she let him know how much this meant to her? How much *he* meant to her. She needed to show him without being needy or clingy.

How is that possible?

He responded to her kisses, his mouth matching hers, his hands touching her until he found places that made her moan and squeal. The emotion she felt for him pushed her higher. She wanted to give herself to him. All of her. His caresses and kisses hadn't stopped and the surge of warmth in her body grew until it peaked like an eruption of shooting stars. Tilly didn't moan or scream. She couldn't make a sound. Silently and with fitful breaths, she held onto the sensations as long as she could.

'Are you ok?' Rafe whispered in her ear.

'Yes,' she managed. 'Very ok.'

'And you want to keep going?'

'Yes.' They couldn't stop now. She craved all of him. Even with all her limerence, neediness and clinginess, she'd never wanted a man as badly as she wanted Rafe now. Her body and soul depended on it.

He shifted a little, leaning over to the nightstand and lifting a condom packet. Thank goodness he was prepared. Tilly mentally chivvied herself for not having thought about it. Was she really that stupid?

Probably.

But she trusted Rafe.

He moved over her, his gaze locked on hers. Was he searching for something? Answers? Truths? Feelings? She met his gaze without flinching. Whatever he was looking for was in her eyes. Not breaking eye contact, she ran her fingers over the hard muscle on his shoulders. Her nails dug into him as he bent over, pressing a kiss at the centre of her neck and easing into her.

'Oh my god...' she gasped. It had been a while, but she let herself relax.

'All ok?' he said, his words like a breath on her neck.

She accustomed herself to the feel of him. 'All good.'

'So good,' he said. 'Too good.'

He lifted her hips off the mattress, holding her firmly, thrusting gently until they found the perfect rhythm.

With every stroke, every hasty kiss, Tilly got closer to the edge, and she couldn't stop smiling. Was that normal? It just felt like such a perfect moment, not like the sex she'd had before, more like bonding. Was this her messed-up past talking again? How could she know?

'I've not stopped thinking about you since the second I clapped eyes on you,' Rafe whispered, kneeling between her thighs, looking down on her like she was the most beautiful thing in the universe. 'You were meant to be here... With me.'

She whimpered through her smile, tremors building inside her, and her stomach coiled in anticipation. He glided his palms over her, around her hips, up her sides, and onto her breasts. Suddenly heat rushed through her veins and she let go of the ledge, unable to hold on anymore. He slid his arms around her, holding her close. She silently shook against him. He thrust again, building the tempo, until finding his own release with a low, satisfied groan.

Digging her nails into him and shaking, Tilly gasped for air.

'You ok?' Rafe kissed her neck, still holding her.

'Yes.' She forced the word out between breaths.

His hot body was one with hers and Tilly wanted to live in this moment forever. So what if she was clingy? Clinging to Rafe now seemed like the most important thing in the universe.

She would replay this moment over and over again in her mind for years to come. She never wanted to forget it.

CHAPTER SEVENTEEN

Rafe

Sunday, December 22ⁿᵈ

Morning

Snowflakes fell past the window, drifting in chaotic angles, mesmerising Rafe as he stared at them from his warm position in the bed. Daylight, huh? They must have slept long. He spooned Tilly, tracing a circle on her bare shoulder, and running his palms gently over her soft, warm body. His right arm was practically dead from having her sleeping on it all night, but it didn't make him want to move. Was this insanity? Hooking up with her at all was insane, given that she worked for a rival business, but it wasn't that. Because this didn't feel like a hookup. Nothing that had happened with Tilly could be dismissed so flippantly.

Being close like this felt so right, so good.

People were moving about outside the room and chatting. But hey, Sunday mornings were made for this and shouldn't be rushed. Rafe couldn't move anyway, not without wrenching his arm out from under Tilly and that would disturb this moment too brutally. This had to be enjoyed at leisure and in comfort.

Mum had made up this bedroom like a log cabin and lying here with Tilly as the snow fell outside was a Christmas dream come true. *If this is what Christmas is all about, then count me in.* Marnie could sing all the Christmas carols she wanted if it meant he could spend Christmas with Tilly like this every year.

She stirred beside him, and he gently nuzzled her earlobe, still smoothing his palm over her silky skin. His body was primed to take this further, and he would happily let the moment develop into more, but *should* he? What in hell's name was he doing? Tilly wasn't actually his girlfriend. She wasn't someone he should be in bed with, cuddling up to and contemplating ways of making love to. He was quite literally sleeping with the enemy... She might be waking up to the idea that working for 1-Quick Getaways wasn't the best idea, but that didn't mean they had a future together. And it was crazy to be thinking stuff like this about a woman he barely knew. He'd had some casual hookups, but none of them had felt like this. He hadn't made time in his life for a serious relationship in a long time, so why was he contemplating it now with someone who shouldn't technically be here at all?

'Hi,' Tilly said quietly, turning her neck a little to see him.

'Morning.' He leaned in and kissed her cheek, slipping his hand under her arm and cupping her breasts as he pulled her close. He was so hot for her. *Christ.* This was what she did to him. She let out a sigh that struck him low in the gut, charging him with more lust.

'How long have we slept?' she asked.

'Dunno. I didn't bring my phone through. I've no idea what time it is.'

She stretched, reaching over to the nightstand, and lifted her phone. 'Nine-thirty.'

'Well, it's Sunday morning.' He nuzzled her. 'Best day for a lie in.'

Tilly let out a little laugh. 'Sounds perfect, but I need to pee.' She threw back the covers, jumped up, and ran to the bathroom. He chuckled, stretching his dead arm and flexing his fingers.

'Don't drop any bottles on your foot,' he called as she shut the door. As soon as it clicked shut, he cringed. Hopefully none of his family were outside the door. They didn't need to know he was in here.

When Tilly came out, he traded places with her, keeping a blanket around his waist as he crossed the room. His arousal had died a little with Tilly gone, but he wasn't sure he needed her to see what was going on and he really needed the bathroom.

A moment of cold dread passed over him when he came out. What if Tilly wanted him to go back to his own room? Maybe that was actually the sensible course of action. But heat returned to his body almost instantly when he spied Tilly back in the bed, wrapped up in a cocoon of blankets, sporting a quite adorable bedhead.

'Staying in bed today, are you?' he asked.

'You did say you wanted a lie in.' She looked a little shy. 'Though I think I'd enjoy it more if you were here too. Will you come back in?'

'How can I refuse?' He got back in beside her and she shuffled over to him. Putting his arm around her, he leaned his head on hers, his focus falling on the little tree they'd decorated yesterday, the silent witness to what they'd done here last night.

They fell into an easy kiss, long and slow. Rafe threaded his fingers into her hair as her hands slid over his chest.

'This has been the best Christmas I've ever had,' Tilly whispered through the kisses. 'Not that my previous ones have been anything much.'

Rafe pulled her close, rubbing his palms over her back. 'Tell me. If you want to.'

'About what?'

'Your not so nice Christmases.'

'You really want to know?'

'Sure, if you want to share.' He kissed her softly on the cheek, then the neck. 'Tell me anything.'

'Well, all my childhood Christmases took place in a care home. Maybe not my first two or three. I must have been at home with my mum then, but I don't remember.'

'Why were you put into care?' He carried on stroking her as she seemed to steel herself to answer.

'My mum was an addict, and she ended up in jail for a bit. We were taken away from her.'

'That's sad.' He kissed the top of her head, holding her close, unable to imagine a life without loving parents. 'You said "we". Do you have a brother or sister?'

'A sister. Ellie. She's a year younger than me. By the time we were put into care, she was really difficult. We got foster homes, but every time we were put with a family, she'd do something stupid, and they'd refuse to have us. She'd get angry and lash out. She stole money, she keyed a car, and one time she attacked someone's cat. It was one thing after another, starting when she was still so young. It never stopped. She's in prison now.'

'Jeez.'

'Yup. I spent my childhood Christmases in care because of her. But I was terrified we would get split up.' She let out a sigh. 'Looking back, I'm not sure I made the right decision.'

'Why?'

'Quite a few of the foster families said they'd let me stay on, but not her, if I wanted to. But I always felt like it was my duty to look after her. Maybe it was just me being clingy, as usual. Clinging to the one family member I still had. It took me until I left school to let go.'

'What do you mean by "being clingy as usual"?'

She huffed out a laugh and pulled away from him. 'It's what happens to people with attachment issues. Look it up and you'll see.'

He frowned. Her voice had gone flat, and her words were full of self-deprecation. 'I've heard of it but...'

'It's who I am. My relationships so far have been rubbish because I'm too needy and clingy. That's what my ex-boyfriend said, and a therapist confirmed it.'

'That doesn't sound like something a therapist should say.'

'Oh, she was nice about it. It just took me time to process. She explained about attachment issues, and I've read loads about it since. There's not really a cure. It's about managing the difficult behaviours. And I'm not exactly managing them very well right now, am I?' She didn't look at him as she spoke, wrapping her arms about herself and shaking her head.

'Well, I'm no expert, so I can't agree or disagree, but I haven't seen you as clingy or needy. Loyal, yes. Keen to prove yourself, yes.' Maybe a little naïve and misguided, but now that made more sense too. 'Somewhat reserved at times, but that isn't surprising, given the bizarre circumstances.'

'You've only known me a couple of days and already we've slept together. That's pretty desperate, isn't it?'

'Takes two to tango, and I don't think I've got attachment issues. I wanted this as much as you.'

She glanced up at him. 'That makes me feel a bit better.'

'You come across as sweet, fun to be with, gentle, and affectionate.'

'Do I?'

'Yes. I think you're a little unkind to yourself at times, and the attachment you're most guilty of is the one you have to 1-Quick. I understand more now. You're loyal because they gave you stability.'

'Exactly.' She stared at him and furrowed her brow a little, like she was surprised by his words.

'It's just a pity the company that provided it is a business with questionable ethics. You really would be better out of there, though I accept it's your call, not mine. But that's my penny worth, for the record.'

'You're right. Work was always an area I thought was safe. I didn't realise the attachment issues extended to that too.' She let out a sigh. 'Here was me thinking I was managing things.'

'I'm sure you are.' He put his arms around her and held her again. 'It's not a crime to need something or desire someone. God, if that's the case, then I'm very needy right now, and I have a serious craving to cling to someone.'

Tilly chuckled. 'Yeah, that's not really what it means.'

'Sorry, I get that. I was being unnecessarily flippant. Maybe you should see a different therapist if it's bothering you. Get a second opinion.'

'So, does that mean I *am* being too clingy?'

He shook his head gently. 'I don't think you are, but if you're worried, then there isn't any harm in speaking to a professional about it.' If she wanted to cling to him, he'd be her rock, but he understood why she was worried. This situation felt odd enough without her added issues. No wonder it was confusing.

'Yeah. I think I'll find a new therapist.' She ran her hand around his cheek and smiled in the way that melted him. 'I'm sorry. I've killed the mood.'

'I'm happy you told me. It's important.'

'You have a way of making me feel important.' She blinked and looked away.

'You are important. And special. I think the Christmas magic is working. It feels like you were sent to me for a reason.'

'What reason?'

'I'm not entirely sure yet.'

'Maybe this.' She glanced back at him, then leaned in and pressed her lips against his. He returned her kiss, falling back onto the soft pillows and pulling her down with him. She lay on top of him, and their mouths worked together. The skin contact was electric but also affirming. It cemented the growing bond between them and strengthened the affection. If Tilly had attachment issues, she wasn't having any trouble attaching to him, and he was good with that. Really good. The closer they were attached, the better.

He wanted to hold her, surround her, kiss her, worship her, and be deep inside her all at once. Blood charged through him as he cupped his hands around her bottom and pulled her close to the source of his desire. Satisfying a physical need was only part of this though, and his heart swooped at the deeply warming sensation that being close to her brought to his whole being.

By the time they were ready to go downstairs, it was almost eleven o'clock. Rafe thought it best if he and Tilly didn't go together. His mum's romance radar was already working overtime, and he wasn't sure he could act normally – not when he'd just spent an hour having beautiful sex with a woman he couldn't stop thinking about. Something would surely give him away. He went first, checking the coast was clear before heading to his own room to grab some clean clothes. If he could as easily put on a clear head, he would, but Tilly, Tilly, Tilly was all that his brain wanted to process.

He'd thought some physical exertion might stop some of his crazy mind games, but instead of satisfying the urges so he could move on, it seemed to have opened more doors and pushed out more questions and possibilities.

Nobody was in the kitchen when he went in, so he grabbed some bread from the bread bin and shoved two slices into the toaster. As he opened the dishwasher to grab a plate, his mum appeared.

'Good morning, sleepyhead.'

'Morning,' he said.

'You must have been tired to sleep this late.'

'It's nice not to have to get up sometimes.'

'Very true.' She glanced at the clock. 'Do you think Tilly's ok? She's not hiding in her room, is she?'

'I'm sure she's fine. I'll check in a bit.' He turned his back to her as he spoke, feigning the need to look at the toaster, but convinced his mum could see right through him. 'I think she squirrelled one of your books up there the other night; she's probably reading it.'

How the white lies flowed.

'Ah, yes. I hope she's not starved for romance while she's here.' She started unloading the dishwasher.

Rafe didn't reply. The little smirk on her face was already too much. He pulled his bread from the toaster and slapped on some butter.

'Leave the dishwasher, Mum. I'll do it once I've eaten. You relax for a bit.'

'I don't mind doing it.' She stacked the plates on the dresser. 'I wonder, do you think?' She turned around. 'You and Tilly.'

'Me and Tilly, what?' Was his face going red? He definitely felt a little warm at the neck.

'Could ever get together?'

'Why are you asking me that?'

'Just hopeful, I suppose.'

'I know you've been trying to engineer it ever since you thought she was actually my girlfriend. But really? Is it a genuine possibility in your mind?'

'Why shouldn't it be? It seems you like her and I'm almost certain she likes you.'

'If only it was that easy.'

'It is.'

'Is it? Of course I like her but... Well, we don't really know each other.' That was true, even if they'd done quite a bit of getting to know each other over the past twenty-four hours. 'Maybe she's happy on her own. Maybe I am too. Maybe we're just two lonely people thrown together who are compatible enough to enjoy a few stolen hours together.'

Hilary sighed and folded her arms. 'Is that what—'

'Morning,' Tilly said from the door. 'Am I too late to have something for breakfast?'

'Not at all.' Hilary spun around with a smile and rushed to greet Tilly. 'What would you like?'

'I can make myself something.'

'No, no. You sit and I'll make it.'

Tilly sat opposite Rafe and gave him a weak smile. He held her gaze, returning her smile, but her eyes seemed a little slack, like she didn't want to look properly at him. Had she heard what he said? It didn't bother him if she had. It wasn't like he'd said anything bad, but what did she make of it? After all, it was true. They were just two lonely people who'd found solace with each other over a cold, wintery weekend. Setups like that were ok. It didn't mean they had to do anything about it. Did it?

Could he walk away from this when it had run its course and go back to his normal life? He sipped on his coffee, watching Tilly over the top of it, and wondering. He liked looking at that face, those wide eyes behind the round glasses, that smile. He enjoyed her company too, her kisses, her vulnerability and her bravery at opening up to him.

Walking away wasn't going to be easy. Definitely not.

CHAPTER EIGHTEEN

Tilly

A plate of toast landed on the kitchen table in front of Tilly. She glanced up at Hilary and smiled, glad for the chance to switch her focus away from Rafe. Not because she didn't like what she saw. God no, she loved it... Literally. How could she not? Her clingy issues were going through the roof since they'd been together. But the look he was giving her was too probing, and she had no way of replying.

'Thank you so much. For everything,' she said to Hilary.

'You're quite welcome,' Hilary said. 'It's been lovely having you here. I feel like you're part of the family.' She gave Tilly a gentle pat on the shoulder.

'Thanks.' Tilly bit into her toast to stop any emotions spilling out in the form of tears. She caught Rafe's eye again and his lip quirked. But it wasn't anything like the way he'd looked at her last night or that morning. The intensity had dulled, and his gaze held more questions than answers. Perhaps he was wondering if she'd heard him say he was happy on his own, and they were just two strangers enjoying a few hours in each other's company. She had heard, and the words didn't surprise her, but they saddened her a little. It also cleared things up in her mind though, and that was good. Now she knew how he felt it was easier to adapt her behaviour. She wouldn't cling to him, but accept this weekend was just that – a weekend. The deep gash in her chest that had temporarily filled with what she'd mistaken for love would heal over again. Infatuation wasn't love, just a phase. Sex was just a physical release, not a bonding session, no matter how close she'd felt to him in those ecstatic moments. Normal people who didn't have attachment issues wouldn't be stupid enough to think Rafe loved her after just a few days. And she didn't love him. Not *really*. She couldn't. No. She just desired him and that made her brain jump to all sorts of conclusions because it hadn't made the proper connections as a child.

The rich aroma of freshly brewed coffee wafted through the air and Hilary sighed, placing a steaming mug in front of Tilly before leaning against the counter. 'I can't believe I'm going to miss the church nativity today.' She broke Tilly's reverie, hauling her into the moment.

'What do you mean?' Rafe asked.

Tilly paused, her toast halfway to her mouth, and looked up.

'Well, I can't get there in this weather, can I?'

'I guess not,' Rafe said. 'I forgot it was today.'

'Such a shame,' Hilary said. 'It's one of the highlights of the year.'

'Is it for kids?' Tilly asked.

'The children take part,' Hilary said. 'And everyone sings. It's not scripted or rehearsed. Whoever turns up gets a part and the minister tells the story. It's always so lovely. We have a new minister. I wanted to see his first nativity with us.'

'Sounds cute. I've never been to a nativity.'

Hilary put her hand on Tilly's arm. 'Poor love, you've missed out on so much. Christmas is a wonderful time with family. I'm so sorry you never had that.' She leaned over and hugged her.

Tears pricked again. Why was everyone so nice? It might have been easier if they were horrible and desperate to get rid of her, then she'd be thrilled to leave. But walking away would be horrible.

'Why don't you show Tilly the video of last year's show? You filmed it, didn't you?' Rafe said.

'Oh, yes. I could.' Hilary retrieved a tablet from a drawer in the dresser. 'It's not the best filming, but you'll get the idea.'

She sat down beside Tilly and flicked through some videos. Tilly leaned over and watched. The church looked quaint, and the children were very cute in their costumes. 'So lovely,' Tilly said. 'I can see why you don't want to miss it. But won't other people be snowed in too? Won't it be cancelled if no one can get there?'

'Maybe, but the church is in Glenbriar, so people in the town will be able to walk to it.'

'It looks magical,' Tilly said. 'Such a shame you'll miss it.'

'At least I get to spend time with my family,' she said. 'The kids are a bit too old to join in and Alexander is a bit too young, so maybe I'm better here enjoying time with them.'

'Speaking of the fam, where is everyone?' Rafe said.

'In the living room. They might be planning another walk or more sledging.'

'I'm not sure I'm going on a sledge ever again.' Tilly glanced at Rafe. Well, she might if he was holding her... Clingy, much?

'It wasn't all bad, was it?' He raised his eyebrow.

'Not all of it.'

'You could stay and help me make a yule log if you want?' Hilary suggested.

'Ok. I've always wanted to bake, but I never really tried.'

'Genevieve is going to help too. She's a wonderful cook. Maybe you've seen her on social media. She's a bit of a star.'

'I'm not sure that I have.'

'She used to be into lifestyle stuff, but now she focuses on cooking and she has her own range of kitchenware.'

Tilly watched as Hilary played a reel of Genevieve cooking.

'She's great,' Tilly said. 'So confident.'

'Are you going to bake?' Hilary asked Rafe.

'I'll pass on that, though I'm happy to do the taste test.'

'Dear, dear,' Hilary said. 'Maybe you could find Genevieve for me. And then you can go for a walk with the others if you're not going to make yourself useful around here.'

'That's me told.' He saluted them. 'Right you are, Mum. I'll fetch little sis number two straight away.'

The decadent scent of dark chocolate was almost as lush as kissing Rafe had been. Tilly was a little lightheaded, though that was possibly due to a combination of everything that had happened this weekend rather than the chocolate.

She, Hilary, and Genevieve gathered around the kitchen counter. Bowls of flour, sugar, and other ingredients were laid out and Tilly felt like she'd been whipped straight onto the set of one of Genevieve's reels.

Hilary tied her Mrs Claus apron at the waist. 'We need to get this sponge just right.' She gestured to the mixing bowl. 'It has to be light and fluffy like a cloud.'

Tilly watched as Genevieve cracked eggs and separated the yolks from the whites.

'I get the feeling that would have taken me hours,' Tilly said.

'It takes practise,' Genevieve said. 'I do it on instinct now. It's like I've forgotten the method.'

'Amazing,' Tilly said.

'You can have a go, if you want.'

'No. I don't think anybody wants bits of shell in their cake.'

Hilary patted her back and smiled. 'Have faith in yourself. Honestly, I've been making cakes with my three since they were knee-high to a grasshopper and some of the mess I've cleared up...' She raised the back of her hand to her forehead dramatically. 'But really, that old saying about not being able to make a cake without cracking eggs? It's true. Just don't worry about it. Even if the process is messy, the outcome can still be wonderful.'

That could apply to more than just this cake. But probably not to her and Rafe. Was that where Hilary was going with this? She didn't know just how messy things had got. Messy but nice. So nice, in so many ways. Something stirred deep inside her, something warm and fuzzy that sat alongside a thought of Rafe coming back, putting his arms around her, and holding her close. A sense of belonging. Only it wasn't real. This wasn't where she belonged. Shaking the thought from her head, she refocused. 'Did everyone else go for a walk?' she asked, taking an egg from Hilary.

'Apparently,' Genevieve said. 'Though I doubt Rafe and Finlay got very far. They'll be in the front garden having a snowball battle.'

Hilary and Tilly laughed. Genevieve came around to show Tilly the best way to separate the egg and she managed it without any mishaps.

'Silly boys are out there throwing snowballs at the window.' Grandma came in and settled at the kitchen table.

'Knew it.' Genevieve cleared away the eggshells.

'But you still made a good choice. Finlay is a wonderful lad.'

'He really is.'

'I adored Finlay the minute I met him,' Hilary told Tilly. 'Though I didn't know he and Genevieve were just pretending to be together at that point. To stop me setting her up with other people, would you believe?' Hilary made a face of mock shock and Tilly laughed harder. How could she not? Apparently, it was the family M.O.

'Cressida is now my only child who hasn't pretended to date someone to get me off their case. But...' She waggled the wooden spoon dripping with chocolate at Genevieve. 'I realised before you did how you actually felt about him and I was right, wasn't I?'

'Yes, Mum,' she said in a low voice.

'I know what's good for my children. And speaking of which.' She turned to Tilly, lowering the spoon. 'Rafe is a good boy. He's got a heart of gold. He's done well in business, and he's a compassionate boss, not a ruthless one.'

'I know that.'

'I would give him a piece of my mind if he ever went that way,' Grandma said. 'No need for those cutthroat methods.'

Hilary let out a sigh. 'He's such a caring soul. I just wish he'd find someone special. Someone who he can be himself with. His last girlfriend only seemed to be attracted to him because of his position and his success; she didn't really seem to care about him. They didn't have much in common.'

Tilly's heart skipped a beat. She and Rafe had a couple of things in common: they both worked in travel, and neither had a great love of Christmas. But was that clutching at straws? It was hardly a long list. 'He's a great guy,' Tilly replied, keeping her voice steady. 'But he's happy on his own, I think.'

'Hmph,' Hilary muttered. 'So he says.'

'Utter twaddle,' Grandma added.

'You know he's divorced?' Genevieve said.

'Yeah. He told me,' Tilly said.

'Do we have to talk about that?' Hilary glanced away. 'I normally don't mind who my children date and have relationships with so long as they're happy, but I never warmed to his ex-wife. He rushed in there when he should have waited. If he had, he'd have been a lot happier in the long run.'

Tilly swallowed. Maybe she and Rafe weren't so unalike. He'd rushed into a marriage, just as she'd rushed into thinking she was in love with the first man who'd been nice to her. Rafe wouldn't want a repeat of that, which was yet another reason she had to keep reminding herself this was nothing but a weekend. The thought of disappointing Hilary preyed heavily on her, but how could she prevent it?

A biting anxiety gnawed its way into Tilly's stomach. She'd already prolonged this 'relationship' enough. She couldn't get away yet, but she had to be prepared. Not only that, she would have to contact her boss soon. The thought of facing the repercussions of this trip made her squirm. She stole a glance at her phone, a silent reminder of the looming task ahead. How was she going to break the news she wouldn't be at work tomorrow because she was still stranded in Scotland? Was that a dog-ate-my-homework standard of excuse or what?

Hilary placed a hand on her shoulder, as if sensing the conflict raging inside, and Tilly wanted to fall into her arms. 'Don't worry,' Hilary said, her voice gentle and kind. 'Everything will work out. You'll see.'

Tilly smiled her thanks but couldn't reply. The well was building up to bursting again and she was fighting hard to hold the floodgates.

'Come here.' Hilary pulled her in for a hug and Tilly's worries momentarily eased. But like everything else this weekend, it would be short-lived, and reality was going to hit hard, very soon. It made her rigid, though she wanted to relax and enjoy the sensation of being hugged by a lovely mum.

'You're so kind,' Tilly whispered, and Hilary released her, but her brow was a little furrowed. 'I need to back out for a moment and message my boss to let him know I'm stuck here.'

'You stick up for yourself.' Hilary gave her another bracing pat. 'And don't feel bad. This weather isn't your fault.'

That was true, but she still couldn't completely shake the niggle that she shouldn't be here at all.

The living room was empty, its huge window walls giving a perfect view of the pristine landscape. No one was in sight, so Rafe and Finlay must have taken their snowball fight somewhere else.

Maybe she should snap a photo and send it to her boss as proof of where she was, but that was ridiculous. She shouldn't have to. Her word should be enough. She was twenty-six and had worked there for nine years. She'd worked hard to get where she was, doing online courses and professional development, though so far it had got her nowhere. Now was the time for them to pay back a little.

She opened her phone and typed out an email.

Hi Arnie

Just to let you know I won't be able to come into work tomorrow. I remained in Scotland on Friday and unfortunately I'm snowed in and can't get back. The trains etc. are also cancelled from the area.

I can work online if that suits, and I'll let you know when I can get back.

Regards

Tilly

There, that was professional and friendly. She'd offered to work from here and covered her back. Surely that would be enough. Now she just had to wait.

She let out a sigh, wrapping her arms around herself, trying to bring back the sensations she had when Rafe had held her close. Her chin dropped to her chest, and she internally cringed. If this wasn't the very definition of needy, then what was? How could she make this stop?

CHAPTER NINETEEN

Rafe

'Look what I found in the shed,' Geoff held out two bright orange snow shovels.

'Knock yourself out, Dad,' Rafe said.

Geoff chuckled. 'Shame I didn't find them quicker or we could have attempted to get your mum out for the nativity. It's too late now.'

'We could still clear some of it,' Finlay said. 'Then at least we could get out in an emergency.'

No doubt they could with a lot of effort, but that would also be cutting a path for Tilly to escape. And Rafe didn't want that. But he wasn't her jailor. She was free to leave whenever it was safe.

'Come on.' Finlay took the shovels from Geoff and tossed one to Rafe. 'Let's do this.'

With a groan, he raised his eyebrow at the shovel. He'd much rather go back to Tilly.

His breath plumed in the chilly air as he puffed his dissent. The driveway sloped uphill; this would need some serious exertion.

'Not exactly a relaxing way to spend a Sunday afternoon,' Rafe said.

'Ready to eat my dust?' Finlay said with a smirk. His appetite for sports was well known and Rafe wasn't sure he could beat him if it came to a competition, but he wasn't going to lie down without a fight.

'You wish. I'll have this driveway cleared before you even break a sweat.'

'Such fighting talk. Come on then, show me.'

As a P.E. teacher, endurance cyclist, member of the tug-of-war team, and rugby coach, Finlay had winning credentials. But Rafe loved the outdoors, hiking, cycling, and skiing, so they were well-matched in terms of fitness, though Rafe didn't have quite the same level of motivation – not for this anyway.

He plunged his shovel into the snow, his boots crunching on the frozen ground with each step. The scraping sound echoed through the silence, punctuated by the occasional grunt of effort as they forged upward. Trees swayed gently in the breeze, occasionally dropping clumps of snow silently to the ground. Snow crystals spritzed in the chill air from the shovels too, swirling around them like a flurry of confetti.

As they ascended the driveway, the incline grew steeper, and the snow seemed to fight back. Each shovelful became heavier, each step more laborious. If this had done one thing, it had stopped him thinking about Tilly. All he could think about was getting to the top so this could stop.

'I need a breather.' He leaned on his shovel, letting out a long, slow breath.

'Yeah.' Finlay stopped shovelling and frowned at what they still had left to do. 'Whose bright idea was this?'

'Some crazy punter.'

Finlay laughed. 'I can almost see the road. Looks like the plough has been down.' He stood on his tiptoes. 'There's definitely black on there.'

Cold air nipped at Rafe's cheeks and icy daggers made their way to his insides as he nodded. With the driveway clear and the main road open, how could he keep Tilly here any longer? If she wanted, she could call a taxi and leave straight away. Even if the trains weren't running from Glenbriar, they might be from Perth and definitely would be from Edinburgh or Glasgow. The snow wasn't widespread. Only rural areas had been badly affected. But now he'd pushed open the door and Tilly could go through whenever she wanted.

He and Finlay continued their uphill battle until they got to the main gate. Despite the physical exertion, there was a sense of achievement as they looked back at their handiwork. The road had indeed been ploughed and getting the Raptor out now would be no problem. His excuses had run out. If he wanted Tilly to stay, he'd have to ask her... Tell her he wanted her to.

But to what end?

What if Tilly's concerns were right? Was she just desperate for someone to attach herself to? Was he enabling her? She was just so easy to love. *Love?*

Do I love Tilly?

Could you love someone after such a short period? *Christ.* He'd been down this road before. He'd fallen in love with his ex-wife about ten seconds after he met her. But that had gone south almost as quickly after their wedding. He'd got it wrong then, and who was to say he wouldn't do it again? Was he doing the same thing now? He needed to slow down and consider things carefully.

Was Tilly worth taking a risk? His gut reaction was yes, but he wasn't sure he trusted his gut.

He and Finlay made their way back to the shed, nursing sore arms and achy legs. 'I need a long soak.' Finlay rolled his shoulders.

'Sounds like a good idea. Let's get back inside.'

Rafe settled for a hot shower. He let the water revive his limbs, tossing back his head and running his hands through his hair. Visions of Tilly popped up in his mind. If she was here... Oh, the things they could do. But where was she? He hadn't seen her when he came in. He wanted to, needed to. His body and soul ached without her. Not the reaction he needed right now. Focus on letting her go... But the opposite was happening. He couldn't get her out of his mind.

He got out of the shower and towelled himself dry before pulling on a pair of soft grey lounge pants. If he couldn't wear these at Christmas, when could he? He added a plain white t-shirt and headed out of the room. As he passed Tilly's door, he heard a soft sound. Was she in there?

He knocked. 'Tilly? Are you there?'

After a moment, the door opened, and she stood before him, her eyes glistening and a little puffy. It cut him to the core to see her so upset.

'What's happened?'

'Work.' She let out a shuddery breath.

'What about it?'

'My boss is furious. You should read his email.'

'I'd like to.'

She stood back from the door, and he came in.

'Oh, Tilly, Tilly,' he said with a sigh, clamping his hands on her upper arms, then leaning his forehead on hers. How he'd missed her. She stayed still, but he sensed she was forcing it. Her surrounding energy seemed to shake. Or maybe it was the powerful force inside him that was buzzing with the desire to hold her close. 'Let's see this email,' he said after a moment, keeping his tone measured and sticking to the subject.

She lifted her phone from the bed, scrolled, then handed it to him.

He read it with a raised eyebrow.

Dear Tilly

I understand from Mitchell that you travelled from Glasgow to Perthshire on Friday on an unauthorised task that involved visiting the private residence of one of our competitors. This was unadvised and undertaken on your own back. The company accepts no liability for this visit, and you won't be reimbursed for it.

As the matter stands, you are expected in the office on Monday morning. If you are unable to be here, disciplinary measures will be taken. I need not add how this will affect your future career prospects.

We are calling a meeting for first thing tomorrow morning, where we will be discussing restructuring. Your attendance is expected.

Arnie Wilcox

'Wow. He sounds an absolute pleasure to work with,' Rafe said with a dollop of sarcasm.

'What can I do?' Tilly's eyes were wide and helpless.

'Let me think about how to reply,' Rafe said. 'I'd like you to throw Mitchell under the bus and quit, but it's better if you keep everything professional, then he won't have a leg to stand on if he dismisses you.' He glanced back at the email and shook his head, then placed the phone on the dresser. Tilly stood alone at the end of the bed with her arms wrapped tight around herself. 'Here,' he whispered. So what if it made more sense to keep his distance? How could he abandon her when she looked so sad? He opened his arms to her. She looked like she might shake her head and turn away, but she yielded and fell into him. He drew her close, and all the muddled thoughts and ideas aligned in a brief moment of peace. 'Try not to worry. I'll help you as much as I can.' He kissed the side of her head, loving the way she closed her eyes like this was a dream. It kind of was. And, all things considered, a rather good one. Just a pity it might only be a short one.

She glanced up at him and smiled gently, her pupils dilating. Then she pushed up on her toes, pressing a kiss on his lips. 'I can't thank you enough,' she murmured.

'You don't have to thank me for anything.'

She kissed him again, slipping her hand around his jaw. He pulled her flat against him, splaying his fingers on her back. His blood rushed south again. Damn these trousers. Soft as they may be, they were also too flimsy to act as a barrier. She'd know just what she did to him.

A knocking sound made them freeze. It wasn't loud enough to have been on Tilly's door... Was it someone looking for him and knocking on his bedroom door? There wasn't anyone in the bedroom on the other side of Tilly.

'Where did that come from?' Tilly asked.

He gave a little shrug as another thud sounded louder than the one before.

'Rafe, are you in there?' Genevieve's voice said, like she was talking into his room and sounding weirdly panicky. Something told him this wasn't the time to be coy about getting caught in Tilly's room.

He let go of Tilly, crossed the room, and opened the door. 'I'm in here, helping Tilly with an email. What's wrong?'

'Alexander slipped when they were outside. He banged his head and has a really big cut. He should go to the hospital, but Cress is worried about driving in the snow. Their car isn't great in it.'

'I'll take him in the Raptor. Just let me grab some clothes.'

'Will you get through?' Tilly said.

'Finlay and I cleared the driveway,' he said. 'And the road is open.'

'It's open? Then I should go too.'

Ice slipped into Rafe's bloodstream. *No.* He didn't want Tilly to go.

You're not her guard. If she wants to go, you have to let her.

'I'll take you later if you want to go,' he said. 'But this is urgent.'

'Yeah, I know. Go.'

He bolted to his room and dragged on some clothes, then hurtled down the stairs.

Cress and Tina were comforting the sobbing Alexander. His beautiful blond curls were now tinged with blood.

'Oh dear,' Hilary said. 'Poor baby.'

'I hope it's a quick fix,' Grandma said. 'We don't want the wee soul in hospital for Christmas.'

'Let's go,' Rafe said. He pushed all thoughts of Tilly from his mind. He had to focus on getting Alexander safely to the hospital.

The Raptor's engine roared to life, drowning out the soft murmurs of Cressida and Tina in the backseat. Rafe glanced over his shoulder, his eyes meeting Cressida's gaze as she held the tearful Alexander's hand. Tina sat on the other side, pressing a bandage to his forehead.

'Don't worry, we'll get him checked out.' Rafe gripped the steering wheel and took off slowly up the track he and Finlay had cleared earlier. Thank goodness they had.

'Thanks so much,' Tina said as the little one sniffled.

'No probs. Hang in there, little buddy,' Rafe said. 'We've got this.' He reached the top of the drive and pulled away from the estate, the snowy landscape unfolding before them, looking more beautiful than he'd ever seen it.

'Is it far?' Tina asked.

'There's a small hospital in Glenbriar,' Rafe replied, eyes pinned on the road. A track had been cleared but in some places drifts from overhanging branches had covered it again. 'There's always a doctor on call. We should be able to see someone.'

'I can't believe it,' Cressida said. 'He was so happy running about and then bang.'

'It happens,' Rafe said. 'We'll make sure he's ok.'

'Your mum said she had you at A&E about five times before the age of ten,' Tina said. 'It must run in the family.'

'I think she was exaggerating, though I was in the rugby team for a bit and that was carnage. I sprained something every time I stepped onto the pitch.'

Lights twinkled beyond as they approached Glenbriar. Even though it was still early afternoon, the light was fading. The Raptor rolled through the town. Christmas trees winked from every shop front, and Cressida distracted Alexander by pointing them out to him.

'Nearly there.' Rafe pulled down a side road and round a sharp bend to the small newly built hospital. 'Hey, wee buddy, we'll soon have you fixed up.'

As he pulled up outside the hospital, his mind wandered back to Tilly. The roads were clear; the town was functioning, and buses would be running soon. If she wanted to leave, she could leave, with or without his help.

'Are you ok to go in yourself?' he said to Cressida and Tina. 'I'd like to grab some stuff in town while I'm here. I'll come back as soon as you're ready.'

'Sure. I'll message you,' Cressida said.

Rafe watched them go in, then jumped out of the Raptor and locked it. He wasn't sure he was supposed to leave the car here, but parking in Glenbriar was bad at the best of times and at Christmas it was even worse. What he wanted was to find something he could give Tilly for Christmas. Even if she wasn't with him, she'd have something. Or she might choose to stay, in which case, he wanted her to have presents to open on Christmas morning. Nice things he'd chosen for her.

Glenbriar was a shoppers' haven if you liked boutique shops and family-run businesses. He could go up the street and get her something from everywhere. A perfect Glenbriar stocking, starting with some treats from the sweet shop, then some hand-made soap. And there was the jewellery shop. He scanned the shelves and displays of pretty pieces. It didn't sell diamonds and wasn't comparable with Tiffany's or even Oliver Bonas, but it was handmade and unique. Tilly would appreciate it... And he wanted to get her something special, because that was what she was to him.

Special.

No matter what happened, she'd always occupy a special place in his heart. Buying Christmas gifts had never been something Rafe enjoyed or even put much effort into. The last time he had was for his ex-wife before they were married, and he'd spent ages trying to find the perfect gift. He'd done that online as he usually did for everyone else, but this felt so much more personal, checking every shop for the perfect item.

Christ! Am I doing it again?

He didn't even remember what he'd bought for his ex in the end. A few years down the line, would this experience be similarly shelved? Maybe he had a serious problem for falling too fast. His eyes roamed over a pretty display laid out on a white table like a mini snow scene. He lifted a silver and rose gold bracelet. A heart entwined with a star dangled from it. Understatedly pretty. Just like Tilly.

If he stopped to think, he'd give up on the whole idea. He shouldn't be doing any of this. But it sparked joy inside him, and he smiled as he looked at the bracelet, imagining it on Tilly. This was what Christmas was all about, wasn't it?

Joy... Love.

No matter which way he looked at it, he was properly done for.

Chapter Twenty

Tilly

Sunday, December 22nd

Afternoon

Tilly lifted her phone from the coffee table in the Harrington's living room. She glanced at the screen, half checking for messages but really just needing an excuse to do something. Everyone was so preoccupied with worry over Alexander. Tilly felt like she was in the way. No one said anything, but she couldn't help it. She was worried too, but only through circumstance. In a few days' time, what would this family be to her? Their concerns wouldn't be hers. She probably wouldn't see any of them again. A wave of cold nausea washed over her at the thought, and she got to her feet, ambling over to the window. How could she bear to leave them? But she must.

Her sister, Ellie, had always been the one to cause trouble when they were young and perhaps Tilly had overcompensated by trying to be extra 'good', sensible or whatever. Anything to fit in and not be rejected. Just as she did at work. The sensible choice here was to get back to London and turn up for work at the job she was paid to do. But that wasn't the choice her heart wanted. Hearts weren't good decision makers though, and she needed to rely on the rational part of her brain to make the correct choice. The one that would be right in the long run.

Not wanting to intrude further on the family's shared troubles, she moved slowly and quietly around the room. Geoff and Hilary were standing on the other side, looking at a photograph on a small console table lit by a beautiful lamp with a stag printed on it. Genevieve was cuddling Mitzi on the sofa next to Finlay, and they were chatting with Grandma. Tilly couldn't make out the exact words but knew they were telling each other everything would be ok. She made it to the door and slipped out of the room.

The house seemed unusually quiet. It was so big that people could be anywhere, and rooms could be empty, even when everyone was here, but Alexander's injury had temporarily dimmed the buzz of Christmas joy. Hopefully he'd be back soon, all fixed up and good as new.

Slowly, Tilly took the stairs up to her room. She trailed her fingers over the garlands, and the fairy lights seemed to respond to her touch like a sensitive plant, gradually lighting up. By the time she'd reached the top, they'd faded again.

Ellie would have ripped the lights off and thrown them to the bottom of the stairs. She'd have knocked over the Christmas tree, run roughshod through the house and terrorised the dogs. Tilly's insides were so screwed up she almost wanted to do it herself. Why should this family enjoy their Christmas without her? The moment passed with a few deep breaths. She'd never sabotage these people. She loved them too much. It wasn't their fault she had to leave.

And she really did have to leave.

If the roads were open, she couldn't in all conscience stay. Duty nudged her to do it. Arnie was already threatening her and, while she'd like to tell him where to shove his job, she couldn't. Getting something else after quitting would be tough. If she had crap references, who would hire her? That meant going back to London and facing the music.

Packing her overnight bag didn't take long. She folded the clothes Genevieve had so kindly washed neatly into her case and zipped it up. With a sigh, she sat on the end of the bed and clutched her face in her hands. The Glenbriar fairytale was about to end. She'd used up all her credits... and her tears. Now she had to be sensible and get on with things the way she always did. No need to cling to the Harringtons. She didn't need them to survive. Wanting them was a different thing, but in life, you rarely got what you really wanted. She'd learned that lesson long ago. Wanting it wasn't enough if you weren't meant to have it.

Taking a long, calming breath, she opened the train app from her phone and tapped the screen a few times. Nothing was yet going from Glenbriar, though there were services from Edinburgh and Glasgow. Should she ask Rafe to run her there? It was quite a drive, and she'd already imposed on the family. She could call the taxi, then try to get buses. Even doing that, she was unlikely to make it for a train that got her to London before work started. Except the sleeper train. She checked it. Seats were still available. She'd be exhausted, but it was possible. Maybe Arnie would be more sympathetic if she made the effort.

A knock on the door made her jump. 'Come in.'

Genevieve poked her head around the door. 'Hi. I just wondered where you were. Are you ok?'

'Yeah...' Tilly shrugged, knowing she wasn't ok at all. Her insides were in bits and her mind was a car crash.

'Oh dear.' Genevieve sat down beside her. 'You look a bit sad.'

'Just worried about Alexander.'

'I'm sure he'll be fine,' Genevieve said. 'Cress messaged and said he's getting that glue stuff put on. Hopefully that'll fix him up.'

'I hope so.'

Genevieve gave Tilly a little pat on the arm. 'This has been one wild weekend.' With a frown, she glanced at Tilly's zipped-up case. Tilly held her breath. Would Genevieve say anything about it? But why would she? Tilly hadn't brought a lot of stuff, so it wouldn't be unusual for her to have everything still in there.

'Are you planning on leaving?' Genevieve asked.

Ok, so she was astute, just like her brother. All three of them, Rafe, Cressida and Genevieve, were alike in many ways – all kind, welcoming and caring. Tilly was glad not to be like her sister. She almost didn't dare think it, but she wished she had Genevieve and Cressida as sisters and not Ellie. Even now, she felt like she was betraying her sister with thoughts like that, but so what? Had her sister ever cared about her? She'd spent more effort ruining their childhood than anything else. Maybe if she'd applied that energy in a more positive way, she'd have made something out of her life.

Suddenly aware Genevieve was watching her, Tilly turned her mind back to the conversation. 'I don't have much choice. I have to leave.'

'Why? We're happy to have you here as long as you want. You can go back after Christmas, can't you?'

'You've all been so kind.' Tilly gave her a weak smile. 'But I can't stay.'

Genevieve tilted her head and made sad eyes, then she leaned over and hugged Tilly. 'You're the nicest girlfriend Rafe's ever had.'

'I'm not even his girlfriend.'

Genevieve patted her on the back. 'I don't think it would take much to make it official if you wanted to. You're so much nicer than his last girlfriend and his ex-wife. Nobody wanted to say at the time that we didn't like her, but she didn't make it easy. We tried to be nice to her, but she was actually really rude to Mum on quite a few occasions. You're such a lovely person, we'd be happy for you to stay.'

'Thank you.' They smiled at each other for a long moment. 'But I need to go back to London,' Tilly said. 'My boss is on my case, and I'm scared I get fired and he won't give me references.'

'But you can't leave right this minute. How will you get anywhere?'

'Taxi, buses, then the sleeper train.'

'That sounds insane. Wouldn't you be better waiting until tomorrow at least?'

'I can't. My boss wants me back for a meeting tomorrow. If I at least show that I'm willing, he might be kinder in his judgement.'

Genevieve shook her head like she was desperately searching for an alternative solution. 'He sounds like a tyrant. Can't you do it online?'

'I suggested that. But I'm already in trouble for being here at all. He wants me there in person.' She got to her feet. 'I should call a taxi.'

'I'll run you into town, if you want, but shouldn't you at least wait until Rafe gets back?'

'We don't know when that will be. What if he's late?'

'Ok. I'll give you a lift, if you're that desperate.' Genevieve stood and paced to the window. 'Are you sure the buses are running?'

'There's a coach that goes from Glenbriar to Edinburgh.' Then she'd get the sleeper train from there and arrive in London in time for her meeting, even if she was beyond exhausted by the time she got there.

Genevieve turned from the window and her eyes travelled across the room, pausing on the nightstand. A wave of heat washed over Tilly as she realised Genevieve's gaze had landed on the condom packet Rafe had left there.

Shit. Shit. Shit.

Bang went any flimsy, phoney excuse or white lie she might want to make up to pretend she and Rafe were nothing but almost strangers who'd ended up stuck together due to a set of weird circumstances. They were all that, of course, but they'd also slept together. And not just that... They'd bonded. Why did she keep thinking like that? But it had felt so strong and so real. Now they were apart, it was like a piece of her had been wrenched out, and she'd never be able to put herself back together again – not without him.

Stop!

This was all nonsense. Clingy and needy like her therapist had warned her.

Genevieve turned to look at her, her expression kind and maybe a little bit pitying. 'My brother hasn't always told the truth about his relationships. I don't know how many times he's fibbed about seeing someone when he isn't really. You are a case in point. I know some of it is just to wind me up, but Tilly, I know he likes you. This might sound utterly ridiculous, but I knew he liked you before he'd even met you.'

'That doesn't make any sense.'

'You weren't there. I believed him, even though my brain was telling me he was making up stories as usual. The way he talked about you and described your smile was so real.'

'That just means he likes my smile, not necessarily me.'

'Maybe to start with, but something drew him to you. You caught his eye, he noticed you, and he was attracted to you. If that had been a photo on a dating profile, you'd have been an instant swipe right.'

Tilly let out a little laugh. No two ways about it; she'd have felt the same if she'd seen a picture of him. She had done! That night she'd looked at photos before she visited and thought he looked kind, generous, caring, and loving. She couldn't have known that from a two-dimensional image, but it had turned out to be true.

'I'm serious,' Genevieve said. 'And really, it's obvious he likes you now. He hasn't even tried to hide it or deny it.'

'But he doesn't really know me.'

'It kind of depends what you mean by that. Of course, he doesn't know everything about you. But nobody can know everything about a person that quickly. All you need to know is how you feel. Sometimes it doesn't take long for people to get together and to know they're right for each other.'

Tilly shook her head. 'That maybe works for normal people, but it doesn't work for me.'

'What are you talking about?' Genevieve sat on the end of the bed. 'You are a normal person.'

'But my childhood wasn't like yours.' Tilly sat next to her. 'I told you before I grew up in foster care. It means I've had abandonment issues all my life. I had to have counselling for it.'

'Aw Tilly. I didn't get how hard it'd been for you. But you're still a normal person.'

'My mind sees things differently. My counsellor told me I attach to other people too quickly because I'm...' She gave a little shrug. 'Desperate, I suppose. She told me not to think I was in love just because I felt good around a person and that it takes time. It could only truly be love once I got to know a person. I'm already guilty of idealising others and putting them on pedestals.' She'd done it at work, with Rafe... This whole family.

'I get what you're saying and I'm not saying it isn't true,' Genevieve said, 'but it doesn't change the fact that my brother cares about you. I can fully understand if you want to take things slowly, but don't go thinking this is one sided.'

'I'm not, but whether I had abandonment issues or not, infatuation isn't love. I'm not denying I'm a bit infatuated with Rafe. He maybe feels the same. And yes, we slept together, but sex isn't love either. They're just phases; they don't mean it'll last.'

Genevieve put her hand on Tilly's arm. 'All true. But I believe love at first sight is real. I believe Rafe saw your photo, and it called to him. The attraction was already there and when he met you, it kept going. I don't think it'll stop unless you want it to... even then, he would respect your wishes, but I doubt he can switch off those feelings.'

'But it's only been what… three days?' Tilly had almost lost track. The crazy attraction had blinded her to everything else.

'Why are there so many rules on love? Who makes them up? Why do people try to tell the rest of the world how they should feel? If you love someone after three days, then that's how you feel. What does it matter how it worked for someone else? Of course people will tell you what you feel isn't love, but infatuation or lust or whatever. But infatuation and lust are parts of love. I'd say it's rare to find love without having felt those things first. I'm not saying they always lead to love, but they can do. And love is love. You can feel it anytime, in any way, for anyone. Sure, it doesn't necessarily mean you're destined to be together. And it doesn't mean you have to know everything about the person. In fact, it doesn't have to mean anything. It's just what you feel.' Genevieve tapped her chest with her fist. 'Your therapist maybe thought you fell too easily, but maybe you're just open hearted. I count you as a friend and I've only known you a few days too. Is that any better or worse?'

Tilly smiled and shook her head. 'I don't know, but I'm really happy to be your friend.'

'Aw.' Genevieve leaned over and hugged her. 'And I'm happy to have you. So, if it's ok for us to be friends, it's ok for you and Rafe too.' She pulled back. 'Why shouldn't a person crave love? It's normal. I did for years before I got together with Finlay. I had all the family love I needed, but it's not the same as romantic love.

Don't close yourself off to something that could be wonderful because of something that one person told you.'

'But…' Tilly let out a sigh. Some of what Genevieve said made sense. But how could she trust herself? 'How do I know it's not just infatuation for one or both of us? Surely that's what takes the time.'

'Maybe, but you'll never know unless you take the chance.'

'I think…'

Voices from the corridor made her stop.

'I think they're back.' Genevieve got up, crossed the room, and opened the door. Tilly followed and peered out. Rafe and Finlay were chatting at the top of the stairs.

'Is everyone ok?' Genevieve asked.

'Fine,' Rafe said. 'Alexander's all patched up, and he's fine. Mum and Grandma are spoiling him with treats now. He's not got concussion or anything. It was all on the surface.'

'Phew. That's a relief.' She turned and smiled at Tilly. 'I'll go see him.' As she reached Rafe, she gave him a little prod. 'Speak to Tilly.'

Rafe's eyes met Tilly's and heat burned through her. Unspoken words seemed to crackle on an invisible wire between them. She wanted to believe he felt everything she did, that his pulse was racing like hers and his heart full to the brim now they were back together. But it didn't take away the fact that she had to get back to London by tomorrow morning.

CHAPTER TWENTY-ONE

Rafe

Tilly backed into the middle of her room, her eyes fixed on Rafe. He closed the bedroom door softly behind him, frowning slightly, the thud of his pulse quickening in his ears. Tilly's lips quirked into the ghost of a smile, but it fell well short of her eyes. Something was up. She sat down on the edge of the bed, her shoulders tense and her gaze fixed on a distant point beyond the window.

Rafe edged closer, tilting his head, trying to catch her eye. 'Tilly? Is everything ok?'

She looked up, her eyes glassy, and shook her head.

'What's wrong?' He sat down next to her. 'Is it that email from your boss? I can help you reply now if you want.'

Tilly's lips pressed into a thin line, her gaze dropping to her hands folded in her lap. 'I... I need to leave.'

'Need to?' Rafe's heart jolted. He should stay calm. This moment was always coming, but they had to be rational about this. 'Tilly... I...' He shook his head. 'Do you mean you need to leave right now?'

She nodded.

'Why? You've already told your boss you're snowed in, and you've given him the option of talking to you remotely.'

'He'll look up the weather himself. He'll see that buses and trains are running. I can't stay here. The guilt will eat me. Please, can you give me a lift into Glenbriar? I need to catch a bus to Edinburgh.' She didn't look up. 'And then the sleeper train to London.'

Rafe struggled to process the words, shaking his head like that would somehow realign everything.

'Sure, Tilly,' he said, his voice barely above a whisper. 'I can do that, but I'm a bit thrown by the urgency.'

'Now I know things are moving again, I can't stay.' Her shoulders sagged. 'I'll feel like I'm doing something wrong or lying somehow. I know I don't owe 1-Quick anything, but I owe myself. This is who I am. I turn up every day and do my job like I'm supposed to. It pays the bills. I might not like it, but I do it. If I don't at least try to get back and then Arnie fires me or refuses to give me references, I'll always blame myself. Everything I've built up will be pointless.' She threw her head back and sighed. 'This kind of thing happened time and again when I was a child. One bad action on my sister's part erased any good I ever did. How can I let that happen here?'

How indeed? 'I understand.' Rafe's mind raced, grappling with her words and knowing how commendable he'd find her desire to get back if he was her employer. Not that he'd ever have put her through this in the first place. His fingers itched to reach out, to hold her close and tell her that everything would be ok. But he didn't have that power. He couldn't guarantee everything would be ok. All he could do was respect her wishes and make this part of her journey as trouble free as possible. 'I'll give you a lift as soon as you're ready.'

Tilly met his gaze and smiled, pressing her lips together, then covering her mouth. 'Thank you.'

He put his hand on her back and rubbed it gently. 'But not to Glenbriar.'

'Where then?'

'Check to see if the sleeper train is running from Glasgow. If it is, I'll give you a lift all the way there and stay in my flat tonight.'

She shook her head. 'I can't ask you to do that. It's too much.'

'You're not asking. I'm offering.' He pulled out his phone. 'Let's see.' Opening the website for the sleeper train, he scrolled until he found the information he was looking for. 'It leaves tonight at eleven-fifteen. I can get you there for that. It'll save you a lot of faffing around on public transport.'

'I really can't thank you enough.'

'I don't want thanks.' His eyes locked with hers. 'I just want to know you'll be ok.'

'I'll be fine.' Her voice cracked and Rafe put his arm around her and pulled her into his chest.

'This doesn't sound fine to me.' It didn't feel it either. The pain in his chest was strong enough to crack it open, but this was nothing to what it would be when Tilly was gone. She was the part of his soul that completed him, a piece he didn't even know was missing until she fell into his life.

'I will be.' Tilly sniffed, rubbing her hand up and down on his chest somewhat manically. 'I'm just sad that I have to leave.'

'You know you'll be welcome at any time. Feel free to come back. I'll give you all my contact details and my mum's and Cress and Gen's too. We're all your friends.' If friends was all they could be, it was better than nothing and it kept a lifeline bobbing on the surface. 'Call or message about anything, ok?' He tilted his head to look at her. 'Yeah?'

'Yeah.' She pulled out of his hold and got to her feet. 'I'm ready whenever you are. My stuff is already packed. I don't know how long it'll take to get there.'

'We've got plenty of time.' He stood up. 'It's only four o'clock. I'll go tell everybody what's happening.'

His eyes met hers and for a moment, they just gazed at each other. Time stood still and all number of visions assailed Rafe's brain, all of them possible futures with or without Tilly, some happy, some sad. None guaranteed. He blinked them away, closed the gap between them, and placed a long, slow kiss on her cheek.

'Come down when you're ready,' he whispered. With one more brief glance, he left the room. His chest cracked like a brick had landed on it, but what more could he do? She'd made up her mind, and it wasn't his place to change it for her. No doubt she was feeling pain too, but he had to respect her wishes. Her loyalty and sense of duty were too strong. They should be commendable, but he was ninety-nine per cent sure her employers wouldn't care one bit. They wouldn't give her the praise and recognition she craved. Their treatment of her was criminal and, like a beaten animal, she crawled back, ready to take all the pain again in the hope of one little fragment of kindness or acknowledgement.

She didn't want to do anything to jeopardise her place there the way her sister had done to them both as children. But surely it would be better to find a new place? Easy for him to say. He wasn't the one with the decision to make. His life was good for the main part. Not having Tilly would be the hardest thing he'd faced for a while, but he could do his best to keep in touch. Show her he wouldn't easily forget her. He wasn't some fleeting person she'd latched onto because he happened to be in the right place at the right time. He was real. He had feelings for her, and they ran deep.

Everyone was gathered at the kitchen table, laughing and chatting. Finlay was tickling Alexander, who looked completely fine apart from the little white wound closure strip on his forehead.

Hilary and Cressida looked around as Rafe joined them, the others still too focused on Alexander to notice.

He sat down with a sigh.

Hilary set down the cutlery she'd been holding and frowned. 'What's wrong?' Her eyes searched him for answers.

He took a deep breath and gave a little shrug. 'Tilly's leaving. Tonight. Heading back to London.'

'What?'

'Did you not talk her out of it?' Genevieve asked.

'I tried, but she has to do this. It's her choice and as an employer myself, I can understand her reasons. I should applaud them.'

'You agree she should go?' Genevieve goggled at him.

He ran his fingers through his hair. 'It's her job and her choice. I don't like it, but it's not my call. I can't keep her here if she wants to leave.'

Geoff's brows furrowed, and he tapped his finger on the table. 'I agree. If I was her employer, I'd expect her to make every effort to get back.'

'She's already offered to work online, but they're not accepting that,' Rafe said.

'Dear, dear,' Geoff muttered. 'I'm sure I've been called all sorts of names by my employees at times, but I hope I've never been that unreasonable.'

'That's pretty bad,' Cressida agreed. 'Did she tell them she was snowed in?'

'Yes, they sound like a right bunch of dicks, but she's worried they'll check up on her and discover public transport is running again. It's her call.'

'That's sad,' Genevieve said. 'She only just got here, but it feels like she's already part of the family. I hate to see her going so soon.'

Rafe nodded. 'Yeah. I said we'd all give her our contact details, so she can get in touch whenever she needs to.'

'Of course.' Hilary's eyes welled with tears. 'Oh, Rafe, I'm so sorry.'

Cressida stroked her back. 'It's ok, Mum. I know it's not what you wanted, but I'm sure she'll keep in touch.'

'Poor girl,' Grandma said. 'There'll be no telling her just now, but when she gets to my age, she'll understand.'

'Understand what?' Cressida said.

'That very little matters in the end, especially a so-called career.'

Geoff frowned and shook his head like she'd completely lost her marbles, but Rafe wondered if there was more truth in those words than any of them dared admit.

'I'm going to take her to Glasgow.' He didn't look at his mum. Her being openly upset was more than he could handle. He didn't trust himself not to crack. The ache inside was so strong. 'The sleeper train leaves at eleven-fifteen, and I want to make sure she gets there safely.'

Finlay patted him on the back. 'Let me know if there's anything we can do.'

'Thanks. You already helped by clearing the drive.' For Alexander's sake, he was glad they had, but a selfish streak inside him was mad. If they hadn't done it, maybe Tilly wouldn't have felt the need to leave so soon. But he couldn't hold on to her indefinitely. What was keeping her here if not the snow?

Me?

Even if he proposed a future for their relationship, it wouldn't bring any guarantees. And it definitely wouldn't be a merry Christmas if she was stressed about her work situation. What had started as one of the happiest Christmases of his life suddenly looked set to become one of the worst.

'Can't she just quit her job?' Genevieve said.

'Sounds very rash to me,' Geoff said.

'Oh, I don't know,' Grandma added. 'Once she learns that family, friendship and love are what truly matter in life, she might decide that's the best move.'

'Listen, it's her choice to make. Not ours. We have to respect that, ok?' Rafe looked around and they all bowed their heads. Grandma looked like she might say something, but she didn't.

They couldn't make the decision for her or put what they would do in this situation onto her. She was capable of making her own choices and doing what was best for herself. Rafe's choice was either to take her or refuse to help her at all. And of course he would help her. He'd do anything for her, even if it meant losing the woman he was falling for.

'I'll ask her to come and say goodbye before she leaves,' he said.

He'd barely left the room when Genevieve caught up with him and dragged him into the empty living room.

'Isn't there anything you can do to make her stay?'

'Like what?'

'Tell her how you feel.'

He shook his head. 'That changes nothing.'

'Really? Tell me, how exactly do you feel about her?'

'I like her... A lot.'

'Uh-huh?'

'What?' He gave a little shrug.

'I know you've slept with her.'

He looked away with a huff. 'Did she tell you that?'

'She didn't need to. You left evidence on the bedside cabinet.'

'Oh for god's sake. You're so nosey. And so what? We're adults. It happens.'

'And you just said you like her.'

'Ok, yes. I like her, but so what?'

'Oh please. You're not going to compare her to one of your hookups, are you? You slept with her because you like her, not because you were both lonely or whatever.'

He shook his head and held up his hands. 'Stop. I'm not denying it, but what do you mean one of my hookups? You make me sound like a manwhore. I don't have that many hookups, you know. In fact, I hardly have any.'

She raised an eyebrow.

'Do you know what it's like to be divorced after just a few weeks of marriage?' he said. 'It messes with you.'

'Obviously I don't know how that feels exactly, but I know how it feels to be dumped and yes, it hurts.'

'It does, but not only that. It's made me wary. I shouldn't have rushed into my marriage. My last girlfriend wasn't really right for me, and I took a long time trying to figure her out and how to make things work. It's confusing when things feel wrong and no matter what you do, you can't fix it.'

'And do you feel like that about Tilly? Does that feel wrong?'

'Not at present, but how can I tell? I don't really know her and I don't have a crystal ball.'

'Nobody does, Rafe.' Genevieve shook her head. 'I've just had almost exactly the same conversation with her. Love is love. Trust your instincts.'

'That's what I did the last time.'

'Did you? You were a lot younger then. You've had a lot more experience now.'

He had. He also had what his heart was telling him. 'Listen, I agree, but I can't stop her from leaving if she wants to, or feels she needs to. What kind of man would I be if I did that?'

Genevieve pulled her lips flat like she was sucking back words she wanted to say. 'Ok, you have a point, but let's not leave her in any doubt that this house will always be open to her.'

'I'll make sure she knows that.'

Every one of his instincts was pushing him to keep Tilly with him, but she wasn't a piece of property. If she wanted to leave, he had to allow that. He would do as Genevieve suggested, and he'd also make sure she knew she could always trust him to support her. Right now, that meant helping her to leave this house, his family, and him.

CHAPTER TWENTY-TWO

Sunday, December 22nd

Evening

The soft jazz version of 'Jingle Bells' coming from a hidden speaker was almost enough to set Tilly off crying as she made her way downstairs with her suitcase. The delicious smell of Hilary's home-cooked food drifted through the house along with the unmistakable sounds of happiness. So much joy had filled her life since arriving here on Friday. How impossible to think it had only been a few days. In some ways it felt longer, but now it was almost over, it was far too short.

'Hey, I was just coming to find you.' Rafe strolled out of the living room with Genevieve.

They were both smiling, but it looked forced. Rafe's lips were pinched and Tilly could hardly bear to meet his eye.

'When can we go?' Tilly asked. Christ, did that sound rude? She just wasn't sure she could prolong this bittersweet agony anymore. How horribly it reminded her of packing up to leave foster homes. Often Ellie chose to pull the rug from beneath her feet just as she'd got excited about being in a place. When she was hopeful and looking forward to having her own room and a kind family to support her was when everything would come crashing down.

Like it was about to do now.

Rafe checked his rather fancy watch. 'It only takes a couple of hours to get to Glasgow. We can go earlyish to make time for the weather and the traffic, but Mum's made dinner, so let's eat first. It'll save having to get something on the road.'

No point mentioning she wasn't hungry at all. Not when they were all being so kind. Just as they had been since the moment she arrived. But how could she eat when her stomach was in knots?

'Ah, Tilly, come here.' Hilary opened her arms, wrapping her in a hug again. Tilly forced herself to be hard as steel to not start crying again. What a wreck she was. She'd never cried as much in her whole life as she had done this weekend… But neither had she experienced so much laughter, joy, and love. Her emotions were going through a revolution, and she couldn't keep up.

'I'm not doing anything too fancy tonight,' Hilary added. 'Take a wee seat. I've done some roast chicken, mashed tatties, and roasted veggies.'

'It smells really good.' And it did, almost good enough to make her feel hungry in spite of the pangs in her tummy.

'It'll hopefully fill you up for the journey. Train food isn't always the nicest.'

'Thank you so much... for everything.' Tilly took her seat at the table, removed her glasses and cleaned them.

'No need to thank me. It's been such a pleasure having you.' Hilary ran her hand over the back of Tilly's hair, smoothing it down, almost like she was stroking a pet, but there was something so motherly about it. Tilly had seen her doing the same kind of thing to her children and Alexander. 'I'm sorry you have to leave, but I understand your reasons. Don't get me started on that horrible boss of yours. I hope he realises what a wonderful and dedicated worker he has in you.'

Tilly knew he wouldn't. 'Well, if I can at least salvage what's left of my career so when I apply for new jobs, I'll have good references, that'll be enough.' She replaced her glasses.

'Sounds like a dreadful place to work,' Grandma said. 'You want to get out of there as soon as you can. Don't waste any more time on the place.'

Rafe sat next to Tilly and Genevieve sat on her other side. Was it possible to mask the sadness in her eyes? Maybe she should just sit and weep openly. Her insides were doing it, after all. She felt more like her child self than ever. Was she having some kind of regression?

'I'm glad Alexander's all better.' She forced her voice to remain level. He was chattering away in his high chair, throwing bits of bread to the floor.

'Yeah, he's all good as new.' Tina ran a finger across his forehead. 'It was one of those cuts that looks a lot worse than it actually was.'

'All that blood was scary,' Genevieve said.

Rafe moved his hand under the table and gently placed it on Tilly's thigh. She inhaled sharply and almost jumped at the contact, but he applied gentle pressure and gave her a little smile.

'We're going to miss you,' Cressida said to Tilly. 'You've adapted perfectly to our family chaos. It won't be the same without you.'

Rafe squeezed her thigh under the table, and it sent her breathing haywire.

'I'll miss you all too. And I'm so grateful for how kind you've been. The way you welcomed me was so nice, especially when I actually came here for... well, a totally stupid reason.'

'It wasn't stupid. Fate brought you,' Genevieve said.

Rafe shook his head. 'Genevieve believes in everything. Maybe it was Santa who brought you.'

It might as well have been. She could almost imagine riding high in Santa's sleigh, watching the dollhouse world below. How often in her life she'd felt like that. Santa only glimpsed the houses for a short moment once every year and Tilly had done that this year too. She'd popped in and enjoyed a fleeting Christmas moment.

'I agree with Genevieve,' Grandma said. 'There were definitely other forces at work here.'

Was that possible? Tilly's heart told her to believe it. Coming here had been a gamble and, even though Mitchell had encouraged her to do it, it was something she wouldn't normally have attempted.

'I wish I had something to give you all to thank you,' she said. 'But I don't.'

'All we need is your phone number,' Hilary said. 'You're always welcome here, but if you can't get back any time soon, please call us.'

'I can write it down if anyone has a pen.'

'If you call me,' Rafe said. 'I can pass it on the family group chat.'

He read out his number and Tilly called it. As soon as his phone vibrated, she ended the call. He tapped his screen and sent a message. Other phones at the table buzzed.

'Now we're all connected,' he said.

Genevieve tapped her phone. 'I'll be messaging you loads. You can't escape.'

Tilly let out a little giggle and Genevieve pulled her in for a one-armed hug.

'I'll be checking you're ok every few minutes,' she said, 'so take care of yourself, ok? And don't let your boss push you around.'

'I'll try not to.'

There was a murmur of collective agreement.

Rafe's eyes fixed on her. 'Don't let him railroad you. You'll stand your ground if I know you. Tenacious.'

She smirked. 'I'm not sure about that.'

'You should be. Coming here at all took guts.'

'It was so silly. I should have thought it through.'

'You did,' Genevieve said. 'You thought you were doing something to prove yourself to your boss, but you had to come because fate was calling.'

'I can't say that to my boss.'

'I wouldn't,' Rafe said. 'But technically, you've done nothing wrong. Unethical maybe, but you were only following company directives. You came here on a colleague's advice after a discussion. I'm perfectly happy to talk to your boss and vouch for your conduct. Call me anytime and I'll speak to him.'

Tilly almost wanted to laugh, but she didn't. She recognised the kindness in his words, but at the same time she couldn't escape what they'd done together. Her boss didn't need to know that.

But I know!

What would Arnie read into the situation? *Rogue employee swans off to visit a rival CEO at home, gets stuck in the snow with him, and comes out with his full backing.* Eyebrows would surely be raised. What had she done to gain his favour? The gossip mill would be churning out all sorts of stories for that one... And she'd not be able to deny any of them.

She was a 1-Quick Getaways employee who had jumped into bed with the CEO of Innova-Travel and that was a fact, not a rumour.

Chewing her food got more and more tricky. Of course, it was delicious. When had Hilary's food ever been anything but? Every mouthful took her closer to the inevitable goodbyes. Although there was plenty of conversation around her, it was oddly subdued, or maybe she just wasn't focusing on it properly. The dollhouse doors were slowly closing and her part in their world was coming to an end.

No one would let Tilly help clear up, or Rafe, for that matter.

'You should get going, in case the roads are bad,' Geoff said.

'Oh dear,' Hilary said. 'I hate goodbyes. I do hope you'll come back.' She gave Tilly a bracing hug and Tilly held on to her.

I wish I could stay. Here. With all of you.

Tilly's eyes filled with tears as memories of leaving foster homes flooded her mind, although it was unusual for the foster families to be this distraught. Typically, they seemed relieved to be rid of Tilly's sister – the little tyrant as she was often dubbed. Occasionally, one of the foster parents would give Tilly a squeeze on the shoulder and tell her to take care, but that was about it.

These hugs were overwhelming. Even Geoff, who had been the least demonstrative of the family, put his arms around her and gave her a pat on the back. She got a slobbery baby kiss from

Alexander and a rib crusher from Finlay. Genevieve and Hilary were openly wiping back tears, and Grandma shook her head with tight lips.

'Safe travels.' Cressida gave her the final hug. 'Let us know how you get on.'

'Bye.' Tilly stepped back from Cressida's hug, giving them all a little wave.

Rafe opened the door and headed for the Raptor. Its lights flashed in the dark driveway as he reached it. Tilly hurried across the snowy ground and hopped in, her throat burning and her head throbbing under the pressure of trying not to let emotions overcome her. She looked back, watching as they wound up the driveway. The light around the door, illuminating the Harrington family, grew smaller and smaller. Finally, it vanished. The dollhouse door closed fully, and Tilly was on the outside again. She shivered despite the heated seats.

Thank goodness for the dark. She could cry silently and anonymously, shrouded by it. Rafe was leaning forward slightly, his eyes fixed on the front, unwavering from the road. Ploughs had cleared a large track down the middle, but there was snow at the sides and on the verges. In places, it had drifted, covering the track again. Tilly half closed her eyes, praying to anyone who would listen to please keep Rafe safe. She'd dragged him out at night in this weather. She'd never forgive herself if anything happened to him. Neither would the Harrington family. How could she bear it if her nonsense caused something dreadful to happen to the most wonderful family?

'So, what will you do for Christmas?' Rafe asked as they reached Glenbriar. How beautiful the street looked all lit up with Christmas decorations on the lampposts and the dimmed shop windows gleaming with little trees.

'Nothing much. Maybe just go for a walk or something.'

He cast her a brief glance, but she didn't meet his eyes. No pity needed. She already knew how lonely it sounded.

'What about you?' she asked. 'I assume you'll go back to your parents' house tomorrow or Christmas Eve.'

'I'll head back tomorrow. Christmas Eve is a fun day. I wouldn't want to miss it.'

'What happens?'

'Ah, you know... The excitement; the build-up of waiting for Santa.'

'And you still get that?'

He huffed out a laugh. 'Not really, but Mum has a way of making it fun for everyone. She sets up hot chocolate and movies. We play games and then we go to the Christingle service at the church in the afternoon. I'm not particularly religious but it's got its own charm, I guess.'

'I don't even know what it is.'

'It's a candlelit service. The kids make Christingles out of oranges decorated with birthday candles and sweets. All the sections represent something, and the kids walk in with them while adults sing Christmas carols. There's something magical about it. Even cynics like me can enjoy it.'

'It sounds beautiful.' Like nothing she'd ever experienced, or maybe would ever experience. 'You're not a cynic. Not really.'

'Maybe not.' He reached over and put his hand on her knee. 'Having you with me has helped to see how much fun this stuff can be. Sometimes I moan and just want it all to be over, but actually when you take the time to embrace it, there's a lot of good in there.'

'There really is. It's all been new to me, and I've loved every minute.'

'That's something to take back, at least. Oh shit!' He took his hand off her knee and slapped the wheel.

'What?' She grabbed the seat. He hadn't braked, so it couldn't be anything on the road.

'Oh... er, nothing. Didn't mean to startle you. I just forgot something, but it doesn't matter.'

Should she pry? What had he forgotten? This trip was of her making, but maybe it was something he needed for his flat that night.

'When I was a kid,' he said, and she recognised a swift change of subject. 'I remember Mum taking us to a Christingle service and giving me strict orders not to let either of my little sisters run when they were carrying them.'

'And did you manage that?'

'Not really. Cress ate all the sweets and then poked Genevieve with the empty cocktail stick. I was too busy trying not to drop mine and set fire to the church because they only had big candles left by the time they got to me.'

'Oh dear.' Tilly laughed and her shoulders lightened temporarily. 'You've just ruined the lovely image you painted a few minutes ago.'

'Sorry.' He patted her thigh again and this time, she seized his hand and squeezed it. A smile played on the corner of his lips before he lifted his hand to the wheel again. The motorway passed in a haze of headlights and taillights. Every so often, they'd skirt the edges of unnamed towns or skirt villages in the valley or on top of hills, visible only by the lights in their windows. Some had flashing Christmas or fairy lights marking the eves. Tilly's mind opened up to her imaginings again. Who lived there? What did they do? Were their lives happy in those little bubbles?

With a sigh, she pulled her eyes from the latest row of roadside houses and checked her phone, hoping for no new emails from work. She still hadn't replied to Arnie. What should she say? If she told him she was coming and then there were delays, it would add to the pressure. If she arrived by surprise in the morning, it would only belittle the effort she'd put into getting there and the trouble she'd put others to, because once she was there, no one would care how she'd got there. Arnie wouldn't even ask. Maybe she should email him and explain she was trying her best, making a big effort.

Was there any point really?

'I hope whatever you tell your bosses at 1-Quick about me will be favourable,' Rafe said. His tone was humorous, but was there a meaningful undercurrent in there too?

'I'm not going to tell them anything about you.'

'How will you manage that? Will you pretend you didn't see me? Because if you tell them the truth, I'm happy to vouch for you.'

'I'm not sure what I'll say. I don't know what Mitchell has already told Arnie.'

'Don't let either of them get away with what they wanted you to do. Tell your boss Mitchell endorsed the idea, and you went along with it because he was the more experienced worker. Or better still, tell them you don't like how they work.'

'I don't think I have the nerve. It's a sure way to get sacked.'

He let out a sigh. 'If i was in your position, I'd leave before they gave me the chance. There will always be jobs for hard workers like you.'

'Yeah.' If she could just be brave. It had taken courage to visit Rafe. Maybe she could invest that energy in doing something for herself. Something she knew was right, but something Arnie and the bosses wouldn't like. She'd devoted nine years to 1-Quick, turned a blind eye to poor management and corrupt practises. The stability had been worth it to begin with. The money was ok, but what was the point of that money? She had nothing to spend it on except her extortionate rent. She had no hobbies apart from enjoying the odd walk here and there, no pets, no family, no one. Her few friends were vague acquaintances from work and not people she spent time with or bought gifts for. The people she loved the most were either at Greenacres or in the car with her right now. She'd finally found her folk, and she needed to find a way to get back to them once she'd sorted out the mess.

CHAPTER TWENTY-THREE

Rafe

Headlights from a taxi illuminated the rain-slicked pavement as Rafe and Tilly hurried down the street towards the dramatically lit-up Central Station in Glasgow. The festive illuminations highlighted the rows of arched windows, reminding Rafe of the black and white films his mum loved. He half expected an old-fashioned car to go by.

The frosty night air bit through his jacket and he kept close to Tilly. Much as he loved this city, he didn't want to be too far from her. Maybe he was being overprotective. Tilly lived in London after all and was used to city life, but he didn't want her to feel alone. A few cars rushed past, slushing through the puddles, but compared to the daytime, it was quiet and near deserted.

As they headed towards the station entrance, their footsteps slapped on the wet pavement. Rafe kept his hand close to Tilly's back. The burn in his chest pushed him to reach out and take her hand. Her grip was firm, almost too tight, like she was trying to crush him, or maybe she just didn't want to let go. He stole a glance at her profile; her eyes were fixed on the ground.

Passing a bench near the entrance, Rafe saw a figure huddled in a makeshift shelter of cardboard and blankets.

'I hate seeing that,' he said. 'It's a bloody crime in this day and age, especially at Christmas. Nobody should be out here freezing and alone.' He let go of Tilly's hand, reached into his pocket and pulled out his wallet, then dropped a ten-pound note into the man's cup.

'Thanks,' the man mumbled, his eyes briefly meeting Rafe's before returning to the ground.

'Take care, mate,' Rafe said. He shared a glance with Tilly as he took her hand again and they started walking again. 'Makes me so sad.'

'Yeah.' Tilly looked back at the man. 'I always wonder how it happens.'

'Could be so many reasons. We give a donation from work every year to a charity that provides Christmas dinners to the homeless. It's only one meal once a year, but sometimes it's little things that make a big difference.'

'I like that idea. When I was in the home, we got Christmas presents people had donated. It wasn't anything fancy, like the big electronic gifts most kids were getting, but it was better than nothing.'

'That's what giving presents should be,' Rafe said. 'Giving to people who have a real need, not just buying expensive gifts for everyone and anyone.'

'I suppose if you have the money to spoil your kids, you should do it though. They're only little for a short time, and those early days are so precious. They can affect us for our whole lives.'

He stopped walking just inside the entrance, looked at Tilly and gently pushed a stray strand of her dark hair off her face. 'You've done alright for yourself considering where you grew up. Better than your sister.'

Tilly nodded. 'Yup. But you know what?'

He shook his head.

'She's got friends. A lot more than I have. How is that possible?'

He glanced around, searching for an answer. 'I'm not a psychologist, so I'm not sure, but my guess is that she's more outgoing than you. She made bad life decisions, but that's because she chose to fight against the harsh upbringing you had. You withdrew, kept yourself to yourself and made a sensible and safe life.'

'You should be a psychologist. That's probably accurate. It just doesn't seem completely fair.'

'Life isn't always fair, unfortunately.'

The overhead speakers crackled with an announcement, and that cold, stale scent of dampness and diesel lingered in the air. Rafe shifted his focus from Tilly to the departure board.

'Platform seven,' he said. 'The train is probably already there if you want to go. They usually let you board early.' Not that he wanted her to leave him any sooner, but she was probably keen to get on her way.

'Yeah, I know,' she said. 'It's how I got here, remember?'

'Sorry, I forgot. It seems so long ago.' But it was only a few nights. So much had happened in between. His eyes shifted back to her again. He could gaze at her all day long and it wouldn't be enough. But short of buying a ticket and going with her, he wouldn't see her for who knew how long.

'Maybe I shouldn't have come to Greenacres.' Tilly's eyes misted over again. 'But I'm glad I did. I'll never regret meeting you.'

Rafe tugged her close, wrapping his arms around her waist and back, pinning her tight to his chest. 'Nor me, Tilly. Nor me.' He dipped in and kissed her forehead, holding his lips there and closing his eyes. 'I found something in you. Something I hadn't found before and I'm not sure I will again.'

She let out a little sob. 'I want to see you again.'

'You will.' He kissed her again with a sigh. 'I don't only exist at Christmas. I'll still be here next week, next month, next year. You've got friends up here if ever you need us.'

Tilly held him so tight she almost broke him in half, but he could take it. He could take so much more because physical pain was nothing compared to the emotional ache tormenting him all over.

Keeping his arm around her, he walked her to the platform. The train was waiting and a sudden urge to get on with her seized him, but he fought it down. He couldn't do that. This was her journey and the chance of getting a ticket this late would be like trying to catch a flight back to Chicago in *Home Alone*.

She turned to him, slipped a cold hand around his cheek, and raised her lips to his. Without question, he returned her kiss, snaking his arms around her and holding her close, probably taking it further than was sensible on a public platform. But only a few people were around, and he couldn't care less if anyone was watching. Rafe groaned as their tongues touched. A hot spark of need woke inside him, but it would soon fizzle out. Tonight, he'd be alone in his flat. Tilly would be rattling towards London and who knew when he'd see her again?

'I'll miss you.' She pulled back.

'Same,' Rafe said, not letting go. 'Message me, ok?'

'I will.' She pushed up and placed a brief kiss on his cheek before lifting her little case.

Other people were getting on the train and Tilly watched them, then took a deep breath.

'I should get on. It's nearly time.'

'Take care.' Rafe stole one last kiss, gave her a bracing hug, then thrust his hands in his pockets as she boarded the train. He ambled along the platform, where he could still see her moving down inside the coach. When she took her seat, he drew level with her, extricating one hand, so he could give her a little wave. The engine kicked into action, and he stepped back, pocketing his hands again, not quite sure what to do with them. Or to do at all. Should he stand here and wait until the train left? Or walk off and let her go? He resisted the urge to barge on, run down the train and pull her back.

Don't go! Stay with me.

But real life didn't work like a Hallmark movie. Tilly had to do this.

Eventually, the train drew off, and he walked along beside it. Tilly looked back, sucking on her lip, then waving. The train picked up speed. Rafe raised his hand to wave.

Wait. He should have told her...

'I love you,' he said, knowing it she couldn't hear him. Could she lip read? He cursed himself for not saying it sooner, but as the train's rhythmic clatter faded into the night with its rear lights, he had a flicker of relief. Maybe it was just as well he hadn't told her before. The waters were muddy enough and Tilly didn't need him messing her up anymore with his rash words. He stood on the platform, watching until the two red specks vanished completely.

Tilly was gone. He sighed. Now he had to go home and clear his head. Maybe he should have paid heed to what Tilly said about love. What felt real in this moment may pass and be little more than a flash in the pan a few days from now.

He walked back towards the exit. A twenty-four-hour shop was open, and he nipped in, buying a hot drink, a sausage roll, and a large muffin. On his way back to the car, he passed the homeless man again and crouched down, handing him the bag of food.

'Thanks, man,' he wheezed.

'Is there somewhere you can go?' Rafe asked. 'A shelter? I can help if you want.'

'Na, you're ok, mate. This'll see me through, thanks. You look after yersel.' The man patted his shoulder. 'Yer a good guy.'

'Take care.' Rafe got to his feet. Good guy or not, he was certainly a lonely guy.

It didn't take long to drive to his flat. He'd only been away a few days, but it felt empty and cold, like he'd been away for weeks. Maybe that was because he didn't decorate it for Christmas and compared to the home he'd just come from, it was so bare. He shook his head, throwing himself down on the sofa in his minimalist living room, not closing the blinds. The city lights twinkled in. It wasn't just the lack of Christmas decorations making the flat feel bare. Laughter, company, and love were absent.

His phone had been vibrating all the way from the station to here and he half hoped he'd find a message from Tilly, saying she'd got off the train and wanted him to come for her and take her home... home to Glenbriar with him. Glenbriar. A place that wasn't home to either of them, and yet it felt like it should be.

None of the messages were from Tilly.

All of them were from his family, hoping he was ok and saying how already the house was quiet and empty without the two of them.

'Bet it's not as empty as here,' he muttered, not sure if he meant in the house or inside his chest.

Other notifications flashed in. Among them he spotted an email to his work address marked *urgent* from an Arnold_Wilcox@1-Quick-Getaways.

He clicked it open and read.

Dear Mr Harrington

As you will be aware, 1-Quick-Getaways has been looking to make connections with various other travel companies across the country. Last week, we sent two employees to Scotland to make first contact with you. It has been drawn to my attention that one of the employees sent to liaise with you took it upon herself to travel to your home in an attempt to conduct a meeting with you when she wasn't able to meet you at your office.

Please let me inform you that this behaviour was not authorised or suggested by myself or any of the other senior managers at 1-Quick-Getaways. We do not condone or sanction this behaviour. We have informed the employee of our take on the matter, and she will be dealt with accordingly.

Please accept my sincerest apologies and rest assured this matter will be taken very seriously.

Arnold Wilcox

Rafe leaned back, and half closed his eyes. Poor Tilly. This was what she was going back to. Nine years of devoted service and she'd be lucky to come out of this with a job at all.

Rafe frowned and tapped the sofa arm. How could he convince her to kick 1-Quick to the kerb and move on? Maybe she could get a job up here. That would take out the problem of a long-distance relationship.

Assuming she wanted that. Hopefully, she wouldn't go back to London and forget he existed. Already she felt like someone he'd invented – perhaps as a story to fool Genevieve. Was she a figment of his imagination he'd spent a couple of blissful days acting out a dream with? Without her close by, his heart hurt, and his mind was foggy. Where did he go from here?

Chapter Twenty-Four

Tilly

The rhythmic clickety-clack of the train pounded in Tilly's head, and she could focus on nothing else. She leaned back in her reclining seat, her eyelids heavy from the emotional whirlwind of the day, but even when she closed them, the irritating lights filtered through. The seat felt cramped, and she kept her head towards the window, deliberately not looking at the person beside her. Sleeping with Mitchell there had been hard enough, especially with his snoring, but having a stranger on the other side was even worse. At least it was a woman. She wouldn't have closed her eyes at all if it had been a man.

Trying to switch off the noise in her brain, she let her thoughts wander back to the platform and Rafe's face as he waved goodbye. Honestly, it had looked like he said *I love you*. But he wouldn't have, would he? That was the limerence talking again, seeing what she wanted to see because she was obsessed and desperate. Would she ever get over it? If her previous experiences were anything to go by, she would, though it would take time. Her insides smarted at the prospect, like they'd been slapped raw.

Beside her, the middle-aged woman folded over the book she was reading and yawned. 'It's not easy to sleep with the lights on, is it?' she said quietly. 'Do they turn them off, do you think?'

'They don't.' Tilly gave her a faint smile. 'I travelled up last week, and they keep them on all night.'

'Oh dear. That's a bit silly for a train you're supposed to sleep on.'

'It's something to do with security.' Tilly held up an eye mask from the complementary pack she'd received. 'It's why they give out these things, apparently.'

The woman pulled a face. 'I don't see that working.' She pulled out her own mask and crinkled her nose at it. 'But then, I'm a psychologist. Maybe I can trick my brain into believing it can sleep... If only.' She smirked as she took off the clear plastic wrapper from around the mask.

Tilly hesitated, her mind lethargic, but something niggled her. The memory of Rafe saying he wasn't a psychologist and her saying he should be. Maybe she should use the one here to ask a question that had burned her for a long time. Normally she wouldn't dream of asking a stranger something like this, but this was important, and the woman had a kindly expression.

'You're a psychologist?' Tilly repeated, just to make sure her tired brain wasn't trying to fool her.

'Yes, indeed,' the woman said.

'Can I ask you something?'

'Please do. I can't promise an answer, but I'll do my best.'

'Do you know about limerence?'

The woman frowned at her for a moment, then gave a brief nod. 'Indeed, I do.'

'Can you explain it to me?' Tilly had looked it up on so many occasions on the internet and it always seemed to fit exactly how she was feeling. But after her chat with Genevieve earlier, and all her interactions with Rafe, she was so confused.

'Well, limerence can take different forms, but it usually plays out in three stages. Firstly, comes infatuation. You might meet, or even just see, someone you like the look of. Maybe they make you feel safe or something about their appearance or behaviour is familiar or comforting to you. You might start to imagine how they would fit into your life and feel a deep connection to them, even if you don't know them that well or even at all.'

That sounds like me. She'd imagined connections with strangers on trains, people she'd passed on the street and even people she'd never seen during her dollhouse fantasies – she was always imagining stuff like that and closing out real life.

'After that,' the woman went on, 'it moves onto what we call crystallisation. It takes all the feelings you get during the infatuation stage to a whole new level. You start to believe that not only would this person fit perfectly into your life, but they would solve a lot of your problems. They're like the answer to your prayers. You might forget the fact they might have problems of their own or reckon you could solve them together and live an amazing life – if only you were together.'

Yup, definitely me. Exactly what she'd done with Mitchell and now Rafe.

'The third phase is deterioration.' The woman gave a little sigh. 'This brings you back down to reality. It's when you find out something real about the person, the one I would call your limerent object. Perhaps you discover they're already in a relationship or find something out about them that completely changes the image of them you've created in your mind.'

Yes, that was what had happened with Mitchell, though not yet with Rafe.

'Once that happens, you'll probably feel rather depressed. After all, people usually invest a lot of emotion into their limerent objects. It's hard to accept the future you've imagined isn't real and isn't likely to happen.'

The woman smiled at Tilly, then frowned a little like she was puzzling something out. 'Why do you ask?'

Tilly wasn't sure she should explain, but she felt a bit like Ebenezer Scrooge after he'd been visited by the three ghosts. The last one had driven the point home like a sharp blade and was now looming in front of a huge heavy tombstone engraved with the words *here lies the future of Rafe and Tilly's relationship*. Was it already dead and buried?

Aware the woman was still looking at her, she gave a little shrug. 'I'm only curious,' she said. 'I won't bore you with a long story, but it's something that's happened to me in the past and I'm not sure how I'll ever know if something is real and not just limerence.' Especially when her limerent object was a man she hardly knew. Genevieve might happily validate her feelings and say *love is love*, but it was hard to believe when all she'd known so far was limerence.

'Well, love and limerence can feel similar,' the woman said. 'The main difference is that limerence is one-sided.'

She remembered the first therapist saying that.

'If you're connected to a person who exhibits signs of feeling the same way, there's no reason why limerence can't become love. If the connection develops, and you solve problems together, rather than hoping the limerent object will solve the problems for you, then it could work. And if you understand the person's flaws and love them anyway, rather than idolising them. If the relationship is comforting and balanced, not one-sided, then you're on the right track. But if it's just a case of you thinking constantly about this person even when you don't want to, it might not be particularly healthy. If you feel at ease with them, rather than scared of being rejected, then it may well be love.'

Tilly took a deep breath. 'So much to think about.' And she wasn't sure what it meant – if anything – for her and Rafe.

'I can't advise you because I don't know your situation fully, but let me give you a few general suggestions that might help, and then you can sleep on it... Quite literally, I hope.'

'Wow, thanks. I have a lot of hard thinking to do.'

The woman gave her a kindly smile. 'The first thing to do is to be kind to yourself. Don't judge yourself harshly. Accept your thoughts about the person and ask yourself some questions. Do you spend a lot of time thinking about them and does it affect your daily life? Is the limerence impacting your life negatively? Or is it perhaps stemming from other challenges connected to your own emotions? Are you focusing on a person who you reckon can solve your problems instead of focusing on solving them yourself?'

Maybe she was. She'd hoped Rafe was the key to the door of promotion and as soon as she realised that she'd latched onto him. Maybe she'd doomed herself to like him before she'd even met him.

'If you want to pursue a relationship with your limerent object, that's ok too, but consider how they feel about you. You might have to ask them, which could be difficult. But also consider what areas of your life would improve if they were in it, or the opposite? Would being with them boost your self-esteem? Would you want to spend time together? What do you have in common? Can you meet these needs yourself instead?'

'That really is a lot to think about.' Tilly smiled at the woman. 'And you've really helped me. I had a therapist before who didn't explain it as well as that. It's always bothered me that maybe it's something in me that's making me feel like this. I've had attachment issues in the past and somehow, I thought attaching myself to people without any real hope of a normal relationship was out of my control. It's so hard to know if limerence is real, or if it might become real.'

The woman placed her hand on Tilly's arm. 'Attachment issues can make people more prone to feeling like this, but the very fact you've identified this in yourself is positive. You're in control; you decide what's right for you. Maybe this chat has given you enough information to help you make informed choices, but I can direct you to some good therapists or websites if you need more.'

'My head's too full for anything else just now, but I appreciate you telling me.'

'Well, you sleep on it and remember, be kind to yourself. You sound very self-aware, so trust yourself. Use some of your awareness and extend it to others around you. If you're afraid of jumping in too soon, then take your time, but don't give up until you're absolutely certain how the other person feels. If you sabotage the relationship before it even has a chance, that's not limerence, but something entirely different.'

Tilly nodded and something cold slipped in her tummy. Was she doing that? Sabotaging a relationship? That was what Ellie had done throughout their childhood. Her methods had been more aggressive, but the outcome was the same. They lost out on the chance of happiness.

'Thank you, so, so much. That's really helpful.'

'You're welcome. Now, let's see if we can get any sleep tonight.'

Tilly smiled as the woman pulled on her sleep mask and leaned back, then she did the same. The blackness helped a little and the clickety-clack of the train shifted into a back section of her mind as the woman's words filtered into the forefront of her consciousness. All of it made sense. Some of it most certainly applied to her, but there was one bit she kept coming back to over and over. The more she thought about it, the more a little bubble of hope expanded in her chest.

The main difference between limerence and love was that limerence was one-sided. What she'd had with Rafe was definitely not one-sided. He'd been an equal partner in everything they'd done. Sure, he could help her solve the problems in her life, but she didn't need him to. She could solve this herself and she bloody well would. He'd given her some pointers and she would follow them.

She wouldn't just be kind to herself this Christmas, she'd be better than Santa Claus. She was about to land herself everything she'd ever dreamed of.

Just keep believing... She could do this, and she definitely wouldn't sabotage it.

Monday, December 23rd

Morning

Tilly came to, but didn't immediately open her eyes. She couldn't. Something was over her face, impeding her vision. For a moment, she didn't move. What was that noise? Oh yeah, she was on the sleeper train. No clickety-clack though, just faint rustling sounds. Why wasn't the train moving? On the way to Scotland, it had stopped a few times. Was this another stop like that? Her body wasn't comfortable, and she was pretty sure she wouldn't get much more sleep, no matter what the time was. Slowly, she peeled back her mask and blinked.

Wait, what? The platform was light. The sun was up. Not bright, but typical of a pale December morning. People bustled around outside. Euston already? Tilly snapped her head round to the seat beside her. Empty. The woman had vanished. No doubt she'd simply got off the train when it stopped and went on her way, but Tilly stared at the place where she'd been. Had she really been there? Maybe Tilly had dreamt the whole conversation, hearing exactly what she wanted to hear.

No, that wasn't the case. Not this time.

Hopefully she'd thanked the woman enough. Pity she didn't know who she was because she'd helped Tilly open her eyes. She pulled her case from under the seat and got to her feet. It was almost eight o'clock. Hardly anyone was left on the train and a cleaner was sweeping around the seats behind, throwing paper cups and used sleep masks into a rubbish sack.

One hour to get to work. She would still make it, though she was a dishevelled mess. Only on the outside though. Inside, her mind was as clear as the bright blue sky that had shone over Greenacres in the snow. She was going to take control, show Arnie and everyone else at 1-Quick Getaways she was worth a whole lot more than they thought. From this day forward, they could find someone else to do their bidding, because she had a better plan.

Chapter Twenty-Five

Rafe

Monday, December 23rd

Morning

Rafe pushed the remote stick to change the radio channel in the Raptor. He seriously didn't want to hear 'And So This Is Christmas'. It hit far too close to home. This was Christmas indeed, and what had he done? Let Tilly go, that was what.

Not that I had any right to stop her.

'Driving Home for Christmas' wasn't a much better option but something about it was more nostalgic, and he kept it on as background noise as he motored down the A9 towards Perth. *Ding, ding.* Round two for this journey was underway. Just last week he'd done it, blissfully unaware 'his girlfriend' was already at his house waiting for him. Now that same woman had gone back to London, and he really would be 'Lonely this Christmas'. Why were there so many festive songs that fit his moods? He could probably make a good playlist for his life round about now.

He'd spent last night in his flat, dedicating a large proportion of his time to replying to Arnold Wilcox's email and then forwarding it to Tilly in a message so she knew what he'd said. So far, she hadn't replied. Hopefully she'd slept ok on the train… though he'd already googled train accidents that morning to check the train hadn't crashed or any other disastrous thing happened to them. He had this seriously bad, no matter how hard he tried to kid himself it would all pass like a snowstorm and melt away after a couple of days.

When he pulled into a service station for fuel, he checked his phone again. His grey mood instantly lifted on seeing a message from Tilly. He flipped up the screen with his thumb and read as he waited in the queue to pay.

TILLY: Hi, sorry for the late reply. I was talking to a woman on the train. She was really interesting. Then I fell asleep and didn't wake up until the train was at Euston, which is a bit of a miracle really. I'm just about to go into the office, but I read your email on the bus. Thank you. I think it'll really help. Maybe you and I could have a business chat sometime? Remember that idea I told you about? Would you be interested in employing someone to develop it for your company?

Wish me luck!

Tilly xx

Rafe smirked at the message and shook his head. What a great idea. The thought had been lingering close to the front of his mind for a while, but it had felt like nepotism to invent a job for her just to save her from 1-Quick. But if she wanted to do it officially, he'd definitely be up for that. Pretty much anything if it meant a good chance of seeing her again. He tapped out a quick response.

RAFE: I wish you all the luck in the world, always. I'm very interested in your proposal and am happy to hear more whenever you want to discuss it, especially if the person is you! xx

The message had been sent twenty minutes before, so she was probably in the office now. Hopefully she was ok and not letting them give her any grief.

He carried on to Glenbriar, still listening to Christmas songs as the backdrop to his solitary journey. They weren't all bad and now he had a ray of hope that he and Tilly might have a working future together. That was something, but with luck, they might have even more.

Greenacres looked so welcoming as he drove down the sloping driveway. Snow still covered the landscape and the lights in the windows twinkled, calling to him. If only Tilly was inside this time, then his heart would light up too.

He entered through the utility room. His ski jacket and trousers were still hanging there from when they'd gone sledging. Memories whipped back as he kicked off his boots. They'd had such fun sledging... And that kiss. So perfect. What a chain of events it had started too. Now it felt oddly like he'd broken up with someone he'd been dating for months. How was that possible? He'd only known Tilly for a few days.

The house was unusually quiet. Was everyone out? Padding down the corridor, he checked the living room, then the kitchen. Hilary turned from the table, wiping her hands on a dishcloth. 'Oh, it's you. I thought I heard someone.'

'I just got back.' Rafe marched over and hugged her. 'Where is everyone?'

'Grandma's resting in the book room. Well, she fell asleep, and I left her to it. The others have all gone out for a walk, but I've got too much to do.'

Rafe shook his head. 'You should rest, Mum. You'll burn out.'

'I enjoy doing it.' Hilary patted his back and returned to the table. 'I just didn't expect to need extra stuff for the church for tomorrow. Turns out the nativity was cancelled yesterday for the snow. It wasn't just me who couldn't get there. Grant, the minister, wants to do it tomorrow on Christmas Eve as part of the Christingle service. It's a lovely idea, but we need extra baking as there's sure to be a bigger turn out.'

Rafe raised an eyebrow. 'You really are a marvel.'

Hilary smiled at him, before her expression fell a little. 'Have you heard from Tilly?'

'Yes. She's arrived safely, and she's come up with a business plan.'

'Oh...'

'That might involve us working together.'

'Oh Rafe.' Hilary let out a little sigh. 'I hope it can be more than just a working relationship. Not that I want to belittle what either of you do, but there's so much more to life than a career, if you give it a chance.'

'Maybe, but I don't want to rush into anything, neither does Tilly.' Not after everything she'd told him. She needed time to reason out where they were going with this, and he could give her that.

'That's all well and good,' Hilary said, 'but don't do the opposite and leave it too late. Tilly is a wonderful young woman. You won't be the only person to notice.'

'True.'

'And she likes you an awful lot. Just as I'm sure you like her.'

He nodded. 'Yes, Mum. I do.'

'Good.' She gave him a little pat on the arm. 'Why don't you come to the church with me? Give me a hand setting up.'

Rafe considered for a moment. It wasn't really his thing at all, but it might stop him thinking about Tilly. 'Yeah, ok. Why not?'

The church in Glenbriar was a relatively plain building with whitewashed stone walls and a small spire containing a bell tower still locally referred to as 'the kirk'. Quaint surroundings made up for what it lacked in grandeur. Its situation atop a small hill, with bare wintery trees surrounding it and a fast-flowing stream tumbling through the churchyard, was both rustic and impressive. Rafe took it all in as he followed Hilary up the path that led to the main doors through the pretty little graveyard carrying a large box of her home baking. Some of the newer graves had Christmas wreaths propped on them and Rafe read a few names of the deceased as he passed by. The scene was Christmas card perfect.

The heavy wooden doors were open, and Hilary went in directly. Another set of double doors led on from the airy stone-floored entry porch to the main body of the kirk. A warm glow from the stained-glass windows illuminated the dark wood pews and burgundy carpets. Hilary led the way along the back and into a small hall.

Plates clinked and two ladies chattered to a young man as they bustled about, arranging trays and crockery.

'Hello.' Hilary put her box down on an empty table. Rafe did the same with his, smiling a hello as the other volunteers greeted him. He vaguely recognised one of the women. The man was wearing a dog collar. Rafe did a small double-take. That was the minister? Maybe it shouldn't have been a surprise, but he looked too young to be a minister. He wasn't the one who'd done last year's service or Genevieve's wedding.

'Hi,' the minister said. 'This looks good.' He peered at the two boxes of cakes on the table.

'Literally just out of the oven,' Hilary said. 'This is my son, Rafe.' She took his arm, almost dragging him forward. 'Rafe, meet Grant, our new minister.'

'Pleased to meet you.' Rafe held out his hand, and they shook. Grant had to be Rafe's age at most, possibly younger. Maybe it was prejudice, or just the way he thought of the church, but Rafe hadn't expected a minister to be so young. *Guess they have to start somewhere.*

'This is Nancy Leitch.' Hilary gestured to the first woman who had short dark hair and large round glasses. 'And this is Dotty Ingenfeld. You might recognise her from the Cosy Bean Café. She owns it.'

Rafe nodded at them both. 'I haven't been to that café for years,' he said.

'You must come again,' Dotty said. 'Though your mum makes some wonderful cakes herself, so you probably don't need to.'

Rafe smiled. 'I'll bring Mum with me and that'll give her a rest from the baking.'

'Good plan,' Dotty said.

Rafe rubbed his hands together. 'So, what should I do? Just boss me about. I'll do anything.'

'Sounds like you're exactly the kind of person we need,' Nancy said.

'Go easy on him.' Hilary rubbed his arm. 'He's had a bit of a rough weekend, poor darling.'

Rafe exchanged a glance with Grant and they both laughed.

'Is something funny?' Hilary said.

'No, Mum. You just make me sound about six.'

'You'll always be her baby,' Dotty said. 'Like my Dagmar. When I talk about her, people assume she's tiny but she's almost thirty.'

Hilary gave him a *you-see* smile.

'What happened to you at the weekend?' Nancy smiled at Rafe. 'Dare we ask?'

Rafe shook his head. 'I honestly wouldn't know where to start. No doubt Mum will tell you better than I can.'

He helped take cakes from the boxes as Hilary launched into the story of Tilly arriving at the house. Some of it was cringeworthy, especially when she kept saying things like, 'They were made for each other, if you ask me,' and 'don't you think it sounds like a Christmas miracle?'

Grant moved over beside Rafe and smiled. 'You, um, really have had an interesting weekend.'

Rafe shrugged with a half laugh. 'You're the minister. Do you think it's a Christmas miracle or just an extremely bizarre coincidence?'

Grant chuckled. 'Haven't you heard? God moves in mysterious ways. Who's to say your coincidence wasn't ordained? Christmas, after all, is a time of wonder. It's a reminder that even in the darkest of times, there's light to be found.'

Rafe arched an eyebrow. 'And do you think Tilly is the light in my darkness?'

Grant grinned, but his gaze drifted around the room and landed on the twinkling tree in the corner. 'Light can be found in many places. In the stories we tell, the traditions we uphold, and the connections we forge. Christmas is a time to celebrate love, hope, and the power of community. If you believe Tilly can bring light and love to your soul, then welcome her, like God welcomes you to His church.'

'You make it sound almost plausible.' Rafe gave Grant a pat on the arm.

Grant's smile deepened. 'It could be. Have faith. Miracles aren't always grand gestures. Sometimes, they're small moments that change the course of our lives.'

Rafe nodded slowly. Maybe Tilly's coming was one of those moments for him.

'Maybe it's time I started believing in Christmas magic.' He returned his focus to the cakes, frowning slightly. He'd never been spiritual or religious, but the minister's words gave him food for thought.

A buzz started up inside him... Was it too late to go after Tilly? She couldn't get back here for Christmas, but he could go to her. He didn't even know where she lived, but she would surely tell him if he asked. Maybe he could fly down tomorrow and meet her somewhere, but getting transport to London on Christmas Eve would be that *Home Alone* style problem all over again.

No harm in finding out though.

'I need to check something.' He nipped into the main part of the church, sat on a pew, and opened his phone. It only took seconds on each website to discover all the flights were booked up, so were the trains... the buses.

Bugger it. Oops, shouldn't even think swears in church.

Unless... It wouldn't be quite the same, but he could go straight after Christmas and spend the whole week with her, including the new year. Public transport should be back to normal by the twenty-seventh. He ran a quick check. Yep, that would have to do...

Now... Should he surprise her or let her know? Call him a sucker for romance, but he really wanted to see the look on her face if he turned up on her doorstep *Love Actually* style.

CHAPTER TWENTY-SIX

Tilly

Monday, December 23rd

Afternoon

Harsh fluorescent lights buzzed overhead as Tilly sat at her desk in the 1-Quick Getaways office in London. She massaged her forehead, feeling a migraine fast approaching. She'd been here all morning, her nerves coiling like springs. Arnie still hadn't called her. Everyone seemed to be avoiding looking at her or talking to her. The Christmas spirit had been sucked from the building and everything was grey and miserable. Would anyone even notice if she packed her bags and walked? How easy would that be? But she wanted to face the music before she made her last curtain call.

Staring at her computer screen, she tried to remember what she'd been working on before going to Scotland. Whatever it was, it didn't seem remotely worthwhile now, but she should at least pretend to be busy. If she didn't, she'd probably fall asleep. The thought forced out a yawn, and she stifled it. She'd had some sleep last night despite thinking she wouldn't, but not enough. The exhaustion inside her was chronic and seemed almost unrelated to sleep. This office was draining the life from her.

Finally, an admin assistant scuttled up to her desk and muttered that Arnie was ready to see her. So much for this early morning meeting she'd bust a gut to get here for. Twelve-thirty-seven displayed on the computer clock. That summed up the way this place worked. Tilly squared her shoulders as she stood and approached the partially open door.

Arnie sat behind his sleek desk, brows furrowed, and eyes fixed on his computer screen. Mitchell occupied another chair opposite; he folded his arms and didn't meet her gaze either. How could it be that this time last week he'd been her limerent object? Rafe would never rudely ignore her like that. He and his family had been the most welcoming people she'd ever met. They were the reason she'd made a life-changing decision that morning. Barely off the train, she'd booked a seat for the return journey later. The woman at the booking office had proudly told her she'd got the last one and was very lucky as a cancellation had just that minute come in.

Luck? Or the miracle of Christmas. Tilly was coming round to the latter.

Keep a tight hold on that magic now! She had to, or she'd sink into the overpowering gloom of this office.

'Sit down, Tilly.' Arnie didn't even bother to look up from his screen.

Tilly took a seat, glancing at Mitchell, who picked at his cuff, focusing all his attention on it. Why wouldn't he even look her in the eye? What was he thinking? She furrowed her brow, pushing her brain back to their last conversation. He'd been cheery then, pushing her to travel north and meet Rafe. She'd done what he suggested. Was he worried she'd got so much info on Innova she'd be a challenge to him? He was in for a shock if he did. The trip had been wasted if that was the goal.

Tilly steadied her breathing. Her heart raced, even though she'd prepped her mind on what she was going to say. Actually doing it was another matter.

Arnie sighed, finally looking up. 'I hope you understand the severity of the situation. Your little escapade to the countryside was not only unprofessional but utterly unacceptable.'

Tilly swallowed hard, her throat dry. 'I understand.'

'Are you sure?' Arnie scoffed. 'Because it calls into question your professionalism and responsibility. You represent this company, and your actions reflect on all of us.'

'Hmm,' she said.

'Mitchell informs me he advised you against the trip.'

Mitchell shifted a little in his seat, and Tilly gave him a brief glance. *He said what?* So this was his game. He was trying to distance himself from her actions. Obviously paranoid about his own job. Or perhaps he'd always known the mission would fail, and she'd come out looking bad, while he remained the star at the top of the Christmas tree.

'And what's this about you basing your whole trip on a photograph in the Innova-Travel office? You were very lucky to even find the right place. Such a foolhardy move.' Arnie tapped his pen on the desk, and Tilly returned her attention to him. What a horrible sceptical tone of voice he was using when talking to her. She almost laughed. If she was a detective, she'd surely have got full marks. But he also had a point. How ridiculous had she been chasing Rafe with so little to go on? Maybe this just added more fuel to Genevieve's idea that this was fate. She was fast becoming a believer, but she was also remembering the woman on the train's words.

You are in control; you decide what's right for you.

That was what she was doing right now.

'Well?' Arnie said. 'Do you have anything to say?'

Mitchell caught her eye, even though she got the feeling he hadn't meant to. His cheeks reddened slightly. How could he sit there and lie about her? Did he expect her just to go along with his version of the story? Normally she would. She hated rocking the boat, and always did what she was told. But things had changed.

'You recall,' he said. 'How I mentioned that picture might not even have been his house.'

Could he be any smarmier? What had she ever seen in him? All he was doing was covering his back and trying to get higher up the career ladder. Good luck to him. Tilly had wasted years in this place. Her promotion chances were now out the window, but it didn't matter because she'd be following them soon... straight out the nearest one!

Arnie's gaze shifted between Mitchell and her. 'Perhaps it was my fault for choosing you to do this job. Clearly you weren't up to the task.'

'Apparently not,' Tilly said. 'Although Mitchell's version of the story is not accurate.'

'Pardon?' Arnie frowned.

'Come on, Tilly. You know what I said.' Mitchell's tone was now whiney and annoying.

'Yes, I do. You said it was a great idea and I should try. That it was exactly the right way to show initiative and approach Rafe Harrington informally. Even when I had my doubts, you pushed me to do it.'

He gave a twitchy little shrug, half glancing at Arnie and clearly attempting to pull a *she's crazy* face. 'That's how you remember it, but it wasn't like that. You were desperate to go and nothing I said could have stopped you.'

Not true. If he'd said not to attempt it, she wouldn't have. Maybe she should thank him. Without his push, she'd never have met Rafe. 'I believe Rafe Harrington himself has emailed you on the subject.' Tilly refocused on Arnie.

'Indeed,' Arnie said. 'He did, and that also worries me. I know him to be stubborn in business and yet somehow you not only get a private meeting with him, you get snowed in with him and then he writes an email about you as though you're old friends. None of it sits well with me.'

'What are you saying?'

'Well,' Mitchell said, as though he'd scored a point. 'It kind of begs the question: did you already know where he lived? And if that was the case, what is your real goal?'

'It smells of gross misconduct,' Arnie added. 'Did you pass any information to him about us?'

Heat flared in Tilly's cheeks. 'You're talking to me about misconduct?' She hated conflict and would much rather run away, but adrenaline was pumping through her veins, pushing her to say her piece. 'How can you make accusations like that? I did exactly as Mitchell suggested. He had previous success with his underhand methods, so I stupidly thought doing the same would give me a step up in here.'

'None of our methods should be underhand,' Arnie said. 'I think you both need to go back to some grassroots training. Mitchell, I need to talk to you further. Tilly, you can consider this a formal warning. Any more slip-ups, and there will be consequences. You may find you no longer have a job here.'

Tilly smiled, and the action caught Mitchell's attention. He gaped at her like she'd grown an extra head, obviously unable to imagine why she'd be smiling.

'That's absolutely fine.' She pushed her chair back and stood. 'Because you know what? I don't need to be here. I don't need a job with such poor management and low standards, where lying and sneaking is common practice. I've given my best to this company for years, taking on extra tasks without extra pay. And what do I get in return? A formal warning for doing what I was advised to and trying to show some initiative.'

Arnie opened his mouth to interrupt, but Tilly raised a hand, silencing him.

'I've toed the line for years, never put a foot wrong, never questioned anything. I've done nothing but try my best and work hard. I've watched others climb the ladder while I stayed stuck in the same position, but got more and more work piled onto me. And you can't even cut me a bit of slack when I get snowed in. You have no idea how much trouble and pain it caused trying to get here in time this morning. But it doesn't even matter, because now I'm here I want to tell you to your face. You can keep your warning and your job. I quit.'

Mitchell's jaw dropped. Tilly turned to him. 'Good luck clawing your way to the top. I hope you enjoy the view and don't fall off and break any bones.'

She turned back to Arnie. 'Oh, and before I go, let me set the record straight on something else. I didn't give Rafe Harrington information about this company because, really, what would be the point? His business skills are light years ahead of everyone here; there's nothing he'd want to steal from 1-Quick. And not only that, he showed me that he believed in me and my ideas. He's given me an opportunity, a chance to pitch a new idea to him at

Innova-Travel. A chance for a fresh start, something I'll never get here.'

Mitchell's lip curled into a sneer. 'You think Rafe Harrington is going to hire you just like that?'

'I didn't say he was going to hire me, but if he listens to me, it's better than whatever 1-Quick has ever offered me. I'd rather take my chances than continue here.'

'Now wait a second,' Arnie said.

'No can do.' Tilly pushed the chair under the desk, her heart pounding. 'I've got a train to catch. Merry Christmas.' She headed straight for the door.

She didn't look at anyone in the office as she collected her red coat and bag from her desk. They might as well think she'd just stepped out for lunch. Arnie and Mitchell could tell anyone who was interested that she wasn't coming back.

As she stepped into the crisp December air outside the office, a weight lifted from her shoulders, and she let out a nervous laugh. Stepping into the unknown was risky for sure, yet it also held an undeniable excitement. For the first time in forever, she wouldn't have to do it alone. She had friends; she had Rafe, and she had his family. Her heart wanted Rafe for everything, but even if she could keep him as a friend, it would be better than anything she'd had before.

With a deep breath, she checked her phone. She still had time to get to her flat, pack more clothes, and then return to Euston.

The thought of yet another ride on that train should fill her with dread, but it didn't.

The streets around her office had never looked so beautiful. Festive displays made her smile, and she grinned stupidly at people in the station and on the tube on the way back to her flat. She got several funny looks as well as the usual non-eye-contact. Here she was on a Monday, going back to her flat in the middle of the afternoon, which in itself felt all levels of wrong. As she looked out of the windows at the passing houses and blocks of flats, she no longer felt the burning desire to join them in their dollhouse worlds. There was only one family she wanted to be with this Christmas, and she was almost certain they'd welcome her with open arms.

A slight niggle had wormed its way into her by the time she reached her flat. Was it possible the Harringtons were just really polite people, and she was no one special to them? What if she went all the way back only to discover she was just a Christmas inconvenience? What if they were all actually delighted she'd gone and they could celebrate Christmas in peace?

Oh god.

She climbed the stairs to her flat, surprised at the lack of music from the people downstairs. Was this just one big mistake? Might she soon be jobless and homeless? Were the family she'd pinned everything on nothing but an unreachable star that would fade away as soon as Christmas was done?

She opened her door, went straight to the living room, and threw herself onto the sofa. The Christmas miracle was losing its shine. Her head was muddled and her thoughts mixed up liked tinsel tangled around a tree. If ever she needed a sign, something to tell her this was real, it was now. But nothing happened.

She'd had messages from Genevieve and Cressida. The words were sweet and kind, but it was hard to know how they were intended. Maybe they were just holding up their end of the messaging bargain for a short while before it fizzled out completely.

Am I just really stupid?

She got up and wheeled her case into her bedroom. Was there any point in packing and making the long journey back to Scotland? Maybe she'd be better just staying here and looking for new jobs.

Her laptop was out of charge, and she plugged it in before getting undressed. She really needed a good wash to rinse off the travel feeling. Her shower was old-fashioned and clunky compared to the luxury of the Harrington's house, but it did the job of making her smell fresh as a daisy again.

With a towel wrapped around her, she returned to her room, still not sure what to do. Her phone flashed, and she lifted it.

RAFE: Hey. How did you get on with your boss? I'm really gutted you'll miss Christmas with us... We all are. Nobody quite as much as me. I'd love to work with you in the new year, but there's so much more. I didn't want to be too forward or too fast, but all I know right now is that my heart hurts so much without you. xx

Tears pricked behind Tilly's eyes. She blinked them back and smiled. That was the sign she'd been waiting for. She was going back to Scotland.

CHAPTER TWENTY-SEVEN

Tuesday, December 24th

Christmas Eve

Morning

Rafe placed a miniature silver sleigh on top of his mum's perfectly iced Christmas cake. Memories of crashing into the bush with Tilly resurfaced along with ones from further back. Christmases from long ago flashed before his eyes. These same decorations had come out year after year. Since the days he'd had to stand on a stool to reach the worktop, he'd been helping decorate these cakes.

One day, would he have experiences like this with a family of his own? He'd missed that opportunity with his ex, but maybe there was a chance with Tilly. Not that he'd asked her. It was one of the many things they'd not had time to talk about. Would that chance arrive? Or was their relationship going to focus on business from now on? Had Tilly been right in her self-assessment and forgotten him as a potential partner already?

Hilary brushed off some icing sugar from the front of her Mrs Claus apron as Alexander got a little enthusiastic with his 'dusting', causing a mini blizzard.

Geoff rolled up his sleeves and scooped up the fallen snow. 'We'll need another plough if you carry on like that, young man,' he said.

'No, grumpy,' Alexander said, and everyone chuckled.

Geoff smirked as he always did when his grandson called him that.

'I don't think you'll ever be grandpa,' Cressida said.

'He suits grumpy.' Rafe winked at his dad.

Geoff frowned and put his hands on his hips.

'See what I mean?' Rafe winked, and they all laughed again.

'Thank goodness none of you ever called me that,' Grandma said.

'Like we'd dare.' Cressida flicked a look at Tina, and they smirked.

Genevieve was adding silver beads to the cake with the total perfection that came from all the cooking videos she made for her social media channels. 'Stop making me laugh,' she said. 'Or I'll make a mistake.'

Finlay mimed nudging her, and she threw him a look.

'Ouch,' Rafe said. 'If looks could kill, you're in trouble.'

Finlay held up his hands. 'I surrender. Do you your worst.' He waggled his eyebrows at Genevieve.

Rafe should be enjoying every second of this, but his heart wasn't fully in it. His message to Tilly from yesterday lay woefully unanswered. Had he completely overstepped in hoping she'd want to see him again? But how could he dismiss everything that had happened between them? Maybe she didn't want to take the risk. Only time would tell, but could it speed up please? Not having her here for Christmas was hurting so bad. How different this would be if she was here, joining in, laughing with them, sharing the fun and the love.

Once the cake was fully decorated, Hilary moved it to the sideboard. Alexander was still eyeing it. Wouldn't be a surprise if later on the little cherub found his way in here and climbed onto the sideboard to start his feast.

The hot chocolate station was out again, and Hilary poured milk into a pan. But Rafe didn't fancy it. He slipped out and went into the living room, sitting in front of the giant windows, gazing at the stunning landscape. One day he'd like to come back here to live. Glasgow was great for work, but this was the kind of place to put down roots. He could commute to Glasgow a few days a week and remote work the rest of the time, but that life would be so much more complete if it featured Tilly too.

He lifted his phone and tapped out another message to her.

RAFE: Hey, sorry if my last message overstepped. Will keep things professional if you'd rather do that.

He laid his phone on the coffee table and sat back with a sigh.

His plans to travel to London on the twenty-seventh had been shoved into a back burner. The doubt riddling his mind blocked him from doing anything that might look too pushy. If he turned up at Tilly's door in London when she only wanted a business relationship, would that be any better than her turning up here last Friday? It was possibly worse.

He ran his fingers through his hair, staring at his phone. Like he'd willed a message to appear, it lit up, and he dived for it.

TILLY: I have lots to talk to you about. Can you answer your door? I've arranged for something to be delivered to you... It's Christmas Eve, after all!

He frowned at the phone, then messaged back.

RAFE: Answer the door when? Do you mean now? I didn't hear any deliveries.

TILLY: Go and check. It should be there now.

What on earth was she up to? And what had she sent? He had some completely terrifying visions of a sexy Santa strippergram before he reached the door. But Tilly would never send anything like that to his parents' house... or at all.

He opened the back door and glanced around. No parcels, nothing.

'Rafe,' Hilary said from behind, making him jump. 'Sorry, son, didn't mean to scare you, but what are you doing?'

'I just had a message and—'

'Oh goodness.' Hilary clapped her hands to her face and stared past Rafe out the door.

He turned around and his heart stopped. Tilly was on the doorstep, smiling shyly, and gently sucking on her lower lip. 'Hi,' she said. 'I'm here to see Rafe Harrington.'

'Oh, Tilly.' Hilary rushed forward and opened her arms, wrapping Tilly in a huge hug. Tears filled both women's eyes and Rafe felt a swelling lump in his throat from deep in his chest. 'Rafe Harrington is right here,' Hilary said. 'And you have my permission to do anything you like with him.'

Rafe raised his eyebrows at Tilly. She gazed at him for a moment, then they both moved, closing the gap and falling into each other. Rafe held her tight, and Tilly put her arms around his back so forcefully she almost snapped him in half. But the pain was exquisite.

Please let this be real.

He stroked the top of her head, then placed a gentle kiss on it. His mum had vanished, possibly to give them space or maybe to alert the rest of the family, in which case the private moment would be short-lived.

'I've missed you so much.' She slid her fingers around his cheeks, and slowly moved her face nearer to his, pausing barely an inch from his mouth. His heartbeat accelerated. 'I brought this.' She dropped one hand from his cheek and fished in her pocket.

When she raised it again, she had a small sprig of mistletoe. 'Just so we're sure this time.'

'Sure of what?'

'Sure that you're the only man I want to kiss under this.'

He took it from her and placed it on top of the door. No time to hang it properly. 'You're definitely the only girl I want to kiss.'

Together, they moved. Her soft lips pressed lightly against his, and she tenderly kissed him, causing bolts of electricity to fire through him. He returned the kiss, reacquainting himself with her gentle touch. It felt so right. So necessary. The most natural thing in the world.

He slipped his tongue into her mouth and his need for her jumped several steps. The kiss deepened, and Tilly's hand wrapped around the back of his head, holding him, making sure he couldn't pull away, which was fine. He didn't want to. Her fingers knitted into his hair, tugging him closer and he held tight, flush up against him, right where he wanted her to be.

Who knew how long they stood like that until they had to come up for air? Who was counting time?

Rafe stroked stray strands of hair from her face, gazing at her like she couldn't possibly be genuine. But she was.

'What are you doing here?'

'Well...' She pulled back and looked at him. 'You said I'd always be welcome... and... um, if it was ok, I'd like to spend Christmas with you.'

'Of course it's ok. I can't think of anything I want more. I just don't—'

'It is way more than ok.' Hilary reappeared. 'It's fantastic.'

'Oh my god,' Genevieve screamed as she rushed out to grab Tilly.

What Rafe wanted to say to Tilly would have to wait. He'd also have to wait to find out how she'd got back here and what had happened with her job. His family weren't going to leave her alone any time soon. And really that was fine because what was the rush? Tilly wasn't going anywhere this time.

CHAPTER TWENTY-EIGHT

Tilly

The warmth around Tilly wasn't just coming from the heat in the house, but from the people who were taking turns to embrace her. The fuzzy feeling inside her chest was like nothing she'd ever experienced before. Here was love. A family. And Rafe.

Finally, Hilary released her, and Tilly stepped outside again to collect her bags. Almost as soon as she got back inside, Geoff took the mistletoe off the top of the door and closed it. Rafe's arms took hold of her. His solid body was a pillar of strength, keeping her upright while her insides wanted to crumple, not from sadness, but from the weightlessness of not having to carry the heavy bulk of work and the stress of life on her shoulders. He stroked her back and rocked her a little.

'How did you get here?' He rubbed his cheek on hers, making her skin tingle at the contact. 'And why aren't you at work?'

'Come into the living room and tell us,' Hilary said. 'It's lovely and warm in there.'

'It's fate,' Genevieve said. 'I've been saying it from the start.'

Grandma patted her back. 'I agree with you.'

'It's mental.' Cressida hoisted Alexander up her hip. 'But good mental. Brilliant, in fact.'

Rafe let Tilly go and she bent down to pat the dogs, who were sniffing around her and wagging their tails. 'Hey.' She gave the two labs a pat first before gently moving them out of the way so that little Mitzi could get her nose in. She instantly dropped on her back and Tilly giggled as she rubbed her tummy. Even the dogs were pleased to see her, and it melted her heart a little more.

'Come on.' Rafe nudged the dogs into the main part of the house. As soon as Horace and Dax went, Mitzi jumped up and tottered after them.

Tilly took Rafe's hand. Heat seeped into her at the touch. He smiled at her and closed his fingers around hers. Together, they headed for the living room and joined the others. When they took their seats, Tilly moved in close, and Rafe put his arm around her shoulder.

'I decided to quit my job. As soon as I did, I got back on the sleeper train and, well, came here.'

'Thank goodness you quit,' Hilary said. 'Sounded like a horrible place to work.'

'I wonder...' Tilly looked at Rafe. 'If you'd be interested in hearing a business proposal?'

He laughed and gave her shoulder a little squeeze. 'I already told you I liked your idea. It sounds right up my street. I kinda wanted to steal it after you told me, but I wasn't going to stoop to 1-Quick levels. We can definitely discuss it in the New Year, and I can help you find a job too.'

'With you?'

'Absolutely. If that's what you want.'

'Oh, I mean, I would do it properly. I don't want to be accused of getting anything underhand.'

'We'll make sure that doesn't happen; we'll do it all officially.'

'Good.' She picked at her cuticles. 'Because I don't want Arnie or Mitchell to think I've... Done anything I shouldn't to get a job.'

'I couldn't care less what they think,' Rafe said. 'But I understand how it might look, so we'll make sure it all goes through the proper channels.'

Tilly leaned into him, and he placed a kiss on her forehead. She wasn't looking forward to anyone at 1-Quick discovering she was in a relationship with Rafe... Assuming she was, and maybe that was still something she had to clarify. Arnie might try to make things difficult, though maybe she shouldn't care. She didn't exactly plan to see him again.

'This is wonderful,' Hilary said. 'We're heading to the Christingle and nativity service this afternoon. I can understand if it's not your thing, but you're welcome to come along.'

'I'd love to,' Tilly said.

'Perfect. Would you like me to take your bags up to your room?'

'I'll do it.' Rafe got to his feet. 'You chill, Mum. You've run after us enough this week.'

Tilly smiled at everyone, then watched Rafe leaving the room. 'Actually, I should go with him... I need to...' She wasn't sure what she needed to do, she just wanted to talk to him.

'On you go,' Grandma said. 'He's only going upstairs, but young lovers shouldn't be separated for too long.'

Heat burned in Tilly's cheeks, but what was the point in denying it? 'Thanks.' She scooted after him.

He was in the hall, lifting her case as Mitzi sniffed around.

'I doubt there's anything in there for you,' Rafe said.

'There might be,' Tilly said, and he glanced around at her voice.

'Don't you want to rest? You've done a lot of travelling these past few days.'

'Nope.' She lifted the smaller bags, not wanting him to look inside as she'd bought presents for everyone, but not had time to wrap them. 'I just want to be with you.'

He smiled his most gorgeous smile. 'I'm really glad you're back.'

They climbed the stairs together and Tilly beamed at the twinkly lights.

'I was worried about you,' Rafe said. 'I pity anyone who works for those 1-Quick cowboys.'

'Me too. I'm glad I'm out, but not as glad as I am to be here.'

He opened the door to her room and paused. Tilly frowned. Was he thinking she might prefer his room? She would, but was that totally presumptuous? What were they really to each other? They'd had one night and one morning together, but that didn't mean they were in a relationship. Was that what he wanted, or had she muddied the water by bringing work into the equation?

'You know, Tilly, I wonder if—'

'Rafe!' Hilary called from the bottom of the stairs.

'Yeah?'

'I just noticed the time. We're going to set off shortly.'

'Ok. We'll be down in a minute.' He smiled at Tilly. 'Are you sure you want to come with us?'

She nodded. 'Definitely. This is like my first proper Christmas, and I don't want to miss anything.'

'Ok. We should get ready though. Mum doesn't like to be late.'

She'd been travelling for what felt like days up and down the country, but Tilly's energy levels were high. Maybe it was adrenaline, but she wanted to believe it was Christmas spirit and it had finally found a home in her heart.

She had presents to wrap later and put under the Christmas tree. Nothing too big, of course. She hadn't had time to do anything special and the shops at Euston Station had been all she could manage, but people liked boxes of chocolates and bottles of wine at Christmas. The thought was what counted after all. And she couldn't stop thinking about this family.

One of them in particular.

It would have been nice to have more time to talk to Rafe before they left, but it still wouldn't dampen her enthusiasm for the afternoon. Once they were all in their coats, boots and winter woollies, the family headed for the cars. Between Rafe's and Geoff's cars, they had enough space for everyone. Tilly even got the front seat while Cressida and Tina sat in the back with Alexander.

Glenbriar church was an extremely cute building raised on a little hill with trees around it and a stream running through the grounds. A small bridge ran over the stream and Genevieve pointed it out to Tilly, telling her she and Finlay had had several photos taken there on their wedding day. Even in the cold, frosty weather, Tilly saw the appeal. Such an idyllic location.

Inside was warm and beautifully lit up, with fairy lights twisted among garlands and strung around the pillars very like the ones on the stairs at Greenacres. Tilly suspected Hilary had been one of the church decorators. Candles around the altar and the pulpit flickered and the Christmas tree gleamed in the corner. Tilly took a seat on a pew with the family, while Hilary bustled off to speak to people. She looked back every now and then to catch Tilly's eye and smile.

'I dread to think what she's telling everyone,' Rafe muttered, tapping a large bible on the shelf in front of him.

Tilly smiled. Whatever it was, she knew it wouldn't be for bad reasons. Hilary was too nice for that.

Gentle organ music began to play, and Hilary rejoined them.

'That's Grant, the minister,' Rafe whispered as a man in a black and purple robe walked to the front. 'Bit young, isn't he? Or am I the only one who thinks so?'

'Do you mean like a government minister?' Tilly said with a frown. 'Who's also the vicar?'

Rafe chuckled. 'No, we don't call them vicars in Scotland. He's the church minister.'

'Ah, that makes sense. I heard your mum talking about the minister before and wasn't sure what she meant. And you're right, he is young for a vicar.'

Rafe nodded. 'Glad you agree. Mum told me not to be a gossip when I said it to her... You know, the same woman who's been saying goodness knows what about you and me to all her church friends.'

Tilly giggled but stopped as the minister reached the front.

'Welcome.' Grant threw his arms wide, his voice resonating through the church. 'This afternoon, we gather to celebrate the greatest gift ever given to humanity.'

Rafe glanced at Tilly and smiled, then put his hand on hers and clasped it. Tilly relaxed into the wonderful sensation of belonging.

'Our story begins in a humble stable, where a young couple, Mary and Joseph, found refuge on a cold winter's night. And there, in the midst of the animals and the hay, a child was born – a child who would change the course of history.'

As Grant spoke, he motioned to the children seated in the front pews, dressed in bathrobes, with tea towels on their heads and clutching makeshift props.

Tilly had also found refuge on a cold, wintery day with a loving family, in a way she could never have predicted.

'And here' – Grant gestured towards the children – 'we have our Mary and Joseph, ready to bring the story to life.'

Tilly clapped with the rest of the congregation as the children rose from their seats and made their way to the makeshift stable at the front of the church.

'And now,' Grant continued, 'as we reflect on the miracle of Christ's birth, let's join together in the song "O Little Town of Bethlehem" which you'll find on your hymn sheets.'

The organ started again, and everyone got to their feet. Tilly had never been much of a singer, but as everyone around her began singing, she found it impossible not to join in. A lump was impeding her throat. The song sounded so beautiful, and the fact she was here at all made her want to weep. She mouthed along, hoping no one would notice her lack of sound, trying to focus on the individual voices, Rafe's low gentle tone, Hilary's strong voice and someone nearby with a slightly off-key but very spirited timbre.

When they all sat at the end of the song, Tilly ducked to the side, pretending to look for something in her bag as she dried her eyes.

Grant continued his story and Tilly watched, laughing with the others when angels' headdresses fell off and the sheep cast great lumps of cotton wool all over the carpet at the front of the church.

'That's right, shepherds,' Grant said, 'keep those sheep in check.'

Tilly didn't remember doing anything like this when she was a child. But this was enough to open her eyes to what she'd missed. The excitement on their little faces, knowing they were going home to wait for Santa and presents after.

Even if all her past Christmases were a flop, so what? She still had a chance to make new Christmases, and that was exactly what she'd do. She applauded with everyone else as the nativity came to a close.

Grant's voice filled the space again. For someone so young, he had quite a presence.

'As we continue our journey through this wonderful Christmas Eve, we come now to a time-honoured tradition: the Christingle. This is a symbol of Christ's light shining in the darkness. Each element of the Christingle holds special significance, reminding us of the true meaning of Christmas.'

Grant picked up one of the Christingles from a nearby table, holding it aloft. 'The orange,' he said, 'represents the world, a reminder of God's love for all of creation.'

Rafe's fingers slipped across Tilly's thigh, and he took hold of her hand, squeezing it gently. A smile grew on her face and she returned the grasp with firm pressure.

Grant pointed to the candle nestled in the centre of the orange. 'The candle,' he continued, 'represents Christ, the light of the world, whose birth we celebrate tonight.' Next, he gestured towards the ribbon encircling the orange, adorned with fruits and sweets. 'The ribbon reminds us of the bonds of love that unite us as one family, while the fruits and sweets symbolise the blessings of abundance and joy that Christ brings into our lives.'

And something had brought a family into Tilly's life. She wasn't sure what, or who, but even one week ago, she'd been lost and alone. *Look at me now!* Here she was, sitting with wonderful people. People who cared. People who loved her.

With a gentle smile, Grant turned to the children, inviting them to come forward and collect their Christingles. 'And now,' he said, 'let us join together in a procession of light, as we carry our Christingles to the altar, a symbol of our collective hope and faith in the Christ child.'

They made their way down the aisle, each one carefully cradling their Christingle. Tilly looked on, barely holding back the tears again. Somewhere in the world, her sister was in prison, possibly alone. Tilly had washed her hands of Ellie after the pain she'd caused in their in childhood. But now was the time to forgive. She'd grown an understanding of Ellie's feelings over the past few days. Maybe they weren't so different from her own.

Sadly, Ellie's choice to fight her pain had ended badly. Tilly had withdrawn. It had avoided trouble, sure, but also everything else. Friendship. Joy. Love.

Holding a grudge took energy, and she didn't want to waste it on something so negative. She'd find a way to contact Ellie and leave her a message. Even just to say hi. They may never be close, but she could still be there – just in case. She knew how hard it was to be lonely.

After the service, Tilly followed the family into a side room for cakes and coffee.

'These are delicious.' Finlay piled several onto a plate.

Rafe gave him a look filled with disbelief but also respect. 'You must have hollow legs or something. Do you like mince pies?' he added to Tilly.

'Guess what?'

'You've never tried one?'

'Correct.'

They both laughed. 'Try one,' Rafe said. 'They're a bit like marmite. You either love them or hate them.'

'And which are you?'

'Love,' he said. 'But Cress and Gen both hate them.'

He handed her one on a small plate and she bit carefully into the buttery pastry, sugary crystals catching on her lips. When she got to the filling, she wasn't sure for a moment, but as the fruits and spices blended on her tongue, she nodded. 'Actually, that's good.'

'Yay!' Rafe gave her the thumbs up. 'Good decision.'

She smiled and took another bite. After she'd chewed it, she said, 'I made another decision during the service.'

'What about?' His eyebrows raised and his brow furrowed slightly.

'About my sister. Ellie. I'm going to call her or leave a message for her.'

'You know where she is?' he lowered his voice. 'Which prison?'

'Yes.'

Rafe cocked his head. 'And you think it's a good idea to contact her?'

'I know what it's like to be in her position. Not jail, obviously, but with the whole attachment thing.'

He nodded. 'And how do you feel about that now?'

'You won't believe this, but I ended up sitting next to a psychologist on the train on the way back to London. We got chatting, and she told me a whole lot of interesting things.'

A little smile played at the corner of his lips. 'Will you tell me?'

'Yeah, but not here.'

'We don't really know that much about each other really, do we?'

'Not yet.'

'I need to teach you about camping.'

Tilly burst out laughing. 'Why?'

'I have a sudden urge to whisk you off somewhere in my rooftop tent.'

'In this weather?'

'Fair point.'

'Tilly, Rafe,' Hilary called them over to meet some of her friends. Tilly's insides were buzzing. Rafe's words all indicated he was looking at their relationship as something for the long term, but she had to be sure.

They returned home and Hilary set up a buffet tea. Tilly couldn't imagine how she managed to cook all these meals and never look stressed. Tilly had bought her the biggest pamper set she could carry on the train. If anyone needed to relax after Christmas, it was Hilary.

They watched *The Snowman* as they ate, and Geoff topped up everyone's glasses. As Alexander went to bed quite early, everyone agreed it was best to hang up the stockings before it got too late. Tilly was prepared to watch this part. She didn't have a stocking, but it wouldn't matter. Just being here was enough.

The fireplace was kicking out some heat in the living room as they gathered around. Geoff had a large box, and everyone was raking about, looking for their own special stocking.

'Do I have one?' Tina asked. 'I think you got me one last year.'

'Of course you do,' Geoff said. 'Everyone has one.'

Tilly held back, knowing she didn't, but it was ok.

Genevieve placed her stocking on the mantel first. 'Why do I still go first?' she said. 'Alexander is younger than me, so is Tilly.'

'You'll always be our baby girl,' Geoff said.

'And the one with no patience,' Rafe added. 'That's really why you were always allowed to go first. Otherwise, we had to put up with an hour-long tantrum.'

'Oi!' She put her hands on her hips as everyone laughed and Cressida and her parents nodded in agreement.

Rafe caught Tilly's eye and beckoned her over. 'Come on,' he said.

Tilly hesitated, feeling a rush of warmth. She'd never been part of a cherished family tradition and she couldn't join in now, unless she ran upstairs and grabbed a sock... But she didn't want to look like she was begging for gifts.

Rafe edged around his family and put his arm around Tilly. 'Don't you want to hang yours up?'

'I don't have one,' she murmured.

'Yes, you do. Of course you do. There's one in the box for you. We wouldn't leave you out.'

She swallowed, her heart so full she might burst. 'I don't know what to say.'

'You don't need to say anything.' He stroked the corner of her eye with the pad of his thumb, brushing away a stray tear. 'Just enjoy it.'

She hung her stocking beside Rafe's, then stepped back to admire the scene. A sense of contentment and wonder settled over her. She was exactly where she was meant to be, and where she wanted to stay.

Chapter Twenty-Nine

Rafe

Tuesday, December 24th

Christmas Eve

Evening

'Come with me a minute,' Rafe whispered to Tilly, leading her away from the fireplace and into the corridor. He opened the door into the little library room where she'd gone on her first day with them.

Cooler air greeted him, and the compact size of the room focused his attention on the heady scent of Tilly's perfume. Something about that fragrance was comforting, but stimulating at the same time.

'What is it?' she asked as he closed the door.

He looked at her, and a powerful bolt of electricity surged through his body. 'Just you.' He moved closer until she was backed against the door and he rested his arms on either side of her head, inhaling her sweet perfume. 'I've wanted to do this since the second you got back.'

'Do what?' she whispered.

'Kiss you, hold you, make love to you. I want you, Tilly. Just you. I want you to know how much. I don't want to leave you with any doubt that you're in the right place with the right person.'

'Even though we know so little about each other.'

'Yes. Because I know how I feel. I know what torture it was being apart from you, even for just one day.'

'Me too,' Tilly said. 'And it's made me realise something. Something really important.'

'What?'

'That I love you.'

Rafe froze, his eyes locked on hers. Then he blinked.

Tilly's heart pounded manically in her ribcage. 'Isn't that what you were saying to me?' She sucked her lip. 'Or have I got it horribly wrong?'

'You've got it exactly right.' He dipped in and pressed a long, slow kiss on her forehead, then brought his head to rest on hers. 'I love you too. I really love you, like so damn much. It seems too much, but that's just how strong it is.'

'That's how I feel too, but I was so scared it was all this attachment stuff.'

'Even if it is, it's fine. I want you to attach yourself to me, please do. And I'll always be here for you, so will my family.'

She raised her hand to her mouth and tears leaked from her eyes. 'You have no idea what that means to me.' Her voice cracked and Rafe drew her close, kissing the tears away gently.

'I do. Because your love means all that to me too. When we're together, good things happen. I feel more alive and happier with you than I ever have with anyone.'

'I know what you mean.'

'It's like the world sits in the right place and everything aligns. We don't need to know everything about each other. There's time for all that. Time to talk, time to learn.'

'Yes,' she said. 'There's no rush, is there?'

'No. In fact, I'd like to take my time getting to know you properly. Because I know whatever happens, my feelings won't change. I've been scared of rushing into things and messing up like I did with my ex-wife, but this is different. This time I'm scared of losing you, scared I waste time, and someone swoops in and snatches you from me.'

She giggled through her tears. 'That's not going to happen. I only want you.'

He held her for a long moment. Words ran dry, but they weren't needed. He and Tilly were together, and they understood each other.

'My mum is likely to come looking for us any second now.' He placed a gentle kiss on Tilly's forehead. 'I just wanted you to know exactly how I felt before anything else happened.'

'And now you know I feel the same.'

'Life is good, huh?' He pulled back and smiled at her.

'The best. And Rafe.' She took his hand just as he was about to open the door.

'Yes.'

'I don't want to be alone.'

'You won't be; that's what I'm saying.' He drew her in for another hug. 'I won't leave you alone tonight or any night. I don't want to be alone either. In fact, I have a very special Christmas present for you, but it only works when we're together.'

She let out a little chuckle and tapped her finger on his chest. 'I like the sound of it.'

'Good, and later on, you can unwrap it at your leisure.'

'Sounds like fun.'

'It's the gift that keeps on giving.' He gave her another gentle kiss. 'Let's get back to the others.'

Once he was back in the living room, he nibbled chocolates until he was stuffed but he declined more wine from his dad. He wanted to have his wits about him. His plans for Tilly that evening were wicked, but delectable.

She'd gone upstairs to wrap presents. Didn't she realise she didn't have to get them anything? But then, of course, she'd want to, and it was kind and sweet of her.

'Son, I hope I haven't put undue pressure on you.' Geoff sat next to him after filling up everyone else's glasses. 'To take over the business. I probably shouldn't have made a big deal out of it. When I retire, I can sell the business or hand over the management to someone else.'

'Yeah.' Rafe sighed. 'I don't want to seem difficult. It's just that I've spent a long time building my own business.'

'It's all good. Just so long as I don't hurt your feelings by selling it when the time comes.'

'It won't hurt my feelings, but I've been thinking things over, and I wonder if there might be a way to keep it in the family by making all three of us owners, only nominally. We'd have the final say in anything huge, but the majority of the day-to-day business would be handled by a manager.'

'Hmm. That might work and I like the idea of the company staying in the family.'

'Then let's look into it in the new year.' Rafe patted his dad on the arm. It might not be the solution his dad most wanted, but it might work as a compromise.

Tilly returned to the room carrying an armful of wrapped gifts. She looked around with an almost furtive glance before heading over to the tree and placing the presents under it. That was when Rafe noticed she was wearing Christmas themed pyjamas.

'They're very festive.' He eyed over the white top with a dog in a Santa hat and the red tartan trousers.

'I bought them before I left London.' Tilly took the seat next to him. 'I thought they might come in useful.'

'They certainly have.' Rafe checked no one else was listening before he leaned in and whispered. 'Though I'll be taking them off later.'

She shushed him with a play slap on his leg and her cheeks flushed quite adorably. When Hilary appeared with hot chocolates, everyone else took that as a sign to get their PJs on too. And when his dad started reading *The Night Before Christmas*, Rafe felt like a child, all buzzed up and unable to wait to get to bed, though knowing he wouldn't sleep for hours... only this time that had nothing to do with Santa's imminent arrival and everything to do with the woman cuddled up beside him.

Alexander was in bed by seven and everyone else snuggled up to watch *Home Alone*. Rafe laughed along with the jokes and one-liners he knew off by heart, but he was more interested in making little circles on Tilly's shoulder with his fingertips. She leaned her head on him, nuzzling into the crook of his neck.

When the film finished, there was some sneaking about as people disappeared to get the gifts for the stockings, pretending not to see each other and laughing when Geoff arrived in a full Santa suit.

'Ho, ho, ho,' he said.

'Merry Christmas, Santa,' Rafe said.

When Tilly went up for her shower, Rafe filled up her stocking. He'd completely forgotten to give her these gifts to take with her when he'd given her a lift to Glasgow for the train, remembering when it was too late to go back for them, and stupidly exclaiming. It had given her a fright. Now he was glad he hadn't given them to her or told her what was up. This would be so much better.

'You got the best present this year,' Hilary said. 'I'm so glad Tilly came back.'

'Me too.'

'I absolutely adore her.'

'Me too,' Rafe repeated.

'Good.' Hilary hugged him. 'So does this mean you and she are officially going to get together?' Her eyes asked the question louder than her words.

'Yes, Mum. We're giving it a try, and I think it'll be good.'

'I'm sure it will be.' Hilary hugged him. 'It started off as a mix-up, but I'm positive it'll end up exactly right.'

'Yeah. I have a great feeling about it.'

Rafe headed upstairs and stopped outside Tilly's room. He knocked on the door and waited until she called for him to come in.

Inside her room, their little tree twinkled.

'Hey,' he said.

Tilly sat on the bed wrapped in a fluffy white blanket. 'I've been thinking,' she said, her eyes wide and her fingers fiddling with the blanket.

'What about?'

'If I do get a job with you and we end up working together... Well, I can't be dating the boss.'

Rafe laughed, sat on the bed and shuffled up next to her.

'What's funny about that?' She stared at him.

'That's not even a rule at Innova because none of my colleagues have ever wanted to date me before. Wait until you meet Marnie. She'll laugh herself silly at the idea.'

'Are you that bad?'

'Apparently so... But we could test that theory if you like?'

'Oh, I do.' Tilly dropped the blanket and straddled him. 'I want to do that, and I also want to make our Christmas magic.'

'Your wish is my command.' Rafe leaned back, crossed his arms over his front and hoisted off his pyjama top. 'It's hot in here.'

'You're not kidding.' Tilly leaned in and kissed him.

His hands cupped her bottom, and he closed his eyes. Their lips met and reacquainted themselves. Tilly tasted better than champagne, mulled wine or mince pies. She was addictively sweet. The faint tinkling of wind chimes in the garden made Rafe smile into the kiss. Was that Santa's sleigh? Maybe he was rushing off with a twinkle in his eye and a flash of stars behind him. Rafe had got everything he wanted for Christmas right here.

CHAPTER THIRTY

Tilly

Wednesday, December 25ᵗʰ

Christmas Day

Shouldn't there be music? Trumpets or something announcing Christmas Day? Well, Tilly didn't really need them. She had Rafe beside her, and that was all that mattered. The best Christmas ever had arrived. All those mornings getting up alone in her flat in London, pretending it was just any other day and getting through it with walks or catching up on work could be forgotten. Even the worst childhood memories could get lost and make way for something new.

'Merry Christmas.' Rafe placed a kiss on her forehead.

She snuggled in closer, loving the skin on skin contact and the heat it brought. He tugged the soft cover over them.

'Merry Christmas,' she said.

'I meant to ask you last night if you'd managed to contact Ellie, but other things kind of took over.'

'I emailed the prison with a message. That's all I feel up to doing just now. I'm not ready for visits yet, but I wanted her to know I'm still here and maybe in the future we can have some kind of relationship again.'

'That's good enough for now.' Rafe stroked her hair. 'But don't cut her any slack. You did that for years. Let her be the one to show you she's changed and is ready to make an effort. I feel sad for the position she's in, and I hope she's getting the help she needs, but you've done the right thing in choosing your own path.'

'Yeah. She's still my sister, and I don't want to cut ties completely, but I can't go back to living my life always worrying about what she's doing, or how her actions might hurt me.' And she was strong enough to do that now. She'd wasted too many years doing what she thought was best for them both, while not looking out for herself. She was doing that now and ready to make a new start.

Be kind to yourself.

The sound of people moving around and wishing each other merry Christmas was the signal for Tilly and Rafe to get up. He nipped back to his own room so they could shower and get fresh clothes before going downstairs.

Alexander had already torn his way into several flashing toys and cuddly animals by the time Tilly and Rafe arrived in the living room.

'Merry Christmas,' they both said together, then laughed.

'Aw,' Genevieve said. 'You're so in tune with each other already.'

They sat down on the sofa and watched the carnage as Alexander ripped open another parcel.

'Merry Christmas, Grandma.' Rafe leaned over and kissed the top of her head.

'I'm counting on it being one later,' she said. 'I hear your father has some first-rate champagne put away for today.'

'As long as no one's drunk it this year.' Cressida lifted her eyebrow as she glanced between Genevieve and Finlay.

They pulled innocent expressions, then smirked. 'If we hadn't nicked that champagne and got plastered, we might never have got engaged,' Finlay said. 'And you'd all have been deprived of my company.'

Genevieve scrunched up a ball of paper and lobbed it at his head. They grinned at each other and burst out laughing.

'We usually open family presents after lunch,' Hilary said. 'But why not open something from your stocking, Tilly?'

'Ok. That sounds like fun.' She crossed the room and lifted her stocking from the mantelpiece. Something inside smelled good, and she inhaled it. 'Is it a candle?'

Rafe laughed, switching his focus to Genevieve. 'Uh-oh, another one who likes to guess everything before she opens it.'

'Why are you looking at me?' Genevieve put her hand on her heart.

'I wonder.'

Tilly sat back down and took out the first gift. With slightly trembling fingers, she opened it. A bar of handmade soap wrapped in floral paper. She held it up to her nose. 'This is divine.'

Rafe smiled as she took out the next one. Each gift turned out to be something gorgeous from a local shop. Artisan chocolates, sweet preserves, candles – she cast Rafe a look; she'd called it. The last one was in a small oblong box. She prised off the lid to find a gorgeous little silver and rose gold bracelet, very delicate, and so pretty. A tiny star linked with a heart dangled from it.

'Let me.' Rafe gently took it from her and fastened it around her wrist. 'It reminded me of you. Beautiful in an understated way.'

She cocked her head and smiled at him. Was anyone as lovely? 'Thank you. It kind of reminds me of us. The heart is how we feel; the star is where it was always written.'

He nodded, leaned over, and kissed her cheek. 'That's so true. That didn't cross my mind when I chose it, but you're so right.'

'This is wonderful.' Hilary clapped her hands together. She was as busy today as always. Even a mid morning trip to the church for the Christmas day service didn't seem to interrupt her flow of cooking and setting up the dining room.

Rafe and Tilly took a short walk and when they came back, Tilly said, 'We should help your mum get ready for lunch.'

'Good idea,' Rafe said. 'Though she might kick us out. Sometimes she says people just get in her way.'

Rafe twirled Tilly in the hallway to Frank Sinatra's 'White Christmas' as they made their way to the kitchen. Tilly couldn't stop smiling. This was a dream come true.

'We're here to give you a hand,' Rafe told Hilary. Geoff was already lifting plates from a cupboard.

'What should I do?' Tilly asked.

'You really don't have to. I've got everything ready. I just need to lift it all into the dining room. Genevieve and Finlay are setting up crackers and some table games.'

'We can lift stuff through,' Rafe said.

'Ah, thank you.' Hilary pulled on a pair of oven gloves and opened the Aga door. A delicious smell wafted through the air. 'The turkey is almost done. Maybe you could take the bottles through. And I'll get a milk jug for Alexander so he doesn't feel left out.'

Tilly lifted some soft drinks bottles and took them into the dining room. Genevieve and Finlay were laughing as they placed something on the table.

'These games are going to be hilarious,' Genevieve said.

Tilly returned to the kitchen, beaming. Even this bit was fun, everyone working together. Rafe was putting glasses on a tray, and Geoff poured some milk into a large glass pitcher. Hilary had on her oven gloves and was unloading more food from the Aga, placing trays on the work surface with a gentle clang. 'Tilly, would you be good enough to pop these pigs in blankets onto that serving dish there?'

'Of course.' Tilly took hold of the tray of pigs in blankets, only realising how hot it was as it scorched her fingertips. She let go with a shriek and the tray spun from her hand, clipping the glass milk jug and sending it to the floor with a clatter. Glass shards and milk flew everywhere.

'Oh my god.' Tilly clutched her face. 'I'm so sorry, so sorry. I'll clean it up. I'll buy a new one.'

Please, please, don't send me away. I didn't mean it. Memories flooded back of the mess her sister had made of foster carers' houses and how Tilly had tried to clean it up or offer to make amends, but it never worked. No one ever wanted her to stay.

Please, don't send me away. Not on Christmas Day. Not from this wonderful family.

'Oh dear.' Hilary placed her hand on Tilly's arm. 'Are you alright?'

'Yes, I'm fine. I didn't realise the tray was hot and when I touched it... Oh, god, I'm so sorry.'

'Tilly,' Rafe said, and his voice was soft but strong enough to break through the turmoil. 'There's no need to be sorry. It was an accident.'

'Don't worry about the silly jug.' Hilary gently patted her. 'As long as you're ok.' She put her arm around Tilly. 'You're what's important, not all this.' She waved her hand at the messy floor.

'I've made such a mess.'

'Don't stress,' Rafe said. 'I'll clean this up. You sit down.'

'Yes, come with me.' Hilary led her to a high stool at the kitchen island.

'Shouldn't I help clear it up?'

'No. You've had a bit of a shock. Just sit for a moment and don't worry.'

Rafe was already brushing up the smashed shards of glass and had towels laid over the milk. 'Don't cry over spilt milk,' he said.

'Absolutely,' Hilary agreed.

'It just...' Tilly took a deep breath. 'Brought back bad memories.'

Rafe glanced up as he pressed a towel onto the damp floor. 'We're not going to send you away for something like this. We're never going to send you away. You're here as long as you want to be.'

'Oh heavens,' Hilary said. 'Of course we wouldn't send you away.'

Tilly laughed through her tears, and Hilary hugged her. 'I know you wouldn't. It just all came back.'

Hilary patted her back. 'I understand. You've had some terrible things happen in your life, but you're safe here.'

'Thank you.'

The tap gushed water and Tilly caught sight of Rafe drying his hands. Then she felt his hand touch her back. 'Mum's right. You're safe here, but we can't guarantee there won't be triggers.'

'Just remember, whatever happens, we won't throw you out.' Hilary took her hand and held it. 'You're one of us now. Heaven help you.' She winked. 'Not sure you know what you've let yourself in for.'

'Whatever it is, I'll take it.'

Rafe wrapped his arms around her from behind, and she relaxed into him. 'I love you,' he murmured.

She rested her head on him and smiled. Genevieve and Finlay peered around the door.

'Games are all set.' Genevieve frowned as she saw Tilly. 'Is everything ok?'

'Perfectly fine.' Hilary went back to the food on the worktop. 'If we get this food through, we can eat. Let's get Christmas dinner underway.'

Once the food was ready to be served, everyone went into the dining room, and Geoff brought the turkey through.

Rafe took a seat beside Tilly. 'You ok?' He smiled at her.

She nodded. 'Sorry about losing it in there. You must think I'm mad.'

'No. I don't. I just think you're Tilly and that's all I want you to be.'

She couldn't hold back her smile.

'I messaged Marnie yesterday to wish her a merry Christmas, and I told her all about you and what happened this week.'

'What did she think?'

'That I've completely lost my mind or been taken over by aliens.'

Tilly pulled a face. 'So, she thinks this is a bad idea?'

'Na, she thinks it's epic. She just can't believe it's all happened since last week and that I'm now dating a 1-Quick spy and am bringing her back with me to work in the office.'

'Is that how you put it?'

'Something like that. She can't wait to meet you and find out how you captured me.' He winked. 'But I told her we'll see her in the office in the new year and not before, because we've not just fallen for each other but we're suddenly mad on Christmas too and we're going to make the most of the rest of the season together.'

'Sounds perfect.'

'Like you.'

'Stop it.' She gave him a little poke.

'I mean it.'

'You realise.' Cressida sat down next to them, speaking as though she'd listened to every word, which she probably had. 'Tilly's stuff is in London. Are you expecting her just to move up here and live with you?' She raised her eyebrow at Rafe. 'Or have you not thought about that?'

'I've thought about it, but we haven't actually discussed it yet. Thanks, sis, for bumping it up the queue.'

'It's fine,' Tilly said. 'Because all that is just stuff. I've never felt more at home anywhere than I do here with all of you.'

'Aw, that's so sweet.' Cressida gave her a little hug on the way to her seat.

'It really is,' Genevieve agreed, wiping away a tear and smiling. Finlay put his arm around her.

'You're so welcome here,' Hilary said.

'Absolutely,' Geoff agreed.

'Yeahhhhhh!' Alexander shouted as Tina lifted him into his highchair.

'Seems like he agrees,' she said. 'And he's only a toddler, so he knows what he's talking about.'

'And I'm a lot older than that.' Grandma tucked her napkin under her chin. 'And I couldn't agree more.'

Tilly fixed Rafe in her gaze. 'I'll always be home whenever I'm with you.'

He leaned in and put his arms around her. 'Then that'll be for a very long time, because I'm not letting you go anytime soon.'

She'd found her way inside her very own dollhouse. The one with people who cared for her and the man she loved. No more looking in the windows. She was inside now and as she nestled into Rafe, her eyes travelled around the room at the smiling faces, then to the window and the snowy landscape. She couldn't imagine being any happier.

'Let's make memories, starting with our first Christmas together,' she said in Rafe's ear, rubbing her cheek on his woolly Christmas jumper.

He pulled back and smiled, then lifted his glass of wine. 'I'll drink to that. And to many, many more Christmases together.'

Tilly raised her glass and clinked it on his as the others did the same, chorusing, 'hear, hear'.

'Merry Christmas, my love,' she said. 'And to all of you... My family.'

The End

MORE BOOKS BY MARGARET AMATT

Scottish Island Escapes

1. A Winter Haven

2. A Spring Retreat

3. A Summer Sanctuary

4. An Autumn Hideaway

5. A Christmas Bluff

6. A Flight of Fancy

7. A Hidden Gem

8. A Striking Result

9. A Perfect Discovery

10. A Festive Surprise

The Glenbriar Series

1. Stolen Kisses at the Loch View Hotel

2. Just Friends at Thistle Lodge

3. Pitching up at Heather Glen

4. Two's Company at the Forest Light Show

5. Highland Fling on the Whisky Trail

6. Snowdown at the Old Schoolhouse

7. Starting Over at the Crafty Bee Barn

8. A Surprise Proposal in the Rose Garden

9. Cutting it Neat for the Wedding

10. A Classy Affair in the Country

11. Mix Up under the Mistletoe

12. A Fresh Start on the Bridle Path

13. Last First Kiss at the Village Church

14. Fight or Flirt on the Scenic Route

15. Love Match on the Road Home

16. Christmas Wishes at the Station Bookshop

17. Faking the Grade at Glenbriar High

18. Summer Nights at Hillview Farm

19. Love Song at the Music Festival

20. Holly Dates at the Christmas Cottage

Love on the Edge – Barra Series

1. The Castle in the Bay

2. The Lighthouse by the Sea

3. The Gateway on the Sands

ACKNOWLEDGMENTS

Thanks goes to my adorable husband for supporting my dreams and putting up with my writing talk 24/7. Also to my son, whose interest in my writing always makes me smile. It's precious to know I've passed the bug to him – he's currently writing his own fantasy novel and instruction books on how to build Lego!

Throughout the writing process, I have gleaned help from many sources and met some fabulous people. I'd like to give a special mention to Stéphanie Ronckier, my beta reader extraordinaire. Stéphanie's continued support with my writing is invaluable and I love the fact that I need someone French to correct my grammar! Stéphanie, you rock. To my lovely friend, Lyn Williamson, thank you for your continued support and encouragement with all my projects. And to my fellow authors, Evie Alexander and Lyndsey Gallagher – you girls are the best! I love it that you always have my back and are there to help when I need you.

Also, a thanks to the editors at Leannan Press for their work on this novel.

Of course a huge thank you goes to the readers who continue to support me in so many ways. I appreciate each and every one of you and hope that I can keep bringing you more books to enjoy! Big love.

Margaret XX

ABOUT THE AUTHOR
Margaret Amatt

Margaret has told and written stories for as long as she can remember. During her formative years, she spent time on long walks inventing characters and stories to pass the time.

Writing books is Margaret's passion and when she's not doing that, she's often found eating chocolate, walking and taking photographs in the hills around Highland Perthshire. Those long walks still frequently bring inspiration!

It's Margaret's pleasure to bring you the **Scottish Island Escapes** series, **The Glenbriar Series** and the **Love on the Edge — Barra** series. Each series features interconnected stories for those who enjoy inhabiting Margaret's world but each and every book can be read as a standalone if you'd rather dip in and out.

You can find more information about Margaret on her website or by signing up for her newsletter

www.margaretamatt.com